OTTO PENZLER PRESENTS
AMERICAN MYSTERY CLASSICS

THE TULE MARSH MURDER

Nancy Barr Mavity (1890–1959) was a legendary newspaper reporter and feature writer for the *Oakland Tribune* for more than a quarter of a century and the literary editor of the *San Francisco Chronicle.* She wrote numerous newspaper and magazine articles on various subjects in addition to producing fiction and nonfiction books, most notably her series of mystery novels featuring crime reporter James Aloysius "Peter" Piper: *The Tule Marsh Murder*, *The Body on the Floor*, *The Other Bullet*, *The Case of the Missing Sandals*, *The Man Who Didn't Mind Hanging*, and *The Fate of Jane McKenzie.*

Randal S. Brandt is a librarian at the Bancroft Library, the primary special collections library at the University of California, Berkeley. He catalogs rare books and has been dubbed "UC Berkeley's Crime Librarian" for his role as curator of the California Detective Fiction Collection.

THE TULE MARSH MURDER

NANCY BARR MAVITY

Introduction by
RANDAL S. BRANDT

AMERICAN MYSTERY CLASSICS

Penzler Publishers
New York

TO

STANLEY NORTON CITY EDITOR

"I learned about murder from 'im"

This is a work of fiction. Names, characters, places, and incidents either are the product of the author's imagination or are used fictitiously. Any resemblance to actual persons, living or dead, businesses, companies, events, or locales is entirely coincidental.

Published in 2023 by Penzler Publishers
58 Warren Street, New York, NY 10007
penzlerpublishers.com

Distributed by W. W. Norton

Cover image: Andy Ross
Cover design: Mauricio Diaz

Paperback ISBN 978-1-61316-583-6
Hardcover ISBN 978-1-61316-582-9
eBook ISBN 978-1-61316-584-3

Library of Congress Control Number: 2024942046

Printed in the United States of America

9 8 7 6 5 4 3 2 1

INTRODUCTION

On April 23, 1959, the *Oakland Tribune* carried the announcement "Nancy Barr Mavity, Book Editor, Dies" and informed readers that Mavity had suffered a heart attack that morning and passed away in her Piedmont, California home "without warning when apparently in good health" at the age of sixty-eight.

She had been at her desk at the *Tribune* the day before—the same as every day of the previous thirty-four years. An accompanying article declared that "in the years to come stories about her will be legendary" and highlighted her career and exploits as a journalist, concluding that she "always will be Mrs. Page One."

Refusing to be confined to a single role, Nancy Barr Mavity led three distinctive lives as a wife and mother, a successful crime and mystery novelist, and a well-respected newspaper journalist. So respected, in fact, that the *Oakland Tribune* literally stopped the presses and printed her obituary and career retrospective on the very day she died and in her usual spot—Page One.

Nann Clark Barr was born in Bridgeport, Illinois, on October 22, 1890, to Dr. Granville Walter Barr, who, in a move that would later influence his daughter, traded a career in medicine for journalism, and Annabelle Applegate Barr. While Nannie (as she was called) was still a young girl, the family moved to Keokuk, Iowa, where her father became City Editor of the local newspaper, *The Gate City*.

At the age of eighteen she earned an A.B. degree from her mother's alma mater, Western College for Women, in Oxford, Ohio. She then went to Cornell University where she was awarded one of the prestigious Susan Linn Sage Graduate Scholarships and earned both a Master's degree and a Ph.D. in Philosophy. With her new doctorate in hand, she obtained a position teaching philosophy at Connecticut College. Her academic career was short-lived, however, coming to an end after she resigned in protest when male colleagues with inferior academic credentials, teaching experience, and publication history were promoted above her.

After leaving academia, she moved to New York City to join a publishing firm and began contributing essays and poetry to a variety of literary magazines. On Christmas Day 1917, she married Arthur Benton Mavity, fifteen years her senior, who worked as a salesman for Henry Holt & Company, and changed her name to Nancy ("Nann C.") Barr Mavity. In March 1919, barely a month after the birth of their first child, a daughter also named Nancy, Arthur was promoted to the position of Pacific Coast Manager and transferred to Holt's San Francisco office. The move was not a welcome one to Nancy, as she had a promising career in progress in New York, but she quickly adapted to her new life in California.

The Mavitys settled in Oakland and in 1920 Nancy went to work for the *San Francisco Chronicle* writing book reviews and literary essays. In 1924, she accepted an assignment from *Sunset Magazine* for a series of articles written while traveling on her own for six months in Japan, China, Indonesia, Australia, and

New Zealand. This was a truly remarkable undertaking, as she had to leave her husband at home alone with two young children—their son John Barr had been born in 1921—in order to pursue this opportunity. Remarkable, yes, but simply a matter of course in the Mavity household.

In 1926, Nancy wrote a highly personal article on "The Wife, the Home, and the Job" for *Harper's Magazine* in which she extolled the virtues of the working wife and mother and fiercely advocated for a woman's right to choose her work and share parenting and housekeeping responsibilities with her husband. (She revisited this theme in a 1951 issue of *Harper's* with a follow-up article, "The Two-Income Family," reflecting on a quarter-century of working outside the home.)

In the meantime, she began writing books—all types of books. Nancy's first effort, *Responsible Citizenship*, a textbook on American politics co-written with her husband, appeared in 1923. This was soon followed by a volume of poetry dedicated to her daughter called *A Dinner of Herbs* and her first novel, *Hazard*, a largely autobiographical roman à clef. She also published a history of newspaper journalism, *The Modern Newspaper*, and a best-selling biography of celebrity evangelist Aimee Semple MacPherson, *Sister Aimee*.

It was when she went to work for the *Oakland Tribune* in 1925, however, that she found her true calling. In the retrospective published at her death, she is quoted as saying, "I went into newspaper work to enlarge my experience of people as an aid to fiction writing, then I stayed in it for its own sake."

Did she ever.

For the next three decades, the byline "By Nancy Barr Mavity" appeared regularly in the pages of the *Tribune*. She wrote colorfully and authoritatively on a myriad of topics—from crime reporting to social reform, from literary criticism to local interest stories—and "won scratches, bruises, scars and accolades as a reporter who let no man beat her on a big story." She covered a solar eclipse, labor strikes, and the Bay Area literary scene; she reported on the 1945 United Nations Conference in San Francisco; and she interviewed physicist Ernest O. Lawrence "when the University of California Cyclotron was but a gleam in his eye."

Nancy Barr Mavity's first mystery novel, *The Tule Marsh Murder*, made the scene in 1929 and introduced ace crime reporter James Aloysius Piper, "commonly called Peter," who is fiercely devoted to his paper, the *Herald*, and succeeds at his job by being relentless in his pursuit of a story, frequently conducting his own investigations without bothering to let the police in on the action. From 1929 to 1933, Peter Piper appeared in five additional novels; Mavity's last mystery, *The State Versus Elna Jepson*, is a 1937 stand-alone courtroom drama about an obstinately independent young woman accused of murdering the wife of the man she loves.

All of Mavity's mysteries were serialized in the pages of the *Oakland Tribune* prior to hardcover publication and are notable for their portrayal of the role of science in the detection of crime. Psychology and forensics frequently provide key clues to the solutions of the crimes. However, it is usually Peter Piper, not the police detectives, who advocates for modern criminological methods.

Over the course of the novels, Peter champions the uses of ballistics and chemistry (*The Other Bullet*), fingerprint analysis (*The Case of the Missing Sandals*), and blood spatter trajectories (*The Body on the Floor*) in uncovering murderers. Newspaper advertisements and book reviews frequently claimed that Mavity's fictions were based on actual criminal cases and true circumstances, and the striking resemblance of the murder victim in *The Case of the Missing Sandals* to Aimee Semple MacPherson did not go unnoticed in the press.

Undoubtedly, *The Tule Marsh Murder* was inspired by a real case that had captivated the San Francisco Bay Area public a few years earlier. In the summer of 1925, a human ear, with bits of scalp and hair attached, was discovered in the saltwater tule marshes of El Cerrito, an East Bay town just north of Berkeley. The subsequent homicide investigation was led by Berkeley's renowned chief of police August Vollmer and was aided by pioneering forensic criminalist Edward Oscar Heinrich, who by this time had earned a reputation as "America's Sherlock Holmes."

In 1910, Heinrich opened the nation's first private crime lab and solved numerous cases using a wide variety of scientific techniques—many unknown or unused before Heinrich employed them. In 1916, Vollmer recruited Heinrich to design America's first "cop college" and the School for Police was launched the following year at the University of California in Berkeley.

With the ear found in the tule marsh as a starting point, Heinrich was quickly able to determine that it belonged to a woman, probably in her twenties, whose natural blonde hair had hints of red and brown dyes. He also correctly determined other East Bay locations where additional body parts were likely to be found, including a pair of jawbones that, through dental analysis, identified her as thirty-one-year-old Bessie Ferguson, an Oakland woman who had gone missing shortly before the ear was discovered.

A few years later, Nancy Barr Mavity interviewed Heinrich and they corresponded for a time afterwards. When *The Tule*

Marsh Murder was published, she sent him a copy of the book and promised to base a character on him in a later novel.

In a lengthy dedication included in her fifth mystery, *The Man Who Didn't Mind Hanging*, Mavity addresses the use of real crimes in her novels. While admitting to incorporating elements of actual events into some of her plots, she downplays the connection between the Bessie Ferguson case and *The Tule Marsh Murder*, stating that "except for the title, there is nothing to suggest that crime."

No, Nancy, not quite nothing . . .

In Mavity's story, Dr. Cavanaugh, a clinical psychologist (who insists "I am not a criminologist"), is drawn into the mystery of a body burned beyond recognition that had been found just above the tule marsh on the slope of El Cerrito hill. A small patch of scalp with a few hairs still attached has escaped the flames, however, and from this Dr. Cavanaugh is able to deduce the following:

"That body belonged to a woman about forty years of age. She patronized an expensive beauty parlour, and had recently had what I believe is a marcel. . . . She was fair of skin, with the brown eyes and vivid colour that accompany this particular pigmentation. Her hair, naturally red, was darkened to auburn by the use of henna, and was worn long. . . ."

Clearly, Dr. Cavanaugh learned a thing or two from E.O. Heinrich. With these physical facts as a starting point, the murdered woman is quickly identified as Sheila O'Shay, an infamous singer recently married to publicity-shy millionaire Don Ellsworth, whose disappearance had been headline fodder for several days, and Peter Piper, who has managed to ingratiate himself into Cavanaugh's confidence, is off and running.

Mavity's fellow journalists praised her mystery novels for being particularly accurate in their portrayal of newshounds and newsrooms—not surprising considering that, as a crime reporter, she covered many of Northern California's most notorious criminal cases. She managed to get an exclusive interview with child murderer William Edward Hickman, scooping all the other papers, after she sneaked onto the train transporting him from Oregon to Los Angeles when it stopped in Oakland. She also provided her readers with extensive coverage of the trials of David Lamson, the advertising manager of Stanford University Press who was accused, convicted, retried twice, and eventually acquitted of murdering his wife, Allene (another of Heinrich's celebrated cases).

She became the first woman ever to spend a night behind the walls of Folsom Prison when she was assigned to report on the pardon hearing of Warren K. Billings who had been convicted, along with Tom Mooney, of the 1916 Preparedness Day bombing in San Francisco.

Although many of Peter Piper's news-gathering antics would never be tolerated by today's law enforcers, anecdotes from Mavity's own career bear notable similarities to those of her fictional hero. During one trial she was covering, she used a ladder to climb through the window of a vacated deliberation room, after the jury had been dismissed for the day, in order to gather up the contents of the wastebasket, writing a story for the next morning's edition on exactly how many ballots had been taken and what the votes were. In another, she risked facial burns by keeping her head next to a furnace pipe so that she could eavesdrop on a jury, and for three days fed the newspaper direct quotes from the deliberations.

Nancy was widowed when Arthur passed away in 1931, leaving her as a working single mother. As challenging as that must have been, she was certainly not going to let her new circumstance hold her back. In addition to continuing her full-time job at the *Tribune*, she also wrote her last three novels before her second marriage in 1938 to photographer Edward Almon "Doc" Rogers, who also worked for the *Tribune* and had photographed the great San Francisco earthquake and fire of 1906. It is unknown why she gave up writing fiction, but she certainly did not give up her association with the Bay Area's literary community.

In 1945, Mystery Writers of America (MWA) was formed to promote the genre and help ensure sufficient pay for mystery authors. But MWA was headquartered in New York, a very long way from the flourishing cadre of mystery writers on the West Coast. So, in 1947, the first regional branch of MWA was established in Northern California.

Its first meeting was held in San Francisco, with critic and writer Anthony Boucher elected chair, Lenore Glen Offord designated secretary, and Alfred Meyers as treasurer. Other Bay Area mystery writers in attendance were Robert Finnegan, Cary Lucas, Mary Collins, Miriam Allen de Ford, Darwin and Hildegarde Teilhet, Dana Lyon, Dora Richards Shattuck (aka "Richard Shattuck"), Eunice May Boyd, and Virginia Rath.

We know all of this because Nancy Barr Mavity was there, too. On March 2, 1947, the *Oakland Tribune* ran a lengthy article with the familiar by-line "By Nancy Barr Mavity," accompanied by the photographs of Doc Rogers, that described the festivities in her characteristic light-hearted prose:

"Crime Incorporated, with murder and mayhem, slow or sudden death and assorted dirty work at the crossroads, has invaded the Bay Area. Its practitioners have banded together to 'hold up' the public, demanding, in two words, more kudos and more kale. Two dozen lively promoters of death met conspiratorially, at the gunpoint of Anthony Boucher . . . to form a Western 'cell' of Mystery Writers of America, Inc., with the flourishing slogan, 'Crime does not pay—enough.' Over dinner and drinks (with or without cyanide) at a San Francisco restaurant, with the butt end of a .44 for gavel, officers were elected and arrangements made for monthly meetings, alternately in San Francisco and the Eastbay."

Many of those subsequent meetings were also documented in the pages of the *Tribune* by Nancy Barr Mavity. In her role as a reporter, she not only highlighted a fascinating aspect of the local social scene, she also legitimized mystery writers as an integral part of the San Francisco literary milieu. Following her death, the Northern California chapter of MWA lauded her contributions in a letter to the editor, "She was not only an outstanding practitioner of our trade . . . she was also one of our most helpful and valued friends, both in her official capacity as chief of your book section, and as an individual whom most of us knew and were proud to know."

Nancy Barr Mavity—as the author of widely-praised stories that stand the test of time, as a groundbreaking (and glass-ceiling shattering) crime reporter, and as a promoter and champion of her fellow purveyors of the detective novel—has certainly earned her place among the classics of the American mystery.

Randal S. Brandt
Berkeley, California

Bibliographical note: The life and career of E.O. Heinrich has been brilliantly documented by Kate Winkler Dawson in her 2020 book, *American Sherlock: Murder, Forensics, and the Birth of American CSI.* The correspondence between Heinrich and Mavity can be found in the Edward Oscar Heinrich Papers at the Bancroft Library, University of California, Berkeley.

Chapter I

THE DISAPPEARANCE of Mrs. Don Ellsworth ("Sheila O'Shay")—it was always printed in this fashion, usually with the addendum that Miss O'Shay's song and dance hit, "Burn 'Em Up," had made half a million dollars in royalties for its composer—had already been front-page stuff for three days.

To be sure, on the third day as on the first, there was no information beyond the stark fact that the ever-spectacular Sheila had spectacularly disappeared. But an essential factor in a big news story is continuity; the city editor's abhorrence of a vacuum far exceeds nature's. Therefore, in pursuance of tactics technically known as "nursing the story along," the newsboys were unintelligibly shouting "Huckstry!" to announce that the Ellsworth mystery still deserved the name.

One of them, at the moment, was roaming the street under Dr. Cavanaugh's window, hoarsely reiterating, "All about the Ellsworth mystery! Latest news of the missing actress! *Her*-ALD! *Her*-ALD!"

Dr. Cavanaugh, reclining on the chaise longue with a smoking stand nicely adjusted at his elbow and the *Journal of Abnormal Psychology* propped with its lower edge resting on the curve of his rotund middle, glanced fleetingly from the page before him to the window. He even let the *Journal* flatten itself out on his waist-coated arc for a moment, while he wondered at a human nature which rushes out to buy a paper, in order to find out that there are no further incidents to relate about people in whom the buyers have no reason to be interested.

As he reached to pick up the magazine, the telephone on the flat-topped mahogany desk across the room set up a series of intermittent summonses, insistent as an alarm clock.

"M-m. I thought so. About time," Dr. Cavanaugh grunted, heaving his large bulk from the chaise longue. Before picking up the receiver, however, he drew a nickel out of his trousers pocket and laid it on the smoking stand. It was a habit of Dr. Cavanaugh's to bet with himself on his own judgment. When he lost, the coin was deposited in a small elephant-shaped box on the desk—but the coins in the box were few.

"Dr. Cavanaugh speaking."

"Dr. Cavanaugh, this is Don Ellsworth. I wondered—may I come and talk to you?" The voice at the other end of the wire was embarrassed and yet urgent, speaking rapidly but with hesitations—the voice of a man who has held an impulse in check, only to act on it suddenly in the end.

Dr. Cavanaugh reached out for the nickel and restored it to his trousers pocket. Then he leafed rapidly through the pages of the memorandum calendar that stood close to the telephone on the desk.

"Certainly. I'm rather full up for the balance of the week. Say Friday—at four?"

Dr. Cavanaugh viewed the mouthpiece of the telephone with a faint smile as he made this test of Ellsworth's patience. From what he knew of Don Ellsworth, Friday at four would not suit him at all. But he did not permit a trace of that smile to colour his tone.

"But—I simply can't wait till Friday." The voice was more sure of itself now. If the speaker had reached his decision to call Dr. Cavanaugh against inner opposition, his impulse, when baulked from without, had gained singleness and strength. "It's urgent. Haven't you read the papers?"

"Only casually."

"It's about Sheila. I tell you, Doctor, I'm almost wild. I'm at the end of my rope. Couldn't I come over now—to-night?"

Dr. Cavanaugh glanced mournfully around the room, its outlines faintly blurred in the gray haze of tobacco smoke. The student lamp which he had brought from Germany in his university days and preferred to electricity as a reading light beamed mellowly down on the comfortably dented pillows of the chaise longue, on the sober gray-and-black covers of the *Journal of Abnormal Psychology*. He had had a hard day, delving persistently, delicately, indefatigably into the dark recesses of the mind of a patient afflicted with hysterical blindness. A hard and baffling day, with nothing to show for it in the way of results—yet.

"The surgeon of the mind—an operation that takes a year—and the need of as steady a hand as if one were extracting a bullet from the heart muscle," he mused as his gaze briefly circled the room.

His thick shoulders heaved slightly in an inaudible sigh. But it was characteristic that, once he had made his decision, he made no play of regret. He had scant patience with the form of self-aggrandizement which in granting a favour makes the recipient uncomfortable.

"All right, Don. Come along." The calm friendliness of his voice carried no hint of his relinquished evening's rest.

"I hate to impose on you like this. But Sheila——"

"If I hadn't been willing to see you, I'd have said so. I'll expect you in fifteen minutes."

And for fifteen minutes Dr. Cavanaugh was lost to the world, deep in an article on focal infection as a factor in dementia præcox.

Except for the outside entrance and separate doorbell, the room had none of the stigmata of a doctor's office. It was furnished as a library, and the books which covered two walls with a mosaic of warm, variegated colour were by no means exclusively technical. The half-dozen pictures that marched in line above the bare tops of the bookcases were noncommittal etchings—only the student versed in this somewhat austere art would have recognized these gray and white crisscrossed lines of ships and harbours and fragmentary streets as extremely valuable and, an artist would add, beautiful possessions. The chaise longue and the easy chairs were not too imposing to be comfortable. The only professional note on the wide desk with its worn green leather fittings was the unavoidable calendar pad—and even this was fitted with a cover and was usually kept closed.

But, for the matter of that, Dr. Cavanaugh was not an ordinary doctor. For his own purposes the room was as carefully equipped as an operating theatre for a surgeon. Besides, though unobtrusively, it expressed his own tastes, and Dr. Cavanaugh had reached a professional eminence which relieved him of the necessity of impressing patients. His treatments were as expensive and as hard to obtain as Freud's—and, he occasionally admitted with a humorous squint in his brown eyes which absolved the remark of conceit, being without Freud's single-minded genius, they were sometimes more successful.

He had now, in the late forties, reached the point where he could afford to take only the cases which interested him. Those cases were as likely as not to be undertaken for no fee at all—to be written up later in one of those terse, stylistic monographs which brought a blaze of light into the dark thickets of bejargoned medical journals. They were also likely to bring him into court as the last resort alienist of a harassed district attorney or a psychopathic millionaire. They had even brought him into the Sunday supplements and the front pages of metropolitan newspapers, where headline writers had been known to refer to him as the "criminal psychologist" and feature writers credited him with an astounding wizardry.

His solution of the Barnes-Hill double murder, three years after the police had given it up, had extended his reputation to the laity and had made his massive figure and his leonine head with its heavy features and surprisingly gentle brown eyes fair game for the cartoonist. What the laity could scarcely appreciate—although the chief of police did—was the skill with which he had contrived to put the explanation of that tortuous cats' cradle of facts into the hands of the authorities without making them appear to have been fools.

"I am not a criminologist," he always insisted. "The study of human motives has been my professional concern for a good many years. What I've picked up on the side is just a hobby—a hobby that happens to fit in with my professional interests. Clues? Well, we can't afford to ignore clues, though I'm no expert in that line. But the most revealing clues cannot be put under the microscope—they are in the workings of the human mind."

The cries of the newsboy had died away down the street when footsteps sounded on the flagged path leading around the side of the house to the office entrance. Dr. Cavanaugh rose and opened the door before the young man on the stoop had lifted his hand to the bell.

"Come in, Don. Take off your coat and have a cigar."

"This is awfully good of you, Doctor. There's nobody else home?"

"Barbara is out for the evening. She will be sorry to have missed you. But if you wanted to talk to me professionally, it's probably just as well."

"Yes—I——" The broken sentence died out in a mumble as Ellsworth turned to lay his coat and hat across the back of a chair.

Don Ellsworth's face, as he turned to the light, was a curious blend of anxiety, embarrassment, and the habitual self-assurance of one for whom money was accustomed to make all rough places smooth. The anxiety and the self-assurance remained, but it was impossible for embarrassment to linger in the impersonal, widely tolerant presence of Dr. Cavanaugh.

Don found himself relaxing in the encompassing arms of the chair and facing the older man with the relief of a child in a scrape who has found an understanding elder to whom to pour out his difficulties. A good part of Don's life, smothered in wealth since he first became known as the "millionaire baby," had been spent in getting into and out of scrapes, but they had all been in the tradition of such misdemeanours. The present situation found him without a code to direct him which way to turn.

"You read about Sheila—that she's gone? She disappeared a week ago without a trace. I've got to find out what has become of her!"

"A week ago," Dr. Cavanaugh said meditatively, clipping the end of his cigar and pushing the smoking stand nearer his visitor. "And the newspapers—which, I suppose, implies also the police—have known it for three days. Isn't your agitation a trifle—retarded?"

Chapter II

"I WISH to heaven the police could have been kept out of it altogether!" Don's heavy black brows drew together in a frown. He looked at the moment like a baulked and sulky boy.

"Indeed?" The doctor's voice barely rose to make the noncommittal word a question. He learned more from his patients by letting them talk than by quizzing them; and by applying the same technic to the normal, or even the criminal, mind, he had listened to some remarkable confessions unattainable by "third-degree" methods.

He waited, in a silence which lapped the room.

"I should have come to you in the first place!" Don burst out at last, tapping his cigar nervously against the ash tray. "Only—well, it's all such a mess. I hoped it could be covered up. I might have known! It's rather a difficult matter to discuss."

"Take your time." Dr. Cavanaugh settled back in his chair with the air of a man who does not even have to be patient.

The effect of this advice was to plunge his visitor into hurried speech.

"It was a week ago—a week ago last night, to be exact. Dinner was as usual. We always kept up a good front, you know.

And Sheila rather enjoyed playing the young matron. It was a new rôle for her—her other marriages, she said, had lacked the brownstone atmosphere. She was in high spirits, as usual. Even when we were alone, she never admitted by word or manner that——Oh, well!" Ellsworth hesitated, and then went on, leaving the sentence unfinished.

"Anyway, I'm sure that she wasn't worried or apprehensive or particularly excited about anything. Sheila isn't the worrying type, and as for apprehension—if she thought there was anything for her to be afraid of, she'd clap her hands together in that way she has, and go after it as a new thrill. But there was absolutely no sign of anything in the wind. I remarked when we had had our coffee that I was going around to the club—though, as a matter of fact, I didn't go, after all. I just took a long drive all by myself into the country, thinking about—things. When I left the house she was on her way upstairs; she said she was going to bed early and get a good night's sleep.

"That is the last I've seen of her. She left all the lights burning in her boudoir—they were still burning next morning. She didn't take anything with her, not even a suitcase. In the morning she just—wasn't there. You know Sheila, of course?"

The doctor had listened without interrupting Don's recital by so much as a nod or a gesture.

"Not very well, unfortunately," he answered easily. "We haven't seen much of you since your marriage, you know."

"No," Don said abruptly, and stopped.

"It was a mistake to be ashamed of your marriage," Dr. Cavanaugh observed impersonally. "It is always a mistake to be ashamed. It creates unnecessary difficulties. What you do, you do. Either don't do it, or stand by it. You always must go on from where you are, you know—not back."

"I did stand by it, didn't I? God knows——" The young man's voice was harsh with feeling.

"Mrs. Ellsworth left, and you want me to find her?" The older man prompted imperturbably.

"I want anything rather than all this blare—the very thing I'd give my eye teeth to avoid."

"You were not the one to report that your wife was missing, then?"

"I certainly wasn't. If you knew Sheila——"

"I saw her several times before she left the stage—and of course, as you know, we've met casually once or twice since. But that's an insufficient basis for determining what she would do."

"She's charming, of course—terribly charming." The savage tone robbed the words of all compliment. "She's—vital. When she wants a thing she simply gets it. And scandal means absolutely nothing to her. It isn't in her world. She wouldn't so much as laugh at it—she'd ignore it. It's been an asset to her, not a liability. She might go like that simply because she knows that there's nothing I could—or would be willing to—do about it. She might do anything!"

"Oh, no!" the doctor protested. "The number of things a given person might do is strictly limited—by that person. But in this case there's someone else involved. If you didn't report her disappearance, who did?"

"Mrs. Kane." Don's animosity toward Mrs. Kane was patent.

"Mrs. Kane?"

"She was Sheila's dresser, I think they call it. A hard-boiled old customer. When Sheila left the stage—when we were married"—his lips twisted wryly on the word—"she brought Mrs. Kane with her as a personal maid. She doesn't fit in at all with the rest of the staff. Her manners are atrocious. She's always resented me."

"Perhaps your manner to her was not exactly placating."

Don swept the comment aside with an impatient wave of his cigar.

"I don't know why Sheila kept her. She's not the devoted-old-retainer type at all. I've heard her speak to Sheila in a way that would cost any proper servant her place at once. Impudent and surly. It was she who found the lights burning in Sheila's boudoir the next morning. She had the nerve to come and ask me where 'Miss O'Shay' was. Nothing on earth could keep her from calling Sheila 'Miss O'Shay.' She knows I don't like it." Despite the anxiety that wrinkled his forehead, Don's injured tone was comically that of a spoiled child who is not used to having people do what he doesn't like.

The briefest of smiles hovered at the corners of Dr. Cavanaugh's lips, and was gone.

"And then?" The calm voice was like a guiding hand, leading Don back from his disgruntled consideration of the failings of Mrs. Kane.

"Of course, when I found she had gone like that, I was upset. And Mrs. Kane kept after me about it. I—I'm afraid I lost my temper." Don flushed uneasily. Those who knew him at all well knew of the futile rages which seized him, often over trivial matters, and seemed so childish in retrospect.

Dr. Cavanaugh glanced at him obliquely under cover of applying a match to a fresh cigar. The child who destroys his toys—and afterward cries to have them returned to him. The worst thing that could have happened to the millionaire baby was that his broken toys always had been restored, or replaced.

"Were you angry with Mrs. Ellsworth for leaving—or with Mrs. Kane for breaking the news to you, let us say, untactfully?"

"I don't know—both, I guess," Don floundered. "To tell the truth, I thought she might have done it just to create a stir. She loved to be the centre of a sensation—it had been her life for so long. It might have been a sudden impulse, the idea that she could plague me into making a search for her, and then show up, laughing, with some fresh newspaper clippings to add to her collection. I wouldn't even be surprised if this Kane woman knew a good deal more about it than she is telling to me or to anyone!"

Chapter III

"You must remember that your distrust of Mrs. Kane may be founded on nothing more objective than your personal dislike for her," the doctor suggested. "You're not much given to discounting your judgments in the light of your emotions, are you?"

Don accepted the mildly voiced criticism with sulky dignity.

"I should hardly say that my wife's maid was important enough for personal dislike," he said.

"She may be very important, indeed, for all we know. At any rate, if her object was to rouse you to a display of wrath, she evidently succeeded. Can you recall exactly what you said to her? I don't mean to be hard on you—your reaction was doubtless quite normal." This time the doctor's smile was definite, even genial. "Whatever it was, I've in all probability heard a good many worse things. And I don't regard it as my job to indulge in moral judgments on my fellows. The most I'm likely to say to you is that you were unwise."

"Well, I—I finally told her I didn't give a damn! She turned her back and left; and the next thing I knew, the police were ringing the front doorbell and asking impertinent questions. I told them as little as I could." There was a grim satisfaction under Don's harassment.

"And did you?" the doctor asked.

Don looked up from a moody contemplation of his shoe.

"Did I what?"

"Give a damn."

The young man leaped to his feet, his hands furiously clenching and unclenching at his sides.

"Look here, you can't——" he began, choking.

Dr. Cavanaugh did not move a muscle from his relaxed position in the big chair.

"Never mind," he said quietly. "I apologize. It was your own statement, you know. Now what, precisely, do you want me to do in the matter?"

"I want you to get me out of it with a minimum of publicity. Everything I've ever done—and it hasn't been much—has been taken up by the papers. If I got lit after a football game at college, or took a chorus girl to dinner, it was spread all over the country. I can't stand any more of it. I can't, and I won't. Just because I happen to have money, my wife can't even leave me without their getting out extras about it."

"If she did leave you," Dr. Cavanaugh amended, so low that he might have been only thinking aloud.

"But——" Don's face was a study in angry bewilderment.

"There are other possibilities. I doubt, in fact, if the one you have mentioned would be the first to occur to most men in your position."

"Well, she couldn't very well be kidnapped from her own boudoir, in a house full of servants. And by the same token, she couldn't have met with an accident, or have been held up by bandits, without leaving a trace. I did not mean to speak harshly of her just now, when I said she might have vanished just to plague me. She wouldn't set out deliberately to hurt anyone—she merely wouldn't notice whether they were hurt or not, if they got in her way. And you must remember that Sheila was used to the most complete freedom of action. She wasn't the sort of person you could put in a bottle and keep there. Suppose she turned up in a week or two and announced that she had merely gone away to pay a sudden visit and that it was purely her own affair, not that of the police. A pretty fool I'd look!"

"Yes," Dr. Cavanaugh agreed softly. "But, you see, she hasn't turned up."

"No-o," Ellsworth admitted slowly, "but I still think Mrs. Kane may know where she is."

"My dear man, beware of obsessions!" The doctor's tone was almost bantering. "However, you may be right, of course; she may."

"I've even thought every day that I might get a letter from Sheila herself, with an explanation."

"And if she did leave you—you'll have to pardon me for being very personal—would she have any reason that you know of? If you let her see as plainly as you have let me see that you regarded your marriage as a failure, the knowledge could not have made her particularly happy, could it?"

"She'd never have left me just because I wasn't enthusiastic about our marriage," Don said with bitter emphasis. "She was getting very much what she wanted out of it—until she decided that she wanted something else. I did think of that, of course—that she might have gone with another man. She could turn any man she wanted blind and crazy. I know, because she did it to me—and the names of some of the others have been public property. Only, unless it was someone out of the past, I don't know who it could be. Sheila had not the slightest desire to give me grounds for divorce. I really think, in a way, that she wanted to settle down—to play the great lady. At any rate, there hasn't been a shred of gossip about her in that respect—and when there isn't any gossip about Sheila, you can depend upon it that gossip looked around pretty closely before giving it up."

"Your own opinion seems to be, then, that your wife must have left of her own free will because there was no way for her to be removed against it; and that, on the other hand, she did not leave either alone or in an elopement because she was satisfied with things as they were. That seems to be rather an impasse."

"It is. And it's just because the more I think of it, the more impossible it all seems, that I've had to seek somebody else's advice on it."

"As I understand it, since Mrs. Ellsworth's departure is already in the public eye, the only way to turn that eye in some other direction is to find out what has become of her; and, if possible, to do it before the activities of the police stir up more publicity. Is that a fair statement of the situation?"

"If you put it that way——"

"I do. That's the bare bones of it, as I see them—and if you come to me at all, you mustn't expect me to put little paper ruffles on them." Dr. Cavanaugh's manner, for the first time, was authoritative. The smile which warmed the sternness of his words did not mitigate the fact that he was laying down terms, to be taken or left. "And why, by the way, did you come to me?" he added.

"I hoped you'd be able to tell me what she'd be most likely to do," Don said meekly.

"I don't know enough about her to do that offhand. I'm no magician, you know. Any science, even such a muddled science as psychology, must have its laboratory material. I couldn't undertake the case professionally. There's too little to go on. But simply as an unofficial adviser, I'm willing to look into it—if you're quite sure you want me to."

"Of course I'm sure! Didn't I tell you——"

"Wait a moment." The limpid brown eyes took on the polished hardness of agate. "If I go into this at all, it is to find out the facts. Suppose the consequences prove even more unpleasant than those you are now facing."

"They couldn't be much more unpleasant." Don looked suddenly tired and white. It is a severe handicap to be brought up to consider the world your tame kitten and then to find that it has claws. "Any fee that you choose to name, of course—and I'll be glad to leave a retainer——"

"There'll be no fee about it; if for no other reason than because you and Barbara used to be pretty good friends."

"You know—about Barbara—I——"

"You did what you had to do—or thought you had to do, which amounts to the same thing. Besides, there is another reason. It is barely possible that this affair may become too big for our private handling. The police have been known to avail themselves of my services. I shall certainly do nothing to invite such a request, but if they should appeal to me, I must feel absolutely free. However, let's cross no bridges. We'll hope it won't come to that."

"I hope not," Don agreed fervently. "Meanwhile, what would you advise me to do?"

"This Mrs. Kane—is she still in the house?"

"Yes. We're on a plane of—of armed neutrality at present. But I couldn't very well ask her to go——"

"Don't. She knows your wife perhaps better than you do,

certainly better than I do. That means that she may be useful, whether she wants to be or not."

"You think——"

"I have no reason to think anything—yet."

Dr. Cavanaugh's leisurely emergence from the deep chair left Don no alternative but to rise also.

"I wish I knew more," he said as they stood in the open doorway.

"Perhaps you know the old Elizabethan recipe for cooking hare. It begins, 'First, catch your hare.' " And with this dubious reassurance Don had to be content.

Chapter IV

"Piper!" The city editor's raucous voice rose above the clack of typewriters and the murmured exchange of jokes in the *Herald* local room.

Peter Piper untangled his legs from the rounds of his chair, caught up a sheet of copy paper and a pencil, and ambled over to the city desk.

"I want you to get a follow story on the Ellsworth case."

"Anything new?"

"There isn't anything new. That's the trouble. We've got to nurse it along till there is. It may blow up any time, of course, but it's a great story while it lasts. And it's still lasting."

The city editor, who on dull days was a man to avoid like a violent and insufficiently caged wild animal at the zoo, was content as a cat in a bed of catnip when a big story broke.

Peter Piper's long, mobile face, which had drooped disconsolately over his typewriter, was slit by a wide grin.

"What's the dope?" he asked, his bright, nearsighted eyes waking up from a bored contemplation of the bulletin board.

"Here are the clippings on the husband. We've used all that stuff, of course. But he'll bear watching. He's not telling all he knows, not by a damn sight. See if you can get anything on him. Meanwhile, you might go out and see if you can get an interview with Cavanaugh."

"Cavanaugh! I didn't know he was in on this."

"He isn't—not yet. But he's likely to be. When the police are in doubt—and they seem to be in quite considerable doubt this trip—they always play Cavanaugh. Besides, he's good stuff any time. Get him on the psychology of why wives leave home, or something like that."

Peter blinked—an exaggerated blink which conveyed a decidedly adverse opinion of the reasonableness of city editors.

"Hell's bells, Jimmy!" he protested. "Cavanaugh's about as easy to interview as the Dalai Lama. He charges forty dollars a look, by appointment only, and then if he doesn't like your looks—good-night!" Peter Piper was a student of law in his off hours, and was entitled to wear (though he never did) a Phi Beta Kappa key, but his office vocabulary was strictly in the vernacular.

"Now don't go off thinking you can't get an interview with Cavanaugh. Because I know you will. Here, take these." The city editor thrust into Peter's hands a sheaf of clippings from the office library, each one pasted on a strip of coloured paper, and turned to the telephone.

"Lord, what an assignment!" Peter groaned aloud. The groan was entirely spurious, because the stimulus of doing difficult things was the wine of life to him. Like all reporters, he affected to be blasé and cynical, and like many of them, though he would never commit the outsider's solecism of calling newspaper work a game, it really was a game to him, played with immense and carefully concealed gusto.

A moment later he emerged from the locker room wearing a soft gray hat—a hat with shapeless crown and brim a series of irregular ripples from exposure to many rains. He was whistling under his breath. What tune there was to this musical performance consisted of two phrases, endlessly reiterated, in a lugubrious, wailing minor calculated to make the human listener long to lift his nose and howl.

"Put it out!" growled the water-front man, whose desk adjoined Peter's. Peter stopped whistling long enough to grin, then absent-mindedly resumed his wailing cadence at the precise note where he had left off. He tossed all the clippings but one into a drawer which already contained carbon paper, cigarettes, a torn bag of peppermints, an assortment of very soft black copy pencils, and an upset box of paper clips. The remaining clipping he thrust into his coat pocket, which already bulged with several sheets of folded copy paper.

"You'll emit that series of sounds once too often some day," the water-front man said, "and there'll be another ax murder. 'Crazed Reporter Slays Mate.' What's the good cheer?"

"Oh, one of Jimmy's wild-goose chases. Nothing to it. It's bound to be a flop. If Jimmy got the idea that there was a cheesemongers' convention being held on the moon, he'd send some poor devil of a reporter out to cover it—and, by heck, he'd get so firmly fixed in the idea that he mustn't come back without the story that the chances are he'd get there!"

Nevertheless, Peter was cheerful.

"Hoo-oo-oo, hu-hu-hu-hoo." The wailing notes were cut short by his efforts to dodge a wadded piece of copy paper hurled after him by the water-front man. He ducked with exaggerated alacrity and made a hasty exit into the library.

"Say, Ben, dig up what we've got on this bird." He thrust the clipping which he had brought from the local room into the hand of the library attendant. "The society department must have run a picture at some time or other. If not, of what earthly use are they, I ask it?"

A few minutes later he had recrossed the local room, still whistling, and slammed the door behind him. He angled his battered car out of the *Herald's* parking lot and favoured the watchman with a hoarse honk of greeting. Peter called his car "Bossy," because, he explained, it had a crumpled horn like the cow in "The House That Jack Built." It also had four crumpled fenders whose waves and dents were only to be matched by the waves and dents in Peter's hat. It was painted bright green, and there were two bullet holes in the side curtains, relics of Peter's rather too prompt arrival on the scene of a shooting fray between the police and a fugitive hold-up man. Peter would not have exchanged it in even trade for a next year's model Rolls-Royce.

Twenty minutes later he parked hastily, with a shriek of brakes, opposite the house of Dr. Cavanaugh. The haste was due to the fact that a small sport coupé, very shiny as to nickel trimmings, was at the moment drawing up at the Cavanaugh entrance. Peter's long legs swung over the door, whose catch had a habit of sticking, and by the time the girl in the sport coupé had alighted and clicked the door shut behind her he was standing on the sidewalk beside her, hat in hand.

Chapter V

PETER SURVEYED the girl with one rapid glance, and took a chance.

"'I'm a poor man, your honour,'" he began.

The girl took one step backward, and stopped. The backward step was the first reaction of one startled by an unexpected voice at her elbow. But Barbara Cavanaugh was a girl who usually stopped to look things over before running away from them.

She saw before her a tall young man in a baggy blue suit. His thick black hair sprang up recalcitrantly from a centre part. His long face was slit by a wide, intelligent mouth which divided a determined out-thrusting chin from bright and peering gray eyes.

Barbara hesitated for a moment, then grinned back.

"'You're a very poor speaker,'" she capped. "And while you're undoubtedly mad enough, you'd never do for the Mad Hatter—with that hat."

"I knew it!" Peter crowed. "You look so exactly like Alice in Wonderland grown up that I had to risk it. I really am in the deuce of a hole, but if you'd said, 'Sir!' or 'How dare you!' I suppose I'd just have had to stay in it."

Peter forbore to tell her that he had diligently studied photographs of Barbara Cavanaugh in the *Herald*'s morgue, and had already decided that she looked like Alice in Wonderland grown up. The clipping at present crumpled in his coat pocket had led him straight from the city editor's desk to the library's photograph files—but there was no use exposing the machinery behind an inspiration.

Barbara did indeed bear a resemblance to Tenniel's immortal child. She was very straight and slender, and so short that her face was habitually lifted a little. Her straight hair, yellow verging to soft brown, was combed smoothly back from her forehead and lifted behind ears that had nothing to fear from exposure. She achieved the difficult feat of appearing quaint, even with a shingled coiffeur and attired, as now, in a white tennis dress rumpled from active play and a sweater of vivid rose. Perhaps the effect was unconsciously favoured by the shy and dazzled look in her wide-set brown eyes. Barbara had lived in an orphan asylum until her fourteenth year, and she had never recovered from the wonder of life, which had begun as an inexorable mechanism and had miraculously taken on the aspect of a fairy tale.

She stood tapping the end of her tennis racket up and down on the sidewalk.

"But you couldn't have been after seeing me!" When agitated or puzzled, Barbara's voice—a low and somewhat breathy voice, like the beginnings of wind in leaves—relapsed into the diction of her orphan-asylum days.

"I just was, though!" Peter asserted. "I'm a newspaper reporter, God help it, and I'm out on the Ellsworth case."

"I know nothing about it!" Barbara said sharply.

Peter's eyebrows lifted slightly. She'd been rather too quick about that. He swiftly reviewed in his mind the information contained in those clippings pasted to coloured slips of paper, with the typed heading, "Cavanaugh, Barbara." It was a slim little file compared with the bulging manila envelope devoted to the exploits of her father, as chronicled in the press. From it emerged a general conception of Barbara as a member of the younger country-club set, more addicted to athletics than to formal social functions. Barbara with a silver cup or two, Barbara as runner-up in the inter-club tennis tournament. Barbara arrested for speeding and naively telling the judge as she paid her fine that she'd "like to leave something extra for the cop—he was such a pleasant cop and absolutely in the right!" (A good little freak story, that had been.) Barbara's name underlined in red pencil in the society chatter of "Suzanne." What did this engaging youngster have to do with Sheila O'Shay, who must have crossed the forty line (though dates were very hard to find in all the stories about her), who boasted in Paris that two men had fought a duel over her and another had committed suicide in despair of winning her favour, all on the same day.

And yet—there was that bit about Ellsworth. It might mean nothing, of course; Ellsworth, wrapped in the glamour of his fabulous wealth, had always been copy. There was Ellsworth's sudden, unheralded marriage to Sheila O'Shay a little less than a year ago, and the equally sudden omission of his name from the lists of parties where Barbara was to be found. Sheila, of course, in her own sphere, was glamorous enough for anybody. In these days only the most faded of dowagers would decline to meet the latest successor to Helen of Troy. Had Ellsworth purposely kept himself and his wife out of Barbara's way? All this was the vaguest speculation—but Barbara's quick and unnecessary disavowal had undoubtedly given him a lead.

"Of course you couldn't possibly know anything about the Ellsworth case," he agreed, as if so foolish a notion had never entered his head. "Nevertheless, it's because of that case that I've looked you up. There's a point on which I think you might help me. If I may talk to you for just a few minutes?"

"And why should I?" Barbara said coldly. "I'm not so very used to stopping on the street and talking to strange young men."

Her face had shut down as if a blind had been drawn across a window. Barbara, who on ordinary occasions could easily have passed for sixteen, suddenly looked all of her twenty-three years. Her lips tightened, losing their childish curve. Her eyes flitted from side to side, from the coupé at the curb to the doorway of the big house. Peter suddenly thought of a chipmunk which he had caught when he was a boy, and had held in his hands. It had lain quite still in his imprisoning fingers, its eyes darting from side to side as hers were doing now.

"I think you should talk to me," he said with slow emphasis, "because the Ellsworth affair may turn out to be a very serious case. As you know nothing about it, it might save you from future annoyance to make that point extremely clear at the beginning."

Her antagonism was an unsheathed sword between them. Her eyes steadied, fixed themselves upon him in a long, considering stare. At that moment Peter became aware that Barbara Cavanaugh was no empty-headed little fool. Whatever he got from her, he would have to win.

She twisted the racket round and round in her hands. Then she turned without another word and opened the door of the coupé, slipping into the driver's seat and holding the door open for him to enter.

The racket clattered unheeded to the pavement. As he stooped to pick it up before seating himself in the car beside her, Peter's eyebrows once again lifted.

Chapter VI

Peter Piper had all the normal susceptibility of a young man to the charm of a pretty girl. The difference between him and the usual young man was that he had learned to gauge its effect, discount it, and lay it neatly on one side where it would not interfere with his judgment. The life of a reporter early teaches the lesson that women—even young and pretty women—are human beings. Peter had looked into more than one pair of wide and innocent eyes, had listened to more than one sweet and persuasive voice, had responded amiably to more than one appealing smile, and had discovered that all these attractions might not prevent their possessor from passing bad checks or engaging in the art of blackmail. Experience tends to dissipate the rosy and distorting mist in which one sex views the other; but the reporter quaffs strong and numerous draughts of experience beyond the limits of his personal affairs. If he cannot carry that brew with a clear head, he is soon advised to seek a more congenial career, in which he will be the only loser if his sympathies run counter to the facts.

Peter's head was very clear indeed. He was aware of the faint, tingling exhilaration of following a lead which had turned in an unexpected direction. The fact that Barbara was attractive to look upon enhanced her newspaper value; it did not in the least befuddle Peter's faculties. He was capable of proceeding precisely as if she were an angular spinster of all too certain years—which may be lack of chivalry or its fine-drawn furthest development.

As he glanced sidewise at Barbara's averted profile and noted the firm curve of her chin and the breadth of brow belying the childishness of her short, tilted nose and delicate colouring, he paid her the unspoken compliment of not underestimating her intelligence. She was, for the moment at least, his antagonist. And experience had taken out of him any masculine conceit that, being a woman, she was therefore too helpless a foeman to be worthy of his steel.

Barbara showed that she deserved the compliment by sitting, quite still and silent, in her corner of the coupé.

"What I really came for," Peter observed conversationally, "was to see if you wouldn't help me by using your influence to get me an interview with your father."

"You said you came on the Ellsworth case," Barbara took him up quickly. Her hands lay quiet in her lap, but there was a tense watchfulness in the poise of her small, alert figure. The years had dropped from her, dropped like pebbles flung soundlessly from a cliff edge in to the sea. She was once again the orphan-asylum child, stamped by the hard, unremitting effort to hold her own, to clutch, bit by bit, at fragmentary advantage in that regimen so inimical to the spirit of childhood.

"So I did," Peter assented. "The office sent me out to get an interview with Dr. Cavanaugh on the case—his views on the psychology of runaway wives, with sidelights on husbands from whom wives disappear—something like that."

"My father doesn't see interviewers—surely you knew?" Barbara faced him now, once again the self-possessed young woman of wealth and position. Her polite, remote voice was calculated to put a presumptuous reporter in his place.

But Peter was not to be intimidated by a society manner.

"You're ever so much more like Alice in Wonderland than Lady Clara Vere de Vere, really," he said with a disarming smile. "Look here! I hoped you'd help a fellow out—it's my job, you know. I came because I was sent; but since I was sent, I've got to use every effort to get what I was sent for. That's reasonable, isn't it?"

"Ye-es," Barbara admitted. "That's your point of view. But I'm much more likely to take my father's. There's a little thing like loyalty, you know. You play on my sympathies to get me to persuade Father, as a favour, to do something he wouldn't do otherwise. Well, supposing that I could—I won't!" The set of Barbara's chin was very firm indeed.

"Not even to help out Don Ellsworth?"

"What—do you mean?" Barbara's voice was little more than a gasp.

"You and Mr. Ellsworth were privately engaged to be married—before he married Miss O'Shay," Peter calmly asserted.

"How do you know?" The words came out before she could stop them. She bit her lip, and a slow flush mounted to her forehead and drained away again.

"Look here," Peter said kindly, "I haven't any ill motive against any of you. I'm quite willing to be frank. I simply guessed it. Whatever Don Ellsworth does has a way of getting into the papers; and one of the things that got in, by way of society gossip from our Del Monte correspondent, was that you and he were seen together a great deal just prior to his sudden marriage. I've the clipping here. But there's no reason why you should mind; the admission is certainly nothing against you."

"But what does it matter? Why did you want to know? You surely don't mean that you're going to drag that in? I was a fool to let you trick me like that!" Barbara's voice was bitter with accusation of both herself and him.

"It matters just this much," Peter said steadily. "There's more in this Ellsworth business than meets the eye—though goodness knows it's been meeting the eye plenty these last few days. Suppose that young Ellsworth had a reason for wishing his wife out of the way. Suppose that you were the reason."

"Gracious, you do leap to melodrama!" Barbara's smile flashed out a moment, and was gone. "If everybody who married somebody else than the first girl whose name the gossips connected with his were to change his mind and murder his wife, the world would be an even more jolly place for the newspapers than it is."

Peter's eyebrows rose.

"Murder?" he murmured gently. "So far as I know, nobody has mentioned that the Ellsworth case involves a murder."

He saw Barbara's teeth catch her lower lip. Then, as if warned against allowing her features to betray her, she released it and turned to him a composed and inscrutable face.

"Your own phrase, I believe, was that Mr. Ellsworth might wish his wife 'out of the way.' Putting someone out of the way is a familiar idiom, isn't it? Pardon me if I misinterpreted your meaning."

Peter beamed upon her with frank admiration. He could discount personal attraction, but he knew better than to discount quickness of wit. Peter disliked fools, even when they made his own task more simple.

"You reserve all your naps for your sleeping hours, don't you!" he commented.

Barbara ignored the tribute.

"I might remind you that your inspired flight of imagination has no string tied to it, to hold it down to mere evidence. You must know that you can't print any such insinuation. Mr. Ellsworth would be after you for libel in no time!"

"I knew you were a bright girl!" Peter's gray eyes shone with enthusiasm. "I didn't suppose society buds had a chance to accumulate that much common sense. The point is, it's a working hypothesis; and working hypotheses sometimes accumulate proof while they work. Now you see why it would be a good thing for you to get your father to give me that interview."

Chapter VII

BARBARA PONDERED Peter's last statement, with its sudden shift of ground.

"No," she said finally, "I don't see what interviewing my father can possibly have to do with it."

"You thought my hypothesis flighty and libellous and a few little things like that—not a nice hypothesis at all. Well, I'm not wedded to it. Only I'm addicted to theories—I really can't live comfortably without one. Your father might present me with a pleasing substitute, devoid of dynamite. Even if he doesn't, he's always good copy. He would distract my attention from these imaginative flights."

"This sounds like a novel sort of blackmail." Barbara's face was white, but her voice was cool. Not for nothing had she spent the first fourteen years of her life on the defensive against the world. "Naturally, I don't care to have the fact that Mr. Ellsworth and I were once—very good friends dragged into print in connection with a sensational story. I should dislike it extremely. The rest of your flight into the blue is sheer piffle, and you know it."

Her voice vibrated in a quick gust of anger; but under that burst of indignation Peter detected a note of anxiety.

"You wouldn't dare print a word of it—you're trying to frighten me with bogies. I used to cry all alone in the dark, because I knew there was a black leopard crouched in the corner of the room, where the broom and dustpan stood in the daytime. Nobody ever bothered to come and console me. Well, it was good training. I had to learn to meet and know my bogies, alone in the dark—and to conquer them. So, you see, I recognize a bogie when I see one—even a grown-up one."

For an instant a whimsical smile flitted across Barbara's eyes, like the shadow of a cloud drifting across a meadow. Then her face hardened again.

"It comes to this, doesn't it? You offer to sell your silence about my personal affairs for an interview with my father."

"Not exactly—though I admit you sound devastatingly logical." Peter remained invincibly debonaire. "But it really isn't so bad as that. Remember, there is an actual possibility—even a probability—that the disappearance of Mrs. Ellsworth involves a crime. At least we'll have to go on that assumption until the lady herself turns up to tell us differently. If that assumption is correct, finding out the facts is a far more important consideration than your very natural dislike of having your personal affairs become public property. I have gained the definite information that you were formerly engaged to Ellsworth; and there's nothing to prevent my making use of the facts gleaned in this interview with you. On the other hand, if I had a chance to talk the case over with your father, he might see things from another angle—turn up something quite different and more important. I'm more than willing to admit that he's a darn sight smarter sleuth than I am. I'd cheerfully let him knock all my flights of fancy into a cocked hat."

The slight figure in the driver's seat turned sidewise, facing Peter squarely, rigidly erect.

"You said you were being frank. Well, I'm going to be frank, too, Mr.——"

"Piper—James Aloysius Piper, commonly called Peter.' "

"Mr. Piper. I'm not a society bud—at least, only a grafted one. I'm a guttersnipe, really. I grew up in a foundlings' home. I was a homely, scrawny little thing, and my hair was straight, so the ladies looking for blue-eyed, curly-haired little darlings always passed me by. They'd come and look us over, you know. And at last they didn't send for me any more, even to be looked over. After you're seven years old, there's not much chance. They put me down as 'unadoptable.' And all the time, as soon as I was old enough to think anything at all, I lived in two worlds. There was no hope for me in the real world, except to be put out to service as soon as I was old enough."

Barbara's eyes were gazing, unseeingly, through the window of the coupé beyond Peter's shoulder. Her voice rushed on, low and breathless:

"But I vowed I wouldn't be a guttersnipe—in my soul. Somebody sent an old set of Howard Pyle's King Arthur books to the orphanage in a Christmas box. I read about those knights over and over. I lived in those stories. I didn't think much about honesty, but I came to care a lot about honour. Loyalty. The aristocratic virtues. The kind that are useless and difficult and that are not calculated to get you anywhere—if you are a guttersnipe. They had a reality beyond the reality of the foundlings' home. Incorruptible. Incorruptible beauty."

The hurried voice died away. Peter crouched forward in his seat, saying nothing.

"Well, when I was fourteen years old, Dr. Cavanaugh was called in as consultant for one of the children, who had what they call a psychoneurosis. Sensory anaesthesia it was—it doesn't happen so very often." Barbara's voice resumed its normal tone. "He is like that, you know. He will take any case, no matter how poor the patient, if it interests him. He saw me in the hall—almost ran over me, in fact, in the dim corridor—and when he had set me on my feet, he stopped to talk to me, casually. I stood there with my back against the wall, and before he left I had told him what I had never told anyone before. I had told him about the other side of me—the side that wasn't a guttersnipe.

"That's all, really—except that the chance stumble over an awkward little girl in an orphan-asylum corridor changed all of life for me. I didn't know then, of course, that Dr. Cavanaugh was a great man, that I was the simplest sort of 1-2-3 problem in his hands. I only knew that I wasn't turned in on myself any more. There was someone else, now, who knew about that inside world of mine. I used to slip around the corridors like a little gray flitter-mouse on the days when he came to visit his patient. I wouldn't have taken a step toward him or spoken to him for the world. But he always found me, and stopped to talk, or to let me talk, rather. I'd save up things in the night to say to him, hoard them, and then pour them all out, pell-mell. He was the first human being, remember, to whom I had ever really talked."

Barbara paused, her dreaming eyes fixed on vacancy. There was no sound from the figure beside her. She might even have forgotten his presence.

"And then, as soon as the papers could be put through, he adopted me—me, the 'unadoptable' child, who had no other expectation in life than to live on in that gray limbo of drab painted walls. He gave me more than luxury, more than education and normal amusements. He gave me life itself. If there happens to be a heaven, the thing that will shine out in Dr. Cavanaugh's record isn't the books that he's written, or the cases he's solved, or the cures he's made. If St. Peter tried to shut him out, there'd be the ghost of a little girl in a gray orphan-asylum frock pulling the gate open with her scrawny, unkept hands." Barbara glanced down briefly at her slim manicured fingers. "So you see"—she leaned back against the side window and turned on Peter the clearest, most ingenuous of smiles—"I'm not likely to try to bamboozle Dr. Cavanaugh for anybody, in any circumstances whatever!"

Peter shook himself. He came, with an inner crash, out of a daze into the bumptious world of reality. His eyes scanned the face, tilted slightly upward, confronting him. There was a trace of inner triumph in that lingering smile.

"Is it possible," Peter mused aloud, "that you were clever enough to tell me all this in order to tie my hands—because you know that I can't possibly write anything about you now without your permission? I'm a bum reporter, I guess," he added disgustedly, "but I couldn't do it."

"It is quite possible," Barbara assented calmly. "I spent the most impressionable years of my life in fending for myself, single-handed. You mustn't forget that I'm still essentially a guttersnipe."

Chapter VIII

PETER PIPER drove Bossy back to the *Herald* office in a state of inner turmoil such as he had seldom known.

"Well—for the moment—you win!" he had said. And Barbara had not refused the hand which Peter extended. At that moment of parting she had looked more than ever like Alice in Wonderland grown up.

Impossible to connect a girl like that with a secret—perhaps a sinister secret. Why, she would not have looked out of place playing house with acorn dishes under a spreading tree! Peter smiled at the picture—a dreamy boy's smile, such as no member of the *Herald* staff had ever seen on his face.

He brought himself up with a start. Because a girl was young and pretty—childlike, even—was no reason at all why she might not be capable of the whole range of human passions and acts. The cleverest woman forger of her time, interviewed by Peter in the city jail where she awaited trial, had been a neat, motherly person, who looked as if she spent her afternoons in baking cookies and her evenings in tatting. Mary Saunders, the "tiger woman," who had killed her rival by inviting her to call and then efficiently battering her skull with the fire tongs, had a sweet, appealing face and the air of one misunderstood by a cruel and captious world.

And there was more, much more, to Barbara Cavanaugh than an attractive face.

"That's where women have the edge on us every time!" Peter growled. "There's something to that Turkish veil idea. If they all wore veils, they'd get away with considerably less."

He forcibly clawed his mind away from the intrusive image of Barbara's yellow-brown hair curving above small, close-set ears. He even shut his eyes, thereby narrowly missing collision with a lumbering truck.

"All that aside——" he murmured aloud.

All that aside, a wave of spontaneous admiration lifted him on its crest.

"Hoo-oo-oo, hu-hu-hu-hoo," he whistled under his breath.

"That girl is no fool," he crowed, and found an inexplicable delight in the admission. Well, he was no fool either, if it came to that. Suppose, with those fantastic, story-book notions of honour in her head, she had felt that Don Ellsworth's defection was an affront to be avenged. Suppose she had taken matters into her own hands to oust Sheila O'Shay as an interloper. Suppose——Nothing to be proved as yet, but a good deal that was worth watching. Peter Piper was seized with a desire to understand Barbara, to know of a surety what unifying reality lay behind that wide brow and tip-tilting nose and firm chin. He wanted to know. He wanted to know, not because it might be news, but because the knowledge had somehow become important to him.

And meanwhile? Meanwhile he had a great follow story. Dr. Cavanaugh, when he had moved west from New York, officially retired—though his reputation made complete retirement impossible—had introduced Barbara as his daughter, which, indeed, she legally was. The romantic Cinderella story of her adoption from a foundlings' home, her secret engagement to Don Ellsworth, the spectacular young multimillionaire—a great story! And written as Peter Piper would write it, delicately, with the fairy-tale quality in it.

"There's a little thing like loyalty." Peter found that, remembering her words, he remembered almost audibly the tone of her voice, like a little wind in the leaves.

But his loyalty was to his paper, not to a girl whom he had seen only once, just as hers was to her father, not to him. Personalities must not interfere. That was the code. He remembered the legend of "Big Joe" McCullen, owner of a paper in Sacramento, who had refused to suppress the story in his own paper when his boy went wrong and was picked up for stealing an automobile in the course of a drunken spree. That was the honour of newspaperdom.

And yet—was it all warped, perverted, narrow, this code that the paper came before all else? There was more to life than the newspapers. This girl's life, for instance——

Peter shot across a boulevard stop sign, and listened with unaccustomed meekness to the irate words of the traffic cop. The neatly printed "Press Car" sign on Bossy's grimy windshield goaded the policeman to fury.

"You reporters think you own the earth!" he bellowed.

But Peter did not respond with the expected retort, and the policeman, somewhat disappointed by a too complete success, retired to his corner.

However, the encounter served to clear Peter's mind. He found that, unawares, he had arrived at a decision. It was a compromise decision, and he admitted with wry honesty that it marked his deviation from the singleness of his newspaper code. Nevertheless, he knew what he would do. He would hold the story, but he would keep an eye on Barbara Cavanaugh. He gave that hostage to his gods. And if it broke big—then there would be no question. If there was a direct connection between Barbara Cavanaugh and the disappearance of Sheila O'Shay, he would have no choice but to act. For the present, Jimmy would have to be satisfied with a report of "nothing doing," and if he didn't like it, he could jolly well do the other thing! At the thought of facing Jimmy Sears, Peter felt unaccountably and most unjustifiably like a champion defending with his body a damsel in distress. And Barbara would have no inkling of this sacrificial heroism. Barbara did not know Jimmy Sears!

When Peter banged open the door of the local room, however, he was immediately aware of fresh hurricanes.

"My God, Piper, I thought you were dead!" The city editor's eye shade was pushed far up on his bristling red hair—a sure sign of excitement. "Where have you been—to Los Angeles? Cop-ee bo-oy!" He snatched the telephone with one hand and thrust a bundle of copy paper across the desk with the other. "Shoot this down. More to come on the tule marsh story!" he shouted over his shoulder to the semicircle of the copy desks, where metal cylinders bearing copy and galley proofs spouted clattering out of their long black tubes, or were sent rumbling down other tubes to the composing room on the floor below.

"You, Piper, get busy on this. Unidentified body found in the tule marsh near El Cerrito. Go over to city hall and get Camberwell of the identification bureau. Find out what, if anything, they know. I've been waiting for you—you're the only man sure to get to Camberwell, thanks to that story you wrote when he was being razzed by the department. Tell him we won't print without permission, of course, but get him to give you something. It looks like murder!"

The city editor pushed his eye shade even farther back on his brow, at the angle, though far from the effect, of a mediæval halo. His harsh voice was jubilant. Anyone would have thought that murder to him was a joyous occasion—as indeed it was.

Peter exhaled a tremendous breath of relief. After all, he did not have to let the paper down. With a new front-page story breaking, the affairs of Barbara Cavanaugh could well afford to wait.

"Hoo-oo-oo, hu-hu-hu-hoo," whistled Peter in a wailing minor, and darted crosswise of the traffic to the city hall.

Chapter IX

AN AIR of triumph was plainly discernible in the *Herald* local room. It manifested itself in the demeanour of the managing editor, who popped in and out of his private office at frequent intervals to confer with Jimmy; in the rushing to and fro of photographers carrying large sheets of cardboard whereon were spread still wet prints; in the Jack-in-the-box materialization of a smudgy-faced boy from the composing room waving a damp page proof over which Jimmy and the managing editor bent with heads that almost touched.

Jimmy jerked the receiver from the jangling telephone at his elbow.

"I don't care what it is!" he snapped. "Unless one of them's murdered, don't bother me. Here, Andy, take this call! Our east-side man wants to unburden his mind about a kid elopement."

Peter, on his return from the city hall, had gone straight to his typewriter.

"Got it!" he flung laconically over his shoulder to Jimmy as he passed the city desk.

"I'll give you twenty minutes—keep it down to three quarters of a column," Jimmy called after his retreating back.

A copy boy stood at Peter's elbow, seizing each page to be set into type as Peter ripped it from the carriage. When he had finished, he strolled over to the city desk, his hands in his pockets.

"Nobody else had got there. It's an exclusive, all right—and it's straight. Camberwell told me with his own ruby lips that Cavanaugh's to be called in on the case. In fact, he was waiting for him to arrive for a conference when I left."

"It's a pretty fair yarn," said Jimmy.

The managing editor darted out of sight again. The local room subsided to a pretence of ordinary routine. Jimmy's watch lay open on the desk, and he consulted it at frequent intervals until a boy appeared with an armload of papers fresh from the presses, the single red line "Extra" in view across the top. The city editor snatched one of the papers from beneath the boy's arm, but his eyes continued to stray to his watch until, a quarter of an hour later, the cries of the newsboys were wafted up from the street below.

"We beat 'em on the street by fifteen minutes!" Jimmy announced in a tone of deep and almost prayerful gratification.

The contentment of the *Herald* office was by no means shared by the two men who sat chatting in a book-lined room on the top floor of the city hall—the room from which Peter had made a whistling exit not long before. The chat was not an ordinary chat, the two men were not ordinary men, and the books, for that matter, were not ordinary books. Several shelves were given over to volumes nearly two feet high labelled with yearly dates instead of titles and containing lists of arrests. Their size and worn covers gave a certain mediæval atmosphere to a room by no means devoted to mediæval concerns.

Camberwell, head of the identification bureau, sat tilted far back in a swivel chair which squeaked rhythmically as he rocked to and fro. His frame was large, but his head was set forward above stooping shoulders—the ineradicable stoop of the farm boy whose strength has been early overtaxed by heavy physical labour. His hands, with their twisted fingers and enlarged knuckles, still bore the marks of that boyhood toil. But his eyes were the eyes of a student. Since the day when, as a lanky youth, an idea had been born in his mind from a chance thumb mark in a farmhouse album, he had pursued that one idea with the zeal which only the born specialist can know. He still looked the middle-aged farmer, but he faced Dr. Cavanaugh with the unassuming equality of a fellow expert.

"I'm not jumping at conclusions," he protested. "I'm just suggesting a possibility to be tested. I wouldn't have bothered you about a mere highway bum, who wandered off into the marsh while drunk, or crept away to die of exposure. There's no doubt at all about it's being a woman. Except for that, we have mighty little to go on. There's just one encouraging bit that I'll show you later. It's only a chance, I know, but it's the first chance we've had, and we can't afford to overlook it."

"It was a mute, inglorious psychoanalyst, living before his time, who coined the phrase, 'The wish is father to the thought,' " Dr. Cavanaugh smiled. "However, that's nothing against the thought. I'm quite willing to take it up. Only, mind, I don't promise anything."

It was Camberwell's turn to smile, a reminiscent smile. He knew from past experience that Dr. Cavanaugh never did promise anything. But the psychiatrist's modesty had not shortened the long list of successful performances, some of them quoted internationally, others—and these included some of the most remarkable—known only to the families of his patients or hidden in the files of police records.

Between these two—the doctor, whose heavy figure was unobtrusively clad in a perfectly tailored suit, whose long pale cigars were manufactured for him individually according to his own mixture, and the grizzled man in plain clothes who swung in the battered swivel chair and rolled in rapid succession a series of Bull Durham cigarettes—there existed none of the antagonism traditional between the police and the independent expert.

Camberwell's admiration for the psychologist was more than professional. He had not arrived at his present office on the top floor of the city-hall tower without a great deal of incredulous and scornful opposition. He had been the first man on the coast to install and classify finger-print records in the old days when criminals were identified—or more frequently weren't identified—by descriptions and photographs only. More recently, he had talked, read, almost eaten and slept "forensic ballistics"—those telltale individual "finger prints" left on a bullet in its passage through a gun barrel. He had forced the detective bureau to take seriously the measurement of reaction time as a test of veracity: a device seized upon with glee by the public press, described with inspired inaccuracy, and captioned the "lie detector."

As a result, he had heard himself described as a freak and his department criticized as an example of newfangled, highbrow "college" police methods. But his methods had held their own in court; and his practice of seeking the collaboration of Dr. Cavanaugh, whom some other members of the department somewhat snortingly referred to as a "nut cracker," had not only contributed to the defence of his pet theories, but on more than one occasion had held him back from serious blunders.

Cavanaugh's association with Camberwell, on the other hand, had led the psychologist to turn his wide-ranging curiosity on the problems of personal identification. It had given him what he always called a "mere hobby"—but it was a hobby which he put to frequent and very practical use. In return, he had given to the policeman, struggling through the thickets of uncharted research, the encouragement of his support in some rather dark and stormy periods. Camberwell's admiration of talents different from his own was intensified by personal gratitude.

"So far," Dr. Cavanaugh reminded him gently, "you have two quite isolated facts to consider: a corpse that has been found, and a woman that hasn't."

"But it isn't a corpse!" Camberwell's chair squeaked with accelerated tempo. "I only wish it were!"

Chapter X

"Oh!" Dr. Cavanaugh said in mild surprise. "My error! I was distinctly under the impression that a corpse was the chief occasion for this conference."

"It isn't as good as a corpse," Camberwell said, as if he had ordered one and it had failed to come up to specifications. "Not nearly so good. It's only—remains."

"Well, then, suppose for the moment we postpone consideration of the corpse which isn't there and concentrate on the lady, who isn't there, either." Dr. Cavanaugh drew several meditative puffs from his cigar before he went on: "Every act, of course, is the expression of a motive, and the motive behind a given act is determined by character, temperament, call it what you will. Conversely, if you know a person's character, you know what motives will operate in him strongly enough to produce actions, and what actions they are likely to produce. Unfortunately, we don't know Mrs. Ellsworth's character half well enough for such prediction. If I had known she was going to disappear," he added whimsically, "I should have made better use of the few opportunities for observation that came my way. What little I do know complicates rather than simplifies the possibilities. Mrs. Ellsworth was a far from conventional person, and her acts, therefore, may not fall into the grooves of conventional conduct."

"I'll say they mayn't!" Camberwell agreed with ironic fervour.

"I've no more to go on than you have," Dr. Cavanaugh went on, scrutinizing the glowing tip of his cigar. "But I've given the case a little thought, a sort of preliminary survey. I've known young Don Ellsworth for several years, and he came to me the other night to see what I could make of it. I declined to take up the case professionally, because I had an idea you might call upon me. It's too bad I had not known about this latest find of yours—if I had, I'd have won a nickel with myself when you called up!"

"You do think, then, that she's been done away with?"

"Not necessarily. We have here—or, rather, we haven't here—a woman entirely free of one of the most powerful restrictions on human conduct: the fear of social disapproval. Sheila O'Shay made herself conspicuous in a variety of ways on two continents. And however disreputable the ways were from the point of view of conventional society, she capitalized them to her advantage. She made a bad reputation pay. She is an exhibitionist, but a canny exhibitionist. Whatever she did contributed to the gate receipts. Now this woman, whose latest and most conspicuous act was her marriage to a multimillionaire several years her junior, disappears. She is excessively fond of money—or rather of what money will buy in the way of a flaunting display of luxury. That has been amply indicated by her previous career. She is also highly sexed—which has likewise been sufficiently indicated."

"It certainly has," Camberwell agreed again.

"If she went away of her own free will, there is the possibility that she was actuated by a strong sex impulse directed elsewhere than toward her husband—I very much doubt if she ever felt any compelling attraction toward a man of Ellsworth's type.

There is also the possibility that Ellsworth put on the screws financially and she found that being married to a multimillionaire did not give her immediate access to all the millions to play with. In either case, she might have left as suddenly and as inexplicably as she did. She would not be hampered, you see, by consideration for Don or by the fear of publicity. She may, indeed, have planned the manner of her exit, knowing the stir it would cause, as preliminary press agentry for a return to the stage."

"But in that case—in any of those cases—we ought to have got some trace of her!"

"I would not underestimate her resourcefulness," Dr. Cavanaugh countered. "In no sense of the word was Sheila O'Shay born yesterday. However, there is the second possibility that she was abducted, perhaps for ransom, perhaps by a jealous former lover. And there is, of course, the third—that she was murdered. So far it's all speculation."

"But this tule marsh business——"

"This tule marsh business may indeed substitute a second mystery for the first—or merely add another unrelated one. By the way, if it were Sheila O'Shay, it would hardly be unrecognizable so soon, would it? Or would it? You haven't told me, you know."

"That part fits in all right as to time. But it makes identification the very dickens of a job. Properly speaking, the body wasn't found in the marsh at all, but above it on the slope of El Cerrito hill. There was a grass fire there a couple of weeks ago that burned the place over. This morning a group of boys playing Indian stumbled on the body. It had been burned beyond recognition. It might have lain there in the tall grass for months or years except that the charred remains showed little sign of exposure to the weather."

"And this fire—how did it start?"

"There you have us. There was a high north wind blowing for several days about that time. I remember it, and anyway the weather reports back it up. Under those conditions, grass fires along that strip are common enough—a cigarette end thrown out of an automobile, a spark from a passing locomotive, embers of a jungle fire made by tramps—any one of a number of things might account for it. On the other hand, the fire came pretty pat to destroy all chance of identifying that body."

"You don't quite mean that." Dr. Cavanaugh leaned back in his chair. He had a way of appearing most relaxed when another man would have leaned forward in strained attention. "You would not have called me away from golf to attempt the impossible—because you're one of the very few people who realize that the impossible is one of the things that simply aren't done."

"You're right!" Camberwell swung the front legs of the swivel chair to the floor with a bang. "There's just one little thing more—and it's beyond me." He pulled a bunch of keys from a baggy trousers pocket, flung his cigarette butt to the floor and automatically stamped it out, and reached down to unlock the drawer of a specially constructed fireproof cabinet that stood beside the desk.

"What do you think of this?" he asked.

Chapter XI

THE OBJECT which Camberwell held out on the extended palm of his hand was a small flat jar of glass with a tightly fitting screw top.

"Fire is always a freakish thing," he mused. "With the brush dry as tinder, as it is at this time of year, it was hot enough to burn nearly all the flesh off this woman's bones. Of course, if it was murder, and the fire was not accidental, there is the possibility that the body was soaked in some inflammable substance first. Yet this one little scrap was left. A flame that veered in a puff of wind, a bit of earth less dry than the rest—we'll never know the how and the why of it, but here it is."

Dr. Cavanaugh deliberately flattened the burning end of his cigar against the side of the ash tray before reaching for the jar. He was capable of rapid action when necessity arose, but he never hurried without reason. His only sign of eagerness was the agate hardening of his brown eyes—a change of expression which Camberwell was quick to note and appreciate.

"I told you I didn't bring you here for nothing," he said. "You can bet one of those nickels with yourself that you'll find this interesting."

Dr. Cavanaugh gravely selected a nickel from a handful of loose change and laid it on the corner of the desk. Then he unscrewed the lid of the jar and walked to the light of the big window.

"Hm!" His only immediate comment was a noncommittal hum, but when he returned to the desk after a somewhat prolonged scrutiny at the window, he pocketed the nickel.

"This goes to the elephant," he said; "but it was hardly a fair bet. I expected to lose. Your finds usually are interesting, you know. Yes," he added, "I can doubtless do something with this—not everything, but something."

"It'll be plenty," Camberwell assured him, "so long as you're willing to take it up. You begin where I leave off, you know. It's too much for me."

"It's only a matter of physiology, which is in my line as a medical man. You started me on this track of investigation in the first place, but it happens to fit in with my previous training. You have here"—he tapped the lid of the jar lightly with a thumb nail—"an irregular patch of scalp about an inch in diameter with perhaps half a dozen hairs clinging to it. And that hair not only belonged, of course, to only one person on earth, but from it we can describe that person, and even, if we have the basis of comparison, can identify its possessor as absolutely as if the one who placed her there had obligingly left for us a full set of her finger prints. We are very ignorant, after all." Dr. Cavanaugh turned the box idly in his hands and looked meditatively into the distance. "It has taken thousands of years for us to discover that the skin of the fingers, and the hair, and the markings on a discharged bullet are unique and individual. Perhaps in a few more thousands of years we shall know that of a million pebbles on the beach each has marks of identification which make it different from every other."

"That would make the keeping of our records even more complicated," Camberwell smiled. He rather hoped the reference to his own work would bring the doctor back to the matter in hand. But Dr. Cavanaugh's mellow voice rolled steadily on:

"Hegel, whom perhaps you have never read, called it the uniqueness of the real. A dime, for instance, he maintains, has what he termed 'an infinite number of distinguishing marks,' even though a million dimes were stamped with the same die and minted with the same machinery. We can never construct in our imagination any idea or image of a dime, or a hair, or a bullet which is as infinitely complex as the real object. Hegel is considered old-fashioned now, but he would have agreed whole-heartedly with your new science of forensic ballistics."

An acute observer might have harboured the suspicion that Dr. Cavanaugh was drifting along the current of this irrelevant discourse with the surface of his mind while his real attention was elsewhere. Under cover of these meanderings, he appeared to be gaining time for some hidden process of thought, reaching some inner decision. But Camberwell was not a psychologist. He twisted uneasily in his chair. With so much to be done, he was in no mood to listen to a lecture in philosophy!

Slight as it was, his impatient movement did not escape the dreamy, inattentive eyes of Dr. Cavanaugh. He shook off his absorption and laid down his cigar, as if that small and definite act were the symbol of his decision.

"I'm as bad as Hamlet's grave digger. He'd never have been allowed to finish his soliloquy if one of you detectives had been present!" he said with a smile which revealed a surprising mobility of expression in the large, deeply chiselled features. "However, I promise not to waste any more time. I'll take this home with me, where I can take a squint at it under the microscope, and give you a report in the morning."

"You think you can identify it?" Camberwell asked eagerly.

"At least I'll narrow the range of possibilities." And Dr. Cavanaugh slipped the gruesome little box into his pocket as nonchalantly as if it had been a package of peppermints.

Camberwell's impatience, perhaps, would again have been severely tested if he had seen the psychologist, several hours later, placidly stretched on the chaise longue and apparently concentrating on the production of the series of perfect smoke rings which floated ceilingward. No one would have suspected that recumbent figure of a preoccupation with crime.

Nevertheless, Dr. Cavanaugh had spent a busy two hours, during which the Florentine leather desk appointments had been relegated to the floor and their place taken by a sheet of glass. The desk, oddly out of keeping with the rest of the furnishings of the room, became a laboratory table, where Dr. Cavanaugh, his big fingers moving with delicate precision, made a number of smears on a series of small strips of glass, protected each one with a cover glass, and marked it with a red-bordered sticker labelled in the doctor's neat, minute handwriting.

His face was impersonally calm and intent, as if the small objects which he manipulated with rapid expertness belonged to the routine of a classroom experiment instead of holding a meaning heavy with life and death and tragedy and crime. He sat almost motionless, hunched over the microscope, occasionally removing one slide to insert another, taking notes on the pad of paper under his hand without removing his eye from the lens. At last, with a faint sigh, he shut the microscope once again into its wooden case and restored the desk fittings to their accustomed places. Even the sheets of faintly pencilled notes were thrust casually into a drawer.

Stretching himself comfortably on the chaise longue, Dr. Cavanaugh devoted himself to watching the procession of smoke rings through drowsy, half-shut eyes. To all appearances, body and mind alike were relaxed in the aimless revery that precedes sleep. But the air of somnolence which hung over the quiet room was illusory. Dr. Cavanaugh was thinking hard, slipping ideas and inferences into place as precisely as he had slipped the slides under the lens of the microscope. Suddenly he heaved himself up from the chaise longue and moved to the telephone; then he returned to his former position, to await, with his usual quiescence, the ringing of the office doorbell.

Fifteen minutes later the door banged open and Don Ellsworth rushed in before the doctor had time to put his feet to the floor preparatory to answering the single sharp announcement of the bell.

"You've found out something!" The momentum of his entrance carried Don halfway across the room before he paused. The words were half a question, half an exclamation.

Chapter XII

Dr. Cavanaugh motioned his visitor to a chair, disregarding the tempestuous manner of his entrance, and waited until Don had flung himself into it.

"I don't believe I said I had found anything," he corrected mildly.

"No, but—I understood——"

"That there was some news in which you might be interested. As a matter of fact, it is impossible to say as yet whether even that really concerns you. However, on the face of it, it seemed worth discussing."

"What is it you have found?" From Don's dry throat the words emerged as little more than a hoarse whisper.

"Not I; I've merely been asked to inquire into it a bit—and, as I told you, I'm still in the dark. Have you read the evening papers?"

"I haven't looked at a paper for a week. I won't read the cursed things, with my name sticking out in headlines all over the place!"

"You have not heard, then, that a body burned beyond recognition by the action of a grass fire has been found on the El Cerrito slope, above the marsh." Dr. Cavanaugh's voice was studiously conversational. He might have been mentioning nothing more important than the finding of a golf ball.

"I don't care whom or what they've found," Don exploded. "So long as it isn't Sheila!"

Don was twisting his hands nervously in his lap. There was the tension of long-continued strain behind the irascibility in his voice. At first glance he looked noticeably thinner than on his previous visit; but a careful observer would have noted that the effect was due not so much to actual loss of weight as to the lines which gave his features a drawn look, and to the dark circles under his eyes.

"Language is an absurdly ambiguous instrument of communication," the doctor meditated, completely ignoring Don's agitation. "For example, that last sentence of yours. On the face of it, it might mean that you are indifferent to all else but Sheila's welfare and her possible danger—or it might mean that you hoped above all things that Sheila would not be found. Naturally, I assume that the first interpretation is the correct one."

"I don't know what I meant!" Don's hand was flung out in a gesture of angry impatience. "I don't feel much like entering on a discussion of grammar."

"Oh, but it sometimes matters a lot—quite a lot," the doctor murmured.

"Well, I'm not in a mood to choose my words very carefully. Suppose Sheila never shows up—simply drops out of sight altogether. I'd still be legally tied to her, wouldn't I? Unless"—a faint gleam of eagerness shone in Don's hollow eyes—"unless I could get a divorce on grounds of desertion. Do you think I could?"

"No doubt. But that's not the particular bridge we are crossing at the moment." Dr. Cavanaugh ruthlessly pulled him back.

"Well, then, suppose she came back—with all the turmoil there's been in the papers. I'd be in a sweet position then, wouldn't I? Things would be as bad as before—no, a hundred times worse, because the things I put my neck into the noose to secure—decency and dignity—would be gone. What a life!" His lips twisted in what was almost a grimace. "I wish I'd been blind and deaf before I ever met that woman!"

Dr. Cavanaugh listened calmly to this jerky, spasmodic outburst, his face as expressionless as that of an image of Buddha. He waited without interruption until Don relapsed into a silence as abrupt as his speech.

"There's still another possibility," he said then. "A cutting of all Gordian knots. I don't say that it is more than a possibility. But I wouldn't be too sure, if I were you, that the activities of our friends, the police, as outlined in to-night's paper, can be disregarded."

With an obvious effort at self-control, the young man forced his hands to cease their nervous clenching and unclenching and lie tightly closed in his lap. Only the involuntary twitching of a muscle at the corner of his eyes betrayed an agitation beyond the power of his will to conceal.

"I don't understand what you're driving at," he said in a low, breathless voice. "You said—the body they found in the marsh couldn't be identified."

"You came here not long ago and asked me to help you," Dr. Cavanaugh went on, as if Ellsworth had not spoken. "But the positions are reversed; I am now about to ask you to help me. I said that the body I mentioned was unrecognizable. It was—except for a tiny patch of scalp." Without raising his tone the doctor's voice took on new emphasis. "That body belonged to a woman about forty years of age. She patronized an expensive beauty parlour, and had recently had what I believe is called a marcel. She was in the habit of using black narcisse perfume. She was fair of skin, with the brown eyes and vivid colour that accompany this particular pigmentation. Her hair, naturally red, was darkened to auburn by the use of henna, and was worn long—in fact, rather surprising in this day, it had never been cut. It was thick and luxuriant, and she took an extreme pride in it. So much for what the microscope tells us.

"From measurements taken of the body itself—Camberwell of the identification bureau was kind enough to supply me with the figures over the telephone, for I have not seen it myself—we are safe in saying that this woman of expensive tastes which she was able to gratify, and a somewhat overweening consciousness of her personal appearance, was rather tall—five feet seven inches. Naturally she would have been of the opulent, deep-bosomed type; but she kept herself trained down to the fashionable slenderness. The articulation of the bones, particularly of the feet, indicates that she was trained in dancing. The formation of the roof of the mouth makes it probable that she was a singer—though she could not have taken her singing very seriously of late, as stains on the teeth show her to have been an excessive smoker of strong Egyptian cigarettes. Does all this convey anything to you?"

The face in the chair opposite might have been carved out of ivory—yellow-white, with burnt-out coals for eyes. Don cleared his throat and ran the tip of his tongue across dry lips.

"You mean—it's Sheila!" His voice was a rasping whisper.

"I mean it was someone who at least bore a general resemblance to Mrs. Ellsworth," Dr. Cavanaugh amended imperturbably. "But there is a way of finding out whether we are dealing with a resemblance or an identity. Under the microscope the cell structure of the hair is as individual as the whorls that make up the pattern of finger prints. I have the hair of the woman who was found dead in the marsh. Will you bring me for comparison a hair belonging to Mrs. Ellsworth, from her brushes, her gowns—any place where you can be sure the hair was hers? That ought to be easy."

For a moment the face before him did not change. Only that twitching eye muscle marred its rigidity. The teeth were clenched so tightly that the line of the jaw stood out sharply. Then a dark flush, almost purple, flooded his cheeks and mounted until even the eyes were bloodshot. His fist crashed suddenly down on the arm of his chair.

"I'll be damned if I will!" he shouted.

Chapter XIII

WITH A single movement that was like the spring of a puma Don Ellsworth catapulted from his chair. His toe caught in the fringe of a rug. He half stumbled, but recovered his balance blindly, hardly noticing the check to his progress. In another instant he had flung himself from the room, leaving his hat forgotten on the table, and the outer door crashed shut, propelled by the backward fling of his arm.

Dr. Cavanaugh's hand paused a fraction of a second, his cigar halfway to his lips. Then the interrupted movement was completed as deliberately as it had been begun. He had not risen to intercept Don, and he made no effort now to follow him.

"Hm!" The sound was half a hum, half a gentle sigh. It was Dr. Cavanaugh's equivalent of half a dozen excited ejaculations. He settled his thick shoulders against the pillows of the chaise longue. But there were no more smoke rings. Instead, he drew from his inner pocket a small leather-bound notebook, propped its lower edge against his arching middle, and proceeded to make notes in almost microscopic handwriting, first on one, then the other, of the two pages open before him.

"Hm!" he hummed again, like a gigantic bumblebee. "On the

one hand we have a young man of undisciplined emotions subject to gusts of rage which he has never been taught to control, unused to delaying his reaction to any impulse, caught by the tremendous vitality and charm of the dazzling Sheila O'Shay—but the attraction evidently soon spent. Query: Why did he marry her?" The query was underlined in the little notebook, and further marked by a star in the margin. "Corollary: Why did she marry him? Money, probably. But did she capture him before he had time to get back his emotional balance, or had she some means of forcing him to it? Not inferable from present data. Leave that out—confuses the present problem." Dr. Cavanaugh accordingly drew a line lightly through the "corollary." He carefully deposited an inch of white cigar ash in the tray, allowing the notebook to flop forward, then adjusted it again at its former angle.

"In general, people will subconsciously choose words that tell the truth, even when it is not the truth they mean to tell at the moment. A great little master of double meaning, the subconscious is!" he mused. "Let's see. Don did not say that he wanted his wife back—he said that he wanted to be rescued from the undesirable publicity aroused by her disappearance. That's quite different. His anxiety was not for her, but for the effect on himself. He resented the interference of Mrs. Kane and of the police. He didn't care what was found 'so long as it wasn't Sheila.'

"On the other hand"—Dr. Cavanaugh's minute scratchings were now scrawled on the opposite side of the facing pages—"his subconscious desire to have his wife out of the way might have a powerful and disturbing effect when the unexpressed wish was suddenly fulfilled. There is also his extreme dislike, amounting almost to phobia, of publicity, by which he feels that he has been victimized. The impulse to run away from an intolerable situation—all the more intolerable if it were to involve him in a sensational murder case—may have become overpowering; and so he ran away without even considering the futility of the escape or its consequences. One thing is certain: Don Ellsworth would not be capable of any carefully devised plot. Unless we have to do with a person clever enough to convey the impression purposely, the whole evidence—what there is to it—does not point to premeditation, either on the part of Mrs. Ellsworth, if she actually left of her own will, or of her murderer, if she was killed. Ellsworth might conceivably act with extreme rashness, follow an instinctive immediate course of self-protection, and then wake up to find himself in a mess, utterly helpless both by temperament and training to devise any sort of scheme to extricate himself."

Dr. Cavanaugh snapped the notebook shut, restored it to his pocket, and heaved himself somewhat wearily erect.

"That hair is beginning to be important," he said aloud; "but it's less important for me to get it than to find out who is unwilling for me to have it—and why. That's what Camberwell and his policemen will never quite appreciate. Which means that I'll have to go after it myself."

Having bet himself a nickel that Don Ellsworth would not have turned homeward after his explosive exit from the office, and verified the prediction by means of a telephone call, Dr. Cavanaugh pocketed his winnings, leisurely shrugged himself into the overcoat which always hung in readiness in the carved Florentine wardrobe that filled one corner of the room, and backed his small, unobtrusive black runabout from its place in the double garage.

The other side of the garage yawned empty. Barbara had driven to a party at the house of friends; and for once Dr. Cavanaugh was glad of her absence. After all, she and Don had been very good friends not so long ago. He might yet have to be glad that the friendship had lapsed. But meanwhile, though she often followed his cases with eager interest, he hoped that he might avoid giving her an account—or, what was just as bad, obviously declining to give her an account—of his progress in this one.

The maid who answered Dr. Cavanaugh's ring at the front door of the Ellsworth house stopped short, her eyes as round as marbles, at the sound of his name. She, at least, was an avid reader of the newspapers; the wonders to be expected of the great Dr. Cavanaugh, who was reported to have been called in consultation on the "tule marsh mystery," had been the theme of delightful flights of imagination in the kitchen not an hour ago. Ethel's expression was a mixture of awe and fright, as if Dr. Cavanaugh, by black magic, was likely to weave a connection between murder and anyone so unwary as to stand in his vicinity.

Dr. Cavanaugh submitted to this fascinated scrutiny with patience. Servants to him were human beings, and he was neither surprised nor offended when they dropped the pretence of being machines.

"I'd like to see Mrs. Kane," he announced with his usual directness, thereby shattering Ethel's conception of the devious ways of criminologists.

The girl's face reflected a shocked astonishment not unmixed with malice and sheer delight in a thrilling situation. Already she could hear herself telling the cook that she had let the great man in, that he had acted "just like you or me, not a bit like a crime-ologist, and no airs at all," and that his request for Mrs. Kane made her feel "just like in the middle of a story, and I hope he's got something on that old fussbudget, and anyway, isn't it exciting, just?"

For the moment, however, she was confronted with a social emergency for which she was unprepared.

"Yes, sir," she stammered. "Come in, sir, and I'll bring Mrs. Kane right down—or would you rather I'd take you to the servants' sitting room?"

"I wouldn't dream of turning you out of your sitting room, with the radio programme not half over," Dr. Cavanaugh said, smiling a little at Ethel's surprised acknowledgment of this evidence of consideration. "Mr. Ellsworth left my house only a short time ago; and though I know he did not come straight home, I think I may venture to take possession of the library in his absence."

"Certainly, sir."

Having opened the door for him, Ethel scurried down the hall. He listened to her footsteps pattering almost at a run up the stairs.

"So Mrs. Kane does not sit with the other servants in the evening. Don was right about her unpopularity, then."

Other steps came down the hall, a resolute, flat-footed thud-thud.

Dr. Cavanaugh picked up a magazine from the table and was leafing its pages when the door opened. He did not look up until, after a moment's hesitation on the threshold, the footsteps, a shade less resolute now, entered the room.

"And what, may I ask, do you want of me?" asked Mrs. Kane.

Chapter XIV

DR. CAVANAUGH finished reading the caption under a cartoon on the open page of the magazine, smiled appreciatively, and returned the periodical with meticulous care to its place in the row on the library table. There was plenty of time to look at Mrs. Kane. He knew the embarrassing effect of a pause; already he had put her on the defensive by forcing her to open the conversation.

When at last he looked up his glance was casual, with no effect of scrutiny. He saw before him a tall, heavy-boned woman whose hair, shinily black like shoe polish, was drawn up from her forehead in a stiff sausage formation—the pompadour in vogue twenty years ago.

"Dyed," Dr. Cavanaugh commented inwardly. "Now why should she bother to dye her hair? Not for beauty, certainly."

Her skin showed a network of tiny blood vessels. Her cheeks and nose had a tight, red, shiny look, even as her hair was tight, black, and shiny. That nose was the dominant feature—a heavy beak overshadowing a sunken mouth.

"False teeth," Dr. Cavanaugh continued his silent observations. "And put in far too late, after the gums had shrunk."

Mrs. Kane's dress, like her hair, followed an extinct fashion. It touched the ground with its dusty hem binding of dingy black. The collar and cuffs were rumpled and showed a faint brown line at wrist and neck.

"A visit to the cleaner's and the laundry would seem to have been indicated—not at all the attire to be expected of a servant in a millionaire's home." With all this, Dr. Cavanaugh's survey had been so brief and unobtrusive as to leave Mrs. Kane with the impression that it was she who stared. It was a hard, belligerent stare from small but by no means dull black eyes.

"I won't take up much of your time, Mrs. Kane," Dr. Cavanaugh began courteously. "But won't you sit down?"

"I'm busy. Besides, I prefer to stand."

A dramatic old codger! Whoever started the idea, firmly fixed in the cheaper sort of fiction, that it was the thing to "prefer to stand" in the presence of an enemy? Had it an anthropological basis as a sign of readiness to give instant physical battle? Dr. Cavanaugh decided to look it up some time. Meanwhile, as a symbol it had its advantages. It showed conclusively that Mrs. Kane was not merely indulging her usual forbidding manner but regarded him definitely as an antagonist.

"Indeed? I should have thought your duties would be considerably lightened by your mistress's absence," he remarked suavely.

"My duties concern myself. I believe you had something to say to me."

Dr. Cavanaugh had some difficulty in restraining his eyes from a fascinated attention to Mrs. Kane's mouth. The false teeth had indeed been installed too late. When she spoke, the upper set moved up and down beneath her lip like a stage drop retreating and appearing behind a lifted curtain. But her manipulation was expert. The teeth moved with a gruesome independence, but they never quite fell out, and when she stopped speaking, the clamp of her jaws thrust them into place with a slight click. The necessity of this constant management gave her sentences a clipped, jerky brevity.

"Well, something to ask you, rather," Dr. Cavanaugh corrected her. "Perhaps you know that Mr. Ellsworth came to me for advice when Mrs. Ellsworth—left?"

"Mr. Ellsworth didn't seem to bother much until the police got busy," Mrs. Kane remarked grimly.

"At your request, I believe."

"He made me mad. I don't say I'd ought to done it, if I'd stopped to think. But when I asked him what he was going to do he said, 'I druther not discuss it.' " Mrs. Kane's thin lips snapped shut, and Dr. Cavanaugh found himself waiting anxiously for the reassuring click. "He 'druther not,' indeed!" The voice rose harshly. "Well, there's other folks as has their druthers, as well as him. I've got my druthers, too, if you want to know!" As if realizing that she was opening too much of her mind to this stranger, she stopped. Her whole face seemed to shut down, to become an expressionless mask.

"I think you did quite right, Mrs. Kane. You showed excellent judgment."

The praise brought a momentary flash from the small black eyes.

"I don't know about that," she said grudgingly. Then the impulse to unload a piece of her mind to a willing listener became too strong. "Fancy losing a lady like Miss O'Shay and paying no more attention than if it was a lost dog that you might inquire for at the pound when you got around to it! An insult to Miss O'Shay it was—her that's had lords of Europe waiting at the stage door for her, and princes begging her to take their strings of pearls, and risking what their high-and-mighty relations would do, which would be a-plenty, if they ever found out. Twist them around her little finger, she would, in them days."

"You must have been with her for a long time," Dr. Cavanaugh ventured, in a voice from which he banished all undue curiosity.

But Mrs. Kane was instantly on guard.

"Oh, you needn't think Miss O'Shay was a has-been! She didn't have to take up with that millionaire whippersnapper because he was a last chance, not by no means. And why shouldn't she leave him, if she had a mind to, I'd like to know!"

"She did leave him, then?"

"I know nothing about it." The click this time was clearly audible. With amused admiration, Dr. Cavanaugh recognized its effectiveness as a means of emphasis.

"Still," he mused, "she might not have meant to go. Did you ever notice in Miss O'Shay"—tactfully he avoided the title "Mrs. Ellsworth," to which Mrs. Kane had shown such marked aversion—"any signs of eccentricity, of instability?"

"You mean, did she act crazy?"

"I should not put it so strongly, but that is the general idea."

"If you doctors would learn to speak plain English maybe fewer of your patients would die. If Miss O'Shay was crazy, or if she wasn't, I'd say it was her own business."

"Yes, it might be." Dr. Cavanaugh's tone was placating. "By the way, do you read the newspapers?" He shifted ground suddenly.

"Do I read the newspapers!" Mrs. Kane repeated the words with indignant scorn. "I've kept Miss O'Shay's scrapbook of clippings since—for years. And those scrapbooks would fill a shelf as long as that"—pointing to the bookcase behind him—"I'm telling you!"

"Then you know"—Dr. Cavanaugh's voice was still unhurried, but he was forcing the pace now—"that an unidentified body has been found in the tule marsh, and that I have been asked to aid in the attempt to identify it. I may be able to make that identification complete if I can secure a hair belonging to Miss O'Shay. I came to ask if you will be so kind as to procure it for me."

For an instant Mrs. Kane's eyes widened, showing a rim of white around the iris. The nostrils of her beak-like nose flared with the sudden intake of her breath. The network of veins on her cheeks stood out against the surrounding pallor like a miniature railroad map drawn in red ink. Her lips worked convulsively.

"I'll do nothing of the sort!" she said in a high, strained voice.

And then it happened—the thing for which everyone who talked with Mrs. Kane watched with horrified expectancy. Those imperfectly fitted upper teeth fell out, and clattered to the floor.

"Oh," said Dr. Cavanaugh gently, "I'm sorry! Allow me."

His heavy bulk covered the space between them with incredible swiftness. He stooped to recover the ghastly white semicircle—and as he rose, the fingers of his left hand plucked, unnoticed, a long auburn hair from Mrs. Kane's skirt.

Chapter XV

DR. CAVANAUGH carefully tucked the hair between thumb and forefinger into the envelope which lay ready in his coat pocket. The gesture was apparently merely that of reaching for a folded handkerchief, with which he dabbed his fingers after restoring the teeth to their owner.

Mrs. Kane with a sublime disregard of germs and complete lack of embarrassment popped the teeth into her mouth.

"But aren't you, to say the least of it, interested in knowing the fate of the lady to whom you have been so long devoted?"

"Devotion's neither here nor there," Mrs. Kane responded cryptically. "I guess I'll find out all I need to know soon enough—maybe sooner."

"Perhaps. And yet I take it you would want to do all in your power to bring the criminal—supposing there is a criminal—to justice." Dr. Cavanaugh spoke with a mild positiveness as if stating an obvious fact.

But Mrs. Kane was not accepting any statement merely because it was positively made.

"Justice!" she retorted with an angry snap of her jaws. "What good would that do? Justice generally is just somebody's fool notion of the way other folks' affairs ought to be fixed for them. Besides, you've got a long way to go to prove that there's any criminal in it at all."

"Oh, yes, quite." Dr. Cavanaugh waved the point aside as if it were not worth arguing.

"I reckon a lady could leave her house without being murdered. There's plenty that does, anyway."

"You're quite right. It isn't certain," Dr. Cavanaugh conceded. "Still, I believe you were the one who was sufficiently worried over Mrs. Ellsworth's absence to notify the police."

"Yes, I did that. I already told you I was mad at the way Mr. Ellsworth acted. And if Miss O'Shay comes back, she may call me a fool for my pains. It wouldn't be the first time she's done that. At any rate, letting the police know she's gone is different from getting her mixed up with the murdered corpse of some nobody that Miss O'Shay probably wouldn't touch with a ten-foot pole. If Miss O'Shay ever got killed, she'd see to it that it was done with more—more—style!"

Dr. Cavanaugh's wandering gaze unobtrusively followed the movements of Mrs. Kane's bony fingers plucking at the folds of her skirt. He was listening more to the modulations of her voice than to her actual words. Was there an undercurrent of acute anxiety beneath these disconnected asseverations?

"Unfortunately, one cannot always control the stage setting in such matters," he said dryly. "I'm sorry you don't feel inclined to help us out; but if you won't, I suppose you won't."

He picked up his hat from the table, and spoke with the mild disappointment of one who has been refused subscription to his pet charity.

"Well, I won't, so you might just as well quit right now!" The click with which Mrs. Kane's teeth dropped into place was very determined indeed.

As he switched on the lights of his car, it occurred to Dr. Cavanaugh that not once had she referred to the missing woman as her mistress, nor addressed him in any other fashion than as an equal.

It was late when he entered the lamplit serenity of his unofficial-looking office, but he lifted the wooden box containing his microscope from a cabinet which looked better suited to liquor bottles than laboratory equipment, deftly transferred the hair to a glass slide, and for a long time sat motionless at his desk, his eye glued to the instrument. Without looking up, he transcribed a series of minute, indecipherable notes on the sheet of paper under his hand.

Barbara, returning from her party, saw the thread of light under the office door. She hesitated a moment, her hand lifted to knock. Then, with a weary little shake of her head, she thought better of it and flitted noiselessly up the stairs.

The next morning, at an hour when most late-hour folk have yet to begin consideration of breakfast, Peter Piper was also experiencing hesitations and head shakings.

"It's one peach of a good murder!" the city editor had said with the appreciation of a connoisseur. "We ought to get Cavanaugh's report in time to make the home edition—Camberwell said he expected it some time this morning. You never can tell about these experts; but if he doesn't turn up anything, play it up anyway as much as you can, and we'll nurse it along. You drop everything else, Piper, and stick to Camberwell. Stick if it takes all day. You might telephone in occasionally."

"Right."

Peter, the inevitable copy paper bulging from his coat pocket, lounged out of the local room. But he was not whistling. He was meditating disobedience to the city editor's orders—with the imminent and definite risk of losing his job, and, what was infinitely worse, of falling down on a story. But if his hunch was right, he stood a chance of getting that report at least a full half hour before the boys gathered in the press room at the city hall—getting it in time to beat the opposition and getting it direct from Dr. Cavanaugh himself.

He stood for a moment outside the entrance to the *Herald* building, and even took a few steps in the direction of the city hall. Then he shook his head and darted across the street, pursued by indignant squawks from the horns of intervening trucks. A moment later the sputtering with which Bossy's engine always preceded going into action was accompanied by a low, lugubrious whistle.

Peter was banking everything on a girl whom he had seen only once, a girl with whom he had matched wits as an antagonist—a girl who would have no idea what it meant to hear Jimmy say, "You may call at the cashier's desk for your money"—a girl who would think it a matter of no importance whether you let your paper down. And yet he was banking on her!

Chapter XVI

"'HE either fears his fate too much or his deserts are small, that dreads to put it to the touch, to win or lose it all,' " Peter chanted under his breath. He did not reflect that the words had been written as a love poem—nor that hard-boiled reporters are not supposed to be given to the quoting of Seventeenth Century lyrics.

Once again he slid Bossy to the curb opposite the Cavanaugh entrance, and waited.

Barbara's tennis dress had not been a fancy sports costume. It was built for real play, and her racket showed signs of hard usage. If she was the kind of girl who got up at eight o'clock in the morning to play tennis, the chances were that she did not merely play occasionally. Peter was placing a long bet that the morning tennis was a daily work-out. Not being a psychoanalyst he was untroubled by the suspicion that his subconscious was arranging a possible opportunity for him to see Barbara again—and that he was pinning his faith to her because he desperately wanted that faith.

But by the time he had waited half an hour a chill grayness had seeped upward from his toes and spread until it absorbed even the pale sunny blue of the sky. He was a fool—a fool without excuse. She was not coming. Dr. Cavanaugh had doubtless sent his report by mail. Even now it had been received at the police department on the morning delivery, and Jevons of the *Record* was pounding out the story.

Peter was so deep in despondency that he did not even see the shiny little sport coupé until the corner of his eye caught a flash of white and rose as Barbara slammed the door of the car behind her. With that, he was across the street.

"Thank God!" he said loudly and fervently.

"Oh, yes?" The corners of Barbara's lips turned upward. "Is that the way newspaper men say 'Good-morning'?"

"You bet it is!" Peter agreed. "Look here," he hurried on, glancing uneasily at the closed front door of the Cavanaugh house. "The other day I asked you to do something for me, and you wouldn't. Now I'm going to ask you to do something else."

"Meanwhile, you've done something for me," Barbara said gravely. "I don't think you reporters are half as inhuman as you pretend to be. I haven't looked in the papers lately, but I'm so sure you didn't write anything about me that I'm going to thank you."

Peter flushed. It was a rare opportunity that the staff of the *Herald* local room missed, for not one of them had ever seen Peter blush.

"I don't know what I'd have done," he said with difficult honesty, "if a big story hadn't broken and let me out."

"I'm glad you said that," Barbara said simply. "I like people who tell the truth—when it isn't necessary. It's one of those impractical virtues—you remember? Now what is it you'd like me to do?"

"It's this"—Peter answered with a directness equal to her

own—"your father is supposed to go to the city hall this morning with a report. I want you to stand here talking to me when he comes out, and introduce me to him. He'd naturally stop to meet one of your friends. I'll do the rest."

"It sounds simple," Barbara said. "The only trouble I can see with your very neat little plan is that I've never been actually introduced to you myself. The friends whom I ask to meet my father are not usually acquired so—suddenly."

"Don't quibble!" Peter said sharply. "The statement, you understand, will be public property in a few hours anyway. If I can get it from your father personally, and get it first, I'll have a whale of a good story. If I don't—well, I'm sunk, that's all. And if he's more likely to mail it than to take it himself, I'm sunk anyway."

"No," said Barbara. "He won't mail it. Father never wastes time."

"Thank God for that!"

"Are you always so devotional, Mr. Piper?" Again that demure up-curving suggestion of a smile.

"Only on special occasions of crisis. Will you do it?"

"Well"—Barbara considered a moment—"I think for the occasion of a crisis you almost might be—one of my friends."

At that moment the front door opened, framing Dr. Cavanaugh's bulky figure for a moment before he descended the steps with his usual air of deliberation covering the speed that comes of avoiding waste motion.

"Can you wait just a minute, Father?" Barbara called out. "I want you to meet Mr. Piper. He's a friend of mine, who works on a newspaper."

Dr. Cavanaugh held out his hand with his grave but friendly smile.

"My dealings with the newspapers have usually been at second hand," he said. "But this younger generation has a way of adding to our education."

"I hoped I might meet you if I came around," Peter said with a disarming grin. "In fact, I'm supposed to be cooling my heels outside Camberwell's doorstep at this moment, but I cooled them outside yours instead. I'm working on the tule marsh story for the *Herald.* We have it from Camberwell that certain evidence was turned over to you for identification, and that your report would be submitted this morning. Would you have any objection to giving me the substance of that report these few minutes in advance? I take it that it will be made public at once, of course; but if I had it from you direct and—well, a few minutes before the other boys got hold of it, it would be a help."

Dr. Cavanaugh paused, his face devoid of expression, while Peter felt his hands grow icy with anxiety.

"Some day," he said at last, "I am going to write a monograph on occupational psychology. So you're trying to work a little gentle graft through Barbara here?"

Peter swallowed.

"Yes," he said, looking rather as if he were backed against a wall in front of a firing squad.

"A queer thing, human nature," Dr. Cavanaugh mused. "If you had denied it, I should have sent you packing. But I see no real harm in telling you that the body found in the marsh is that of Mrs. Don Ellsworth!"

"Whoopee!" Peter's face was illumined with an incredibly wide grin. His wide-set gray eyes were sparks of excitement. He turned to Barbara, his arm extended for an eager handclasp.

But Barbara was leaning against the side of the car, her knuckles white where her fingers clung to the door handle for support.

Her eyes were closed. Her lips were only a faint compressed line against the pallor of her pinched, wan face.

Then, with an effort that summoned the last reserves of vitality, she opened her eyes.

"I'm glad—you got your story, Mr. Piper," she said, and crumpled to the running board.

Chapter XVII

Dr. Cavanaugh, despite his age and his position on the steps several feet farther away from the curb, was the first to reach Barbara's side. Peter, in fact, was rigid with astonishment, his face a blank mask of amazement. Only the sight of Cavanaugh's dark figure bending low, obscuring Peter's vision of the little heap of rose and white on the running board, brought his feet into tardy action.

Dr. Cavanaugh turned his head as Peter reached his side.

"If your reaction time is always as slow as that," he observed, "you'll be at a disadvantage in a number of situations."

"What—do you think——" Peter stammered inanely.

"It's nothing to be upset about," Dr. Cavanaugh assured him. He did not add that the degree of Peter's concern was rather excessive. The sight of a faint could hardly be in itself alarming to an experienced newspaper reporter. "Too much tennis before breakfast. I've warned her before that she played too hard," he continued, extracting a small bottle from his pocket. He withdrew the cork and waved the phial under Barbara's nose. "She'll be all right in a few minutes."

Peter abstractedly picked up the tennis racket from the sidewalk and stood turning it in his fingers.

"But can't I—do something?" he asked miserably.

Barbara's eyes opened wearily and closed again. In another moment she had struggled unsteadily to her feet.

"Don't be in a hurry," Dr. Cavanaugh advised. "You've gone at things a little too hard and you paid the penalty in a fainting attack. Nature's way of enforcing withdrawal from the scene of activity. A day's rest in bed will set you up finely."

"Mayn't I carry her in?" Peter had never in his life felt so incompetent.

There was a hint of humour in Dr. Cavanaugh's glance.

"No such romantic measures are necessary, young man," he said. "My arm will be quite sufficient—though less spectacular. I'm not saying this to hurry you, but wasn't there something about your trying to get a story to your office ahead of time?"

"Suffering cats!" Peter exclaimed. "I forgot all about it. You're right, I've got to beat it."

He was halfway across the street when Dr. Cavanaugh called him back.

"By the way," he said, "you might return my daughter's tennis racket."

For the second time that morning Peter blushed as he looked down and saw the racket unconsciously clutched in his hand. He bounded back to the curb and tilted it against the side of the car.

Barbara said nothing. She leaned against her father's encircling arm; and, so far as Peter could judge, was oblivious of any other presence.

"If you're sure there's nothing I can do——" Peter said hesitantly. It seemed somehow heartless to leave her like that. It did not occur to him that he had left bodies strewn by the roadside after a wreck in order to rush to the nearest telephone with his story, without a similar qualm. He wanted Barbara to look at him. He wanted to know whether her eyes would be those of Alice in Wonderland grown up, or of the wary, defensive orphan-asylum girl, or of the self-possessed young woman who drove an expensive sport coupé.

"I assure you, there's no cause for anxiety." Again Peter had to submit to the doctor's grave scrutiny with its undertone of amusement.

Feeling very much like a small boy who has made a blundering nuisance of himself, he once again crossed the street and jerked Bossy into gear. It was only with the familiar hard smoothness of the wheel under his hand that his mind lurched into clarity. It was a clarity so disturbing that he fought it off with an almost physical sense of struggle. But it was no use.

Peter's brain, temporarily numbed, was once again functioning alertly. His emotional bias—and he admitted wryly that only an emotional earthquake could make him forget that Jimmy at the city desk was waiting for his report—was powerless against the relentless chug-chug with which the events of the morning fell into place.

Barbara did not look like the kind of girl who would faint easily. She had not seemed in the least exhausted when he talked with her. She admitted that she had not read the papers recently—therefore she probably knew nothing of the body found in the marsh. His memory raced back over the words of their conversation. He had mentioned a big story but had not said what the story was. Of course there were plenty of people who paid little attention to the papers. On the other hand, might she have deliberately kept away from them through fear of what she might read? It was a futile but very common defence which led people unconsciously to act as if what they did not know for certain was therefore nonexistent.

She had fainted just after her father's announcement that Sheila O'Shay had been murdered. Was there a connection there? She had once been engaged to Don Ellsworth—and she did not want the fact to be known. Was she protecting Don? Or was her father—who, come to think of it, had been very anxious to get rid of Peter before Barbara should fully regain consciousness—protecting her? Was he afraid of what she might say when she once again realized the discovery from which she had recoiled into unconsciousness?

Peter faced with tightened lips and sick eyes the last question of all. Was her friendliness toward himself a deliberate device to secure him on her side—because he might find out too much? Was she using the age-old chicanery of women to beguile and confuse men? He recoiled, despising himself for the suspicion. But his dislike of the idea did not make it any the less possible. After all, the method, if it was a method, had been disconcertingly effective! But he knew the danger of believing what you want to believe, and he forced his mind to meet squarely the image of her face.

"Damn it all," he grunted. "I don't know—but I've got to find out!"

Chapter XVIII

PETER'S FACE, minus its usual bisecting grin, looked longer than ever when he dragged himself wearily across the local room to Jimmy's desk. He felt physically battered. The familiar din of the local-room typewriters, the shouts of "copy boy," the "bling" of telephone bells, which usually were unregarded elements of a normal atmosphere, smote his ear as separate sounds, distinctly, as if he were hearing them for the first time. All this rushing to and fro seemed futile and unimportant, like the scurrying of mice across a barn floor. What did it matter, anyway, whether the *Herald* beat the *Record* by an edition?

Jimmy caught sight of Peter's tall, angular figure over the head of the society editor who had just succeeded in claiming his attention.

"Talk to me about it later," he said brusquely.

"But she's on the telephone," the society editor explained.

"I don't care if the Angel Gabriel is on the telephone! Well, Piper?"

Peter leaned his elbow against the wire mail basket, tipping it at a perilous angle.

"I didn't go to the city hall——" he began nonchalantly.

"The hell you didn't!"

The familiar elixir of the local room was having its effect on Peter. He felt a faint resurgence of his customary enjoyment in baiting the excitable city editor, who leaped after news like a dog tearing after a rabbit.

"No," he drawled, "but I got an advance statement direct from Dr. Cavanaugh. He has identified the body as that of Sheila O'Shay."

Jimmy wasted no time in congratulations.

"Boy!" His voice was a raucous, joyous bark. "Go to the library and get all the pictures we have of A. G. Cavanaugh—Cavanaugh spelled with a 'C.' " He peered across the room at the office clock, pushing his eye shade back over the hedge of upstanding red hair. "Go to it, Piper. We'll hold the edition fifteen minutes over the deadline. Give us a short lead. Then get the clippings on Cavanaugh and write a good follow story for the home edition."

Peter lounged across the room to his desk, thrust a sheet of copy paper into the carriage of his typewriter, and typed his name in the upper left corner.

The face of Barbara wavered before his eyes: the face of Barbara, white, with closed eyes; the face of Barbara with the broad, childlike brow and the smooth hair drawn straight back; the face of Barbara with the determined chin telling him that she was a guttersnipe. The face of Barbara——

"Piper!" the voice of Jimmy at his elbow was a rumbling growl. "This is a daily newspaper, not a biennial edition of *Who's Who*. We're holding the presses for you!"

Peter thrust the face of Barbara out of his mind. When a story had to be written, it had to be written—"despite of Day and Night and Death and Hell." The line, forgotten since high-school days, flashed out of the darkness. Resolutely he summoned the old habit of concentration. But it was easier to ignore the world outside—the room with its voices and bells and clattering confusion—than to blot out that other, inner confusion which made his thoughts a clamour of questionings.

He hammered out a lead—jerked out the sheet and tore it up—flung the wadded scraps on the floor in the general direction of the wastepaper basket—and began again. His fingers pounded rapidly, steadily—clackety-clack, pause, clackety-clack—on the keys of the battered typewriter. As each sheet of copy paper was whipped out of the carriage, with "more to cum" typed at the bottom, a copy boy at his elbow whisked it out of his hand and ran with it to the city desk, waited for Jimmy's rapid perusal, and ran again to the copy desk, where he sent it hurtling down the tube to the composing room. The city editor bent over his desk, with a man from the art room, arranging a layout—Cavanaugh, Don Ellsworth, Sheila O'Shay.

Peter himself took the last sheet from the typewriter and laid it before Jimmy.

Jimmy looked up.

"That's a pretty good yarn," he said.

It was the highest pinnacle of praise to which a member of the *Herald* staff could be lifted. Jimmy reserved his superlatives for the unimportant. He unloosed the full intensities of his vocabulary on a misplaced initial in a two-inch item; but when by a juggling of captions the mayor of the city was labelled "Bank Embezzler," all that he had said was, "Oh, dear!"

"You look all shot to pieces," he added. "Go out and get a good lunch and then walk around for half an hour. Here!" He thrust two silver dollars across the desk to Peter. "The lunch is on the house." He had remembered that it was the day before pay day—a day on which the members of the local room staff were likely to lunch on a sandwich and five-cent coffee.

"Thanks," Peter said indifferently. "I'm all right."

"Do as I tell you!" snapped the city editor. "And your follow story will be page one—and sign it."

Peter drifted past the desk where the society editor was indignantly, though in cautious tones, discussing the shortcomings of Jimmy with the water-front man.

"Mrs. Ames is one of the most prominent women in town—the Van Alstyne Ameses, you know."

The water-front man did not know, but he grunted sympathetically.

"When she wants her picture in Sunday's paper it's got to go. And what was I to tell her? That Jimmy didn't care how prominent she was, compared with somebody that got murdered, I suppose! I guess Mrs. Van Alstyne Ames is just as important as any corpse. But Jimmy's positively inhuman."

"I'll say he is!"

It is the custom of all local rooms to agree on the inhumanity of city editors. Peter jingled the dollars in his pocket and nodded briefly to the two in passing. How important everybody thought his own concerns! Barbara didn't read the papers—she probably didn't even know what it meant to get a signed story on page one. Besides, Barbara——

He ought to be elated instead of tired, and dry in the mouth as if he had been eating chips. Peter had written good stories before. But for the first time in his life he had written a good story—and did not care.

Chapter XIX

"SUSPECT HELD IN TULE MURDER."

The banner line in heavy black type that streamed across eight columns at the top of the first page caught Peter's eye as the copy boy flung the city edition across his typewriter.

Something in the pit of his stomach seemed to perform a sickening flip-flop—the same feeling which always seized him when a rapidly rising elevator jerked to a stop. The reaction was instantaneous and unreasonable. It could not possibly be——

He snatched the paper from the desk and sank slowly into his chair, his eyes leaping from line to line of the brief story which announced that Mrs. Nellie Kane, former dresser and maid of Mrs. Don Ellsworth (Sheila O'Shay), was lodged in the city jail.

"No charges have been placed against the woman, according to Captain of Inspectors L. B. Davis, but it is alleged that she is suspected of holding important information which she has declined to divulge and which, in the opinion of the police, may have a bearing on the case."

"Thank God!" breathed Peter. And added, "Idiot!"

He was ashamed of his own relief—a relief which left him light-hearted to the pitch of giddiness. Had he lost all sense of proportion, of probability? He decided, ruefully, that he evidently had. But his absurd buoyancy persisted, as if a heavy rock had come hurtling down in the direction of his head and had then miraculously missed him.

"Because she's old and poor and probably dowdy, they call her 'the woman,' " he mused with a sardonic smile. "If she'd been young and belonged in the fur-coat class, she'd have been 'Mrs. Kane' throughout. Lord, what snobs these mortals be!"

"Mrs. Ellsworth, whose disappearance on the eighteenth of last month——" There followed a resumé of the case, which Peter scanned anxiously. The name of Barbara Cavanaugh was not mentioned.

"Of course it wouldn't be—it couldn't be, without me," he reminded himself. "I'm going positively cuckoo. I ought to be psyched. And by jiminy, the old bird pretty nearly did it, just by the way he looked at me." Thus disrespectfully did Peter refer to one of the foremost psychiatrists of the United States.

"Piper!" The voice of the city editor blared, like the blast of a trumpet considerably off key.

At the sound Peter was his alert, nonchalant, lounging self again.

"Present or accounted for," he grinned, as he strolled over to the city desk.

"I want you to get an interview with this Kane woman. Get her picture if you can. You can take a camera man with you, but you'd better leave him outside. Davis may baulk, but see what you can do with him. They've nothing on her, I understand, but they ran her in last night. Probably thought jail would scare her into coming through. Anyway, stick around and see what you can pick up."

Peter ran his long fingers through the hair which promptly sprang up again from its centre part in an incorrigible cowlick.

"Cheerio!" he said gaily. "In other words, you betcha."

The city editor had already seized the desk telephone and jerked it toward him, but he turned to survey Peter.

"Don't play hopscotch on the way," he admonished. "The cops might get you."

But Peter was already on his way to the locker room for his hat, whistling dolefully.

"Temperamental kid!" Jimmy growled. "Low as the seventh circle yesterday, and now he's ready to kick the moon. Talk about prima donnas! But a damn good newspaper man, at that. Lord, the better they are, the worse they are. Andy!" he bawled, after this brief period of reflection. "Get busy on that annulment case. Nine o'clock in Judge Wood's court. And get a picture of the mother and baby."

The tumult of the local room was in full swing as Peter banged the door behind him.

Whatever Mrs. Kane knew had nothing to do with Barbara. If the old lady really knew something—Get it? You bet he'd get it! If that dame knew something that would let Barbara out——Peter's enthusiasm for Mrs. Kane would have astonished that somewhat unprepossessing person if she had been aware of it. It mounted so rapidly that by the time he reached the steps of the city hall he was almost running, leaving the camera man, dragging his black box and tripod, to pant along behind him.

Captain Davis, however, was unresponsive to Peter's carefully veiled eagerness.

"Nothing doing," he said decisively, as Peter leaned over the edge of his roll-top desk. "Wait till she's charged—if she ever is."

"Maybe if I talked to her she'd let something slip," Peter suggested.

"No chance," Davis reiterated. "Our men have been talking to her all night. She's about as likely to slip as the Rock of Gibraltar."

"Do you mind telling me—not for publication—what you've got?"

"I don't mind telling you that we've got nothing at all. But that's not saying that there's nothing to get. She knows more than she's telling, that's certain; and we've got to sweat it out of her. So far"—the captain of inspectors smiled grimly—"our men have been doing most of the sweating. I guess you'll just have to wait, Peter. Cavanaugh's going to have a try at her this morning. I don't think much of these new-fangled psychological methods myself. But there's no denying the old bird has a way with him. Camberwell got him in on the case in the first place and persuaded him to follow it through. They're two cranks together, and thick as thieves. But I should worry if they deliver the goods."

Captain Davis was well accustomed to the persistence of reporters; moreover, though he had learned to hold firm against that persistence, he was not averse to a little chat with Peter. Somewhat to his surprise, however, Peter hunched himself upright and showed no inclination to linger in the captain's office; nor was there any sign of disappointment visible on his mobile countenance.

"Well, see you later," he remarked with a fine casualness, as he drifted out into the hallway.

He did not, however, leave the city hall. Instead, he leaned against one of the pillars at the side of the entrance door, looking very much like a young man with nothing to do and all day for the doing of it. Yet Peter had a strong hunch that he had never earned his pay envelope more assuredly than by the wasting of that hour.

At last his vigil was rewarded, after a period in which an elevator man, a uniformed policeman from the traffic bureau, and two reporters from the press room had variously commented on his low, breathy, and monotonous minor whistle as something to be taken to the morgue, to be the equivalent of an injured cat and a banshee, and to be deserving of ninety days in the cooler.

That whistle lapsed abruptly into silence as a tall figure mounted the steps before him.

"Good-morning, Dr. Cavanaugh." Peter extended his hand with the engaging smile of a small boy hoping for a peppermint. "I hope you remember me?"

Chapter XX

"You are the young man who gets—and forgets—his stories. I begin to regard you as a suspicious character. What do you want this time?" The doctor's smile took the sting from his words, as it had a way of doing.

"You're right—both ways." Peter was unabashed. "I've got to get a story and I do want something from you. I'd like to go with you when you interview Mrs. Kane. I want to get a light on her personality. As to what she says, I won't use anything without your permission, of course."

"Several other persons share your desire for light," Dr. Cavanaugh observed, "but I understand that so far it hasn't been gratified. Why don't you get your interview direct?" he added crisply.

"Because Captain Davis won't let me. But of course, if I went with you, there'd be nothing said."

"That's the second time you've told me the truth when subterfuge would have seemed easy and more profitable. I almost suspect it's a habit with you." Dr. Cavanaugh's deliberate, unemphatic voice was almost a drawl. "Well, young man, you've flattered one of my weaknesses. I had sufficient curiosity to read your story. If anybody tells you that he never reads what's written about him, you may put him down as a liar or a colossal egotist who thinks that God alone is qualified to have an opinion on him besides himself. And you didn't once call me a criminologist. Perhaps a scientific training makes pedants of us all. I confess to a twinge of resentment whenever I am called a criminologist."

"Sheer luck," said the grinning Peter.

"Call it luck—or inspired accuracy. Anyway, I'll admit I liked it. You see, I never disguise myself or my purposes. I lay all my cards on the table—and let the other fellow play them. I'm not even interested in catching criminals, as such, though I'm interested in understanding my fellow human beings. This little hobby of identification merely helps sometimes to locate the subject whose mental processes interest me. I suppose," he went on without change of tone, "since I've inflicted all this explanation on you, the least I can do is to let you come along."

"Whoopee!" crowed Peter.

With a smile half indulgent, half wistful, the doctor led the way down the corridor to the jail elevator. Youth! When a man looks thus tenderly on the ebullience of youth, Dr. Cavanaugh reflected, he is growing old. The time had long passed when any of life's incidents could make him shout "Whoopee!" The greatest psychiatrist in America glanced briefly at the newspaper reporter whose pay envelope held $50 every week, and breathed a sigh of reminiscent envy.

The long, bare room in the women's quarters of the city jail smelled vaguely of whitewash. The matron, with clanking keys at her belt and an air professionally maternal, ushered in Mrs. Kane and faded into a corner. Peter grinned. It must be rather a strain to assume a motherly air with the redoubtable person who marched to the table where the two men had seated themselves and faced them with a belligerent stare.

"Mrs. Kane," Dr. Cavanaugh began with an air of kindly severity, "you have made a mistake in judgment."

"You ain't got a thing on me, not a thing," Mrs. Kane snapped, her teeth flashing up and down with more than usual rapidity. "They can talk till doomsday, and I'll say the same. You got that hair, by hook or by crook, but how can you prove that it belonged to Miss O'Shay? Answer me that!"

"A good point," Dr. Cavanaugh conceded blandly. "But if the hair which I took from your dress does not connect you with Miss O'Shay, it does connect you with the woman found, supposedly murdered, in the tule marsh. Things might be rather uncomfortable for you if you refuse to admit that the hair is hers."

Mrs. Kane's mouth opened, closed again with a click, and finally reopened.

"Anybody that thinks I'd harm Miss O'Shay is a fool," she muttered. "All you policemen are fools, anyway."

"Not necessarily," Dr. Cavanaugh argued cheerfully. "But I'm not a policeman. Let us suppose that you have Miss O'Shay's best interests at heart—that you believed you were best protecting her by refusing to tell any of her affairs to outsiders. In the circumstances, I still think that you made a mistake in judgment. The police are bound to find out—or at least to try to find out. And in trying they may uncover—all sorts of things."

Mrs. Kane, who had stood rigidly erect, sat down very suddenly in the chair by the table, as if a scaffolding under her voluminous garments had collapsed. She had had a sleepless night, and, despite her determination, she looked badgered and perturbed. The doctor made no move to go to her assistance, but continued to look across at her with steady, placid gaze. He didn't fuss; he didn't shout at her and point his finger; he didn't put words into her mouth and demand, "Isn't that so?" He seemed to have some sense. Why not tell him—a little, anyhow? Enough to get those questioning men away from her—those men to whom she would not talk though they kept at her for a year!

"They'd better have left things alone," she protested sulkily. "What good does it do to rake everything up? If that was Miss O'Shay who was found in the marsh, you can bet there was some scandal back of it. There always was," she added bitterly, and followed her words with a vehement click, like the snapping spring of a trap.

"Still," the doctor suggested tranquilly, "some scandals are worse than others."

"I suppose they are," Mrs. Kane admitted grudgingly.

The doctor continued to gaze serenely into space. Peter was scribbling indecipherable notes on a sheet of copy paper held under the table. The heavy breathing of the matron, who was indulging in the corner, in what she euphemistically called a cat nap was the only sound in the room.

Mrs. Kane also closed her eyes for a moment; but when she opened them they were alert, with the sharp glint of jet.

"I'll tell you this, if you want to know," she said acridly, "though I never thought as I'd live to tell it to a single soul. That whippersnapper, Mr. Ellsworth, didn't want to marry Miss O'Shay. He was wild about her at first—and he wasn't the only man who was that, I'm telling you—and then he cooled off and wanted to back out. They had a terrible fight. But anybody that gets into a fight with Miss O'Shay knows he's been in a real scrap. He flung out and said he never wanted to see her again. And then she went to a lawyer, she did, and drew up the nicest little breach-of-promise suit you ever saw. You bet she'd got it all down in writing, too, and had kept the letters. It took just one good look at that paper and the evidence to bring him round. She kept the papers, just to remind him if he ever got funny, and they're in the wall safe in her bedroom to this day. If you're looking for one person that wouldn't be too displeased to have Miss O'Shay out of the way, it strikes me you'd better page Mr. Don Ellsworth!"

Her long skirts swishing, Mrs. Kane rose to her feet with what could be described only as a flounce.

"Thanks," said Dr. Cavanaugh, quite unruffled by this outburst. "I'll do that. I am sure that your information will prove extremely valuable."

Peter had also risen to his feet. There wasn't a chance in a hundred, he told himself, but you never could tell till you tried.

"By the way, Mrs. Kane," he said, speaking for the first time, "I've a camera man waiting just outside the door. I'm a newspaper man, and you know we always have to have attractive pictures to go with our stories. So long as this case is in the papers anyhow, won't you let us have your picture to dress it up a bit?"

With an amazement that almost robbed Peter of the power of action, he saw Mrs. Kane pat her sausage roll of varnished hair.

"Well, now," she said, "I ain't rightly fixed for a picture."

But Peter was already shaking the matron by the shoulder.

"Hurry up and open the door for the man in the hall, Ma," he whispered. "Your prize prisoner is going to pose for a flash!"

"I suppose you'd like me to smile? Dear me, that flashlight thing is sure to make me jump a foot!"

"Sure!" said Peter irrepressibly. "Look pleasant, right toward the camera, please. That's it—shoot!"

As the jail elevator rumbled downward Peter turned to Dr. Cavanaugh.

"Whoever would have thought she'd fall for a line like that?" he exclaimed. "Gee, human nature's funny, isn't it?"

"So I've observed," Dr. Cavanaugh agreed imperturbably.

"But if you'd looked at her hair, you wouldn't have been so surprised. No woman dyes her hair without a reason—or shall we say without faith? You're the first person, I suppose, who has flattered Mrs. Kane for a long time. You justified her faith. And now, I suppose, she'll be pursuing you, to make sure of her conquest."

"God forfend!" gasped Peter. "I hope they keep her safely parked in jail!"

Chapter XXI

Peter Piper stood with his finger hovering over the doorbell, in a state of acute and unaccustomed embarrassment. Peter's finger usually attacked doorbells without hesitancy. He cocked his head slightly to one side and observed that tentative member with detachment, as if it did not belong to him.

"Shucks!" he admonished it with a shake of the head which tilted his disreputable soft felt hat even farther over one eyebrow. "Punch, you idiot, punch! You can only get kicked out, and heaven knows, that's no novelty."

The doorway where Peter stood was rather impressive, as doorways go; but Peter was unimpressed by grandeur. Too many mahogany doors had swung open to him—swung open upon suicide, murder, embezzlement, the downfall of ambition, the price of folly. The glamour of wealth had long ago lost all power to affect him—he had followed the same story too often across Khorassan carpets and splintery bare boards. Yet for some reason Peter was undeniably nervous.

But then, Peter had never before attempted a formal social call on a young lady.

In Peter's set you did not make calls. If you liked a girl, you said casually, "What do you say we stay downtown to dinner tonight and do a show?" Then you bummed two tickets from the drama editor, and that was that. But Barbara bothered him. You couldn't say a thing like that to Barbara. Barbara probably went to her shows in box parties without the intervention of a drama editor. He felt as uncertain of Barbara as if she belonged to a strange and probably hostile savage tribe. He had no particular respect for her tribal customs, whatever they were—in fact, he had an extremely upstanding respect for his own; but he had to see her again. And for the first time in his varied life Peter was greatly at a loss as to how to proceed.

Well, the only way to do a thing was to do it. He ought to have asked her first, of course. But you couldn't very well say, "By the way, may I call?" to a girl who has just slumped to the running board of a car in a dead faint. Neither the etiquette books, which Peter hadn't read, nor the novels, which he had, provided for a situation just like this. She'd probably take him for a cheeky rough-neck. Maybe he was! But still, he had to see her. He couldn't make her out. She kept playing hide and seek with his imagination at the most inconvenient times; when he was dead tired and trying to go to sleep, for instance, or when he was halfway through a story that had to make a deadline. That was the devil of having an imagination! If he saw her again, she'd drop into place, and he'd discover that he'd been making it all up. The best way to lay a ghost was to face it.

"Yes, sir?"

Peter jumped. The door stood open, framing a maid done in India ink and Chinese white. The tone of her voice indicated that the door had been open and the maid standing there for an interval long enough to require patience.

"I'd like to speak to Miss Cavanaugh." Peter spoke with his best *Herald* dignity, to cover that absurd start.

"Yes, sir. What name shall I give, sir?"

A small shining tray was whipped into play before him. Peter had never possessed a calling card in his life. The only cards he owned were printed, with *"Evening Herald"* in large Old English letters in the middle, and "J. A. Piper" in small block letters in the lower left-hand corner. He looked haughtily past the small shining tray, damning it into invisibility.

"Tell her it's Peter Piper of the *Herald*." His tone challenged the India-ink-and-Chinese-white automaton to make the most of it. The tilt of his long chin even indicated that for two cents he'd knock her block off. The automaton stood her ground, undeterred by this display of arrogance.

"I don't think——" she began.

"Well, you needn't, need you?" There was something sudden and disarming in Peter's wide smile. "Suppose you put it up to her? I'll bet you two bits she sees me. Are you on?"

The faintest flicker of responsive friendliness rippled across the automaton's face.

"Will you come in and wait, sir?"

Peter dropped into the nearest chair in the hall, and lapsed into unplumbed depths of discomfort. It was like sliding down an inclined plane. "Peter Piper of the *Herald*" had slid from his lips by habit. What did he want to say that for? It sounded unbelievably silly—like "Lord Raven of Ravenswood." What had he come for, anyway? He and this girl had absolutely nothing in common. Curiosity—that was it! Curiosity was said to be fatal to cats. "Cats—bats—bats—cats!" Alice in Wonderland. The immortal wonder-child of Lewis Carroll's imagination. Was she really like that—Alice in Wonderland grown up? Or was he betrayed by that trick of drawing her fair hair straight back from her round forehead? The real Alice probably grew up quite differently. She wasn't mixed up in a murder, anyway! Lewis Carroll made fools of us all—he made you love his Alice so.

Peter Piper brought himself up with a start. That word was dangerous. He was walking straight into danger—a danger that befogged clearness of vision in a mist of sentimentality. Peter had a deep distrust of sentimentality. It was all right to be sentimental over Alice; you couldn't very well help it, and Alice was safely out of harm's way, in fiction. But this was reality, the Twentieth Century, and Sheila O'Shay was dead and Barbara Cavanaugh had fainted at the news of the discovery. There were too many Barbaras—the Alice Barbara and the orphanage Barbara and the young lady Barbara with all those strange tribal customs he knew nothing about. And was there another Barbara—a deep, clever, wits-about-her Barbara whom he didn't know at all? Well, he had wits of his own if it came to that.

Curiosity. Let it rest there. If curiosity made a fool of him, he wouldn't be the first cat to succumb. It brought him up in his downward slide toward despondency to insist on the singleness of his motive. Curiosity. He turned his back resolutely on that other, more dangerous word. And she couldn't do more than turn him out—in which case he'd remember to slip the black-and-white automaton her two bits. He needn't mind—he'd been turned out of plenty of houses before.

But he would mind—he would mind quite sickeningly. The other times it was the *Herald* that was turned out—just Peter Piper of the *Herald*. But this time it would be Peter Piper himself. Aghast at his own egotism, it dawned—with curses—on Peter that there wasn't a chance in the world that Barbara had been consumed with any curiosity about *him*.

He wiped his hands on his handkerchief—they were cold, and damp with perspiration—and bunched the handkerchief into his already sagging coat pocket. He snatched his hat from the bench beside him. She'd know what a fool he'd been—it was too late to help that now—but he'd salvage the remnants of his folly. He'd get out before she turned him out. He had already taken a step toward the door when he remembered the automaton and hastily clawed two dimes and a nickel from the chewing gum, rubber bands, and paper clips in his trousers pocket. The little shining tray winked up at him from a small table. He laid the three coins in a neat row on its gleaming surface, the nickel, being the largest, in the middle. Then he glared at it balefully.

"Damn!" he said softly, addressing the tray. "Damn! Damn! Damn!"

"Well, if it isn't Peter Piper, swearing at the world!" Laughter rippled through the voice, through and under and around, like broken lights playing across water.

For the second time that day Peter jumped at the sound of a voice.

Then he jerked the little tray a foot into the air, tossing the coins high, scattering them to the corners of the room.

"She's lost her bet! Bless Pat, the automaton's lost!" he carolled.

Chapter XXII

Barbara stood slim and straight in the doorway. Her clothes, Peter noted, were slim and straight, like herself. So were the clothes of every other girl on the street, but the fact had escaped Peter's observation. She was a girl who never bothered with being surprised. The cascade of coins on the hall floor passed without immediate comment.

"Nellie needn't have put you in Coventry like this—out in the hall," she said. "Come on in, won't you?"

She held aside a curtain, and they were in a small, rather jolly little room, which seemed to be full of a fireplace and orange marigolds. Peter followed the casual wave of her hand toward an armchair. He was already in it before he noticed that Barbara remained standing, her elbow crooked across the corner of the fireplace. Another of the tribal customs! He ought to have waited till she sat down. But it was too late now—he couldn't very well jump up again.

"Well," said Barbara, gazing down into the fire and addressing the glowing heap of coal, "I don't suppose you came on purpose to play with the card tray. Don't tell me you're after another story!"

Peter rose from his chair with deliberation. He was more angry than he had ever been in his life before. Anger broke over him, wave upon wave, and left him trembling. He forgot that he had ever in his life gone after a story and been proud of it. He stood over her, tall and menacing, by the fireplace, with less than a foot between them. His clenched hands were drawn back, the arms slightly bent. Barbara stared into furious gray eyes. If she had been a man, she knew that he would have knocked her down. She squared her shoulders ever so slightly.

"Story—be—damned!" Peter said slowly, striking each word a separate blow. "What do you take me for? I came to see you, I tell you! I came to—to make a call!"

"Oh! Oh! Oh!" Barbara's laughter was not polite, controlled, musical laughter. It was the helpless, choking, clutching laughter of one seized and shaken by an irresistible hurricane of mirth. "So—so that's the way you make a call, is it? Do you—do you—do it like this—very often?"

She leaned her forehead against the mantelpiece, her shoulders shaking. Against the mighty wind of such laughter there was no defence. Peter was caught up in it, helpless. Barbara lifted her face, scarlet from chin to brow, and wiped the tears from her flooded eyes.

"No," said the grinning Peter, "I never made a call before."

"Let's begin, then. The first thing people usually do in the course of a call is to sit down. Suppose we do that." But before she turned from the fireplace, standing very straight and small before the towering Peter, she held out her hand. It was a small, slim hand, and yet somehow not incompetent—a hand that would be accurate and sure in all its movements, a hand that would never flutter or fall helplessly or make futile, bungling gestures. Its clasp was very firm, very alive.

"I want to thank you," Barbara said, her face grave now and sharpened into the withdrawn yet alert look which Peter remembered. "I haven't laughed like that since—for a long time."

The instant's hesitation brought Peter's mind leaping back to forgotten reality.

"You're feeling quite all right again after—your illness, the other morning?"

"Quite." The word fell like a pebble dropped very gently into deep water. Barbara had sunk into the second of the two fireside armchairs. Her hands were clasped lightly in her lap, but something in the poise of her body was wary rather than relaxed.

"Please don't look like that," Peter blurted. "I like you ever so much better when you're Alice in Wonderland. I like you that way best of all."

"But this isn't wonderland." The sad little voice was barely a murmur, from very far away. "Besides"—the voice had come back this time, was near and crisp and firm, like watercress just out of a brook—"you mustn't like me that way, in pieces. I won't be a character that you've made up for yourself. I'm just—I. If that's not good enough——"

"It's quite good enough." To his surprise, as if it belonged to someone else, Peter heard his voice shaking. "I'm sorry I made such a fool of myself, and got mad a minute ago."

"You were, rather," Barbara agreed. "After all, the only times I'd ever seen you you'd been after a story. I thought it was the only thing you ever did. I'm glad it isn't." Her eyes, lifted to his, had the undisguised beaming friendliness of a child's.

Peter made a decision. It was rather a momentous decision, inasmuch as it sacrificed his gods—the gods of the *Herald*—without a quiver.

"Look here," he said solemnly, "I promise that I'll never mention the Ellsworth case to you again. I guess that'll show whether I'm always 'after' something."

"Oh, but don't do that!" There was a touch of panic in the hurrying protest. "I want to know all I can about it. The newspapers never tell anything until it's—too late. Don't shut me out, please!"

Peter's hand reached out in a gesture of warning. She was giving herself away—and she mustn't; not to Peter Piper of the *Herald.* The small face turned up to him was harried.

"Look here," he said again, "are you taking me for a friend?"

"Yes," she said quietly. "I've no business to, I suppose. But I think I am."

Peter sighed—a heavy, gusty, and by no means chivalrous sigh with which to greet an offer of friendship.

"It complicates things, rather. But it's worth it."

"Thanks." That was said as a small boy might say it, hiding feeling with an abrupt casualness.

"I can't help knowing that you are—interested—in this case."

"I am that." In the remembered Irish inflection of her voice he heard again the gamin, the guttersnipe, the girl of the orphanage, the girl who had been like a little wild thing in a hostile wood. If she had bared her small sharp teeth and struck, in circumstances he could not know, he for one would remember that girl of the orphanage. He would not blame her for it. Never. But she did not know what she was up against. He didn't know, either, for that matter. He'd have to know, if he was to help her.

"I won't shut you out," he said gently. "I'll tell you anything you want to know. But believe me, it's for your sake I ask you not to shut me out, either. Let's go at it together."

"I—know." She closed her eyes. Her face became a sharp white mask against the dark chair back. For a moment he wondered if she were going to faint again. But her eyes, when she opened them, were intent and very steady. "I'm willing to help you in any way I can," she said. "I'll help you with my father. If there are things I can't tell you, I'll say so. But I'm asking you to be frank with me when all I can promise is to be as frank with you as I can. It doesn't seem a very fair bargain."

"It isn't a bargain at all—I'm not dealing in bargains. Did you think I was holding out for a *quid pro quo?*"

"No," Barbara said hastily. "Now don't go and get angry again. You're so—unpredictable."

"Goodness knows what I'm letting myself in for. I may be compounding a felony for all I know. Not that I care, only I generally prefer to compound my own felonies, with my eyes open. But I'm going to trust your judgment—because I believe you've got judgment. Only there's just one thing. I'm willing to tell you anything you want to know—only you must never ask me to withhold anything from the paper unless you can give me a perfectly clear and complete reason for it. And even then you must leave it to me, absolutely. If you use anything I tell you, to keep somebody else two leaps ahead of the sheriff—well, that just adds to the complications of existence. By the way, the one bit of news you probably don't know is that Don Ellsworth married Sheila O'Shay under threat of a breach-of-promise suit."

"Oh, I am glad!" Barbara's face was lit with sudden, incredulous delight. "No," she added thoughtfully, "I didn't know that."

"You seem rather pleased about it." The room, for all its dancing firelight, seemed gray and chilly, tricked out in the flaming mockery of orange marigolds. Don Ellsworth belonged to her own tribe.

"I am. Up to the very day that I got his wedding announcement, I thought Don and I were engaged. I just had to believe there was some explanation—he wasn't the sort of person who could let you down without a reason. Of course I'm glad to know he didn't do a thing like that of his own free will!"

"You care—such a lot?"

"That isn't the point at all. He would cut his tongue out sooner than acknowledge that he was forced into marriage. It's the one thing I never understood—and couldn't ask."

"Well," said Peter wearily, "I don't think he'll share your transports at having it known. It rather puts a crimp in him as the bereaved young husband of an adored wife."

"You mean—they'll suspect him?"

"They'll suspect everybody they possibly can—you can bet on that."

Barbara opened her mouth as if for furious protest. Then she closed it again and merely squared her shoulders against the back of the chair.

"Don's all right," she said at last. "Only I suppose there isn't any use shouting about it. But if you go after him with any of your strong-arm methods, be sure you know what you're about. Don doesn't like newspaper reporters—not one little bit, he doesn't."

Chapter XXIII

PETER PARKED Bossy in the gloom of a large shade tree at the corner, and extinguished the lights.

"If you do get bumped, it can't hurt you very much. You've got to take your chances in this game, Bossy old girl," he remarked. Then he marched debonairly up the gravelled driveway and rang the doorbell of the Ellsworth house. When on business, Peter lost no time over doorbells. And he was on business now—on detail to cover the Ellsworth house and not to come back till he got something. That it was now nine o'clock in the evening, and Peter's working day supposedly closed at four, meant nothing to Jimmy. To be fair, it meant very little to Peter, either. His gray overcoat was worn smooth at the cuffs so that the crisscross of threads was plainly visible to the observing, and one pocket was ripped halfway down by the jamming of copy paper, folded magazines, and large apples into its capacious maw, but he wore it as jauntily as if it were an opera cape. Peter on an assignment was not to be intimidated by men, angels, or butlers.

The door opened with surprising promptness and revealed a young man with eyebrows done in charcoal, a sullen mouth, and eyes puffy from lack of sleep, whose hat and overcoat indicated that he was just leaving the house. He had the air of one not so much answering the doorbell as accidentally coinciding with it.

Peter stepped at once into the shaft of light that streamed from the open door.

"Oh, you rang? Someone will answer the door in a minute." The young man would have brushed past if Peter had not obviously and bulkily stood in the way.

"I rather think you're the person I want to see," Peter remarked easily, with one of his friendliest grins. "In that case, mayn't we consider the door already answered? You're Mr. Don Ellsworth, I think."

"What did you want to see me about? I'm in rather a hurry." The voice was brusque and noncommittal.

"I think it would be worth your while to wait for a few minutes," Peter said firmly.

"I don't believe I know who you are——?" The young man, defensive but puzzled, peered at Peter's kindly and quite unabashed countenance.

"You don't. I'm Peter Piper of the *Herald.* I'm sorry to have to trouble you at this time, when I know you must be busy and worried, but if you can give me a ten-minute interview it will help greatly in putting your position in a proper light before the public."

"I have nothing whatever to say in which the public is interested." The voice was controlled, but the heavy brows drew together in a single line across Don Ellsworth's forehead.

"I'm sorry, but the public already is interested. It's painful to you, but you can't help it. Certainly I can't help it. It's news. That news will be printed, despite you and me. If it were news about somebody else, you'd read it. It happens to be news about you, and other people insist on reading it. Believe me, I'm not invading your privacy because it's my personal idea of fun. But if you answer my questions frankly, what you say will derive an immense advantage from being said by you of your own free will. You can't keep the public out of it, so you'd better have them on your side. I'm giving you your chance."

Peter spoke rapidly, emphatically, but without raising his voice. His head was thrust a little forward, his bright, near-sighted gray eyes steadily fixed on the dark face before him. He saw that face whiten about the lips, saw the veins bulge at the temples—and stepped back just in time to avoid the lunging sidewise blow whose impetus brought Ellsworth through the open door, which crashed shut behind him.

Don required Peter's steadying touch on his elbow to recover his balance and prevent his plunging forward down the steps. He was not even conscious of that briefly supporting hand.

"I may not keep the public out, but I can keep you out!" he said, turning toward the vague blot of shadow on the darkened porch which was Peter. "And every other newspaper reporter, too. I've not one single word to give to the press now or at any other time. That's my answer!"

"Very well," said Peter imperturbably; but he said it to Don Ellsworth's back, rapidly losing its form as a shadow among other shadows as he dashed down the driveway, his feet scuffling with vicious force on the unoffending gravel.

"And the worst of it is," mused Peter as he followed at a more leisurely gait, pausing to light a cigarette from a crumpled package which he exhumed from his overcoat pocket, "he may have to give all those words to men from the district attorney's office, and they'll pass them along to us; and by that time they may not sound so well—not half so well. But Barbara's tip was certainly a good one. I almost think he doesn't like reporters—not one little bit he doesn't!"

Peter's evening assignment was by no means concluded. He returned to the dark and almost invisible Bossy at the corner, and looked carefully up and down both streets before he decided that he might properly venture the glow of his lighted cigarette behind the side curtains. He did not know precisely what he was waiting for, but he waited in a state of alert quiescence.

If the police should force the pace and come with a warrant to search the house, Peter was going to be there. They might let the Kane woman out—though that was unlikely; she was fairly sure to be held as a material witness unless Ellsworth gave bail for her, and Peter was of the opinion that Ellsworth would bear with equanimity Mrs. Kane's absence from his house. Or something altogether unforeseen might break. You never could tell. He might better have followed Ellsworth; but after all, he had nothing to go on there—and anyway, his present job was with the house.

It was neither the returning Ellsworth nor Mrs. Kane whose appearance brought Peter leaning forward in the front seat an hour later, but a small black runabout from which emerged the broad shoulders and rotund form of Dr. Cavanaugh. He walked up the driveway with long, leisurely strides, and stood in parley for some minutes with the maid at the entrance.

Peter had closed Bossy's door gently behind him and was halfway across the street when he paused.

"After all, I can't very well trail the doctor like a faithful pup," he pondered. "He's been pretty good to me, and I don't want to break the charm. It's just possible I might be in the way." While he still hesitated, the front door closed and the house turned to him a shut, impenetrable face.

Peter, however, did not recross the street. Instead, he turned the corner and gazed upward at the dark side of the house. A pergola led to a garden at the rear, and above the pergola to the left a faint gleam of glass indicated what was probably a sunporch. A few lights still shone from the lower floor at the back—"servants' rooms," commented Peter—and a dimmer light, as if penetrating a dark room before reaching the street, indicated the front hall.

"Hm," meditated Peter. "Now where the dickens did the great Cavanaugh go to?"

As if in answer a light—bright, definite, unshaded—flashed on in the room over the pergola, on the second floor.

"Now I wonder. Suppose I have a look-see. If it's none of my business, I can just climb down again. If it is, I'll crash the front door, ask for the doctor, and trust to him to let me in on it. Of course, if I'm caught on that pergola-thing, it may take a fair bit of explaining."

It was the idea of that possible explanation that determined Peter. Jimmy would not back him up in any such performance—Jimmy, having told him to cover the Ellsworth house and not come back till he got something, would merely take his copy and read him a lecture if he got into difficulties. But the lecture would not be nearly so hard to take as if he didn't turn in any copy. He could hear himself arguing with a bevy of frightened, indignant, incredulous servants, who would thoroughly enjoy the excitement of capturing a burglar red-handed. He could see himself submitting with sang-froid to a ride to the police station in the jangling patrol wagon, and then confronting the irate, sputtering, and friendly Captain Davis, who would ask him if he expected to get away with murder. Decidedly, such a culmination would not be without its points.

Neither, Peter discovered, was the pergola without its points.

They were the sharp half-inch points of a particularly stalwart variety of climbing rose. They made long claw-marks on his calves, and his hands seemed to encounter them with unerring and painful precision.

"Gosh, what a cat fight!" breathed Peter. "If I don't claim damages under the workmen's compensation act for this——!"

He began his climb at the farther garden end of the pergola and walked, crouching, along the top, where progress was easier, except when his foot slipped through the squares of the lattice. And then, in a state which it seemed to him must be one of fluttering ribbons, he reached the house wall at last, and, squatting on his thighs, looked into the brightly lighted boudoir of Sheila O'Shay.

Chapter XXIV

DR. CAVANAUGH'S broad back loomed directly in the field of Peter's vision. He was seated somewhat absurdly on a very small chair whose long spindling legs and short back gave it the distorted look of something that had started out to be tall and had stopped growing. It was the sort of chair peculiar to ladies' dressing tables, but as this was the first time Peter had ever seen a lady's dressing table, it appeared to him something of a monstrosity. Dr. Cavanaugh's solid bulk, clad in its usual sober black, projected beyond his insufficient seat; he looked, Peter thought, rather like a block of granite balanced on the top of four far too slender stakes.

The dressing table itself—a glass-topped, triple-mirrored affair on which at the present moment the doctor rested a nonchalant elbow—was covered with a surprising multitude of objects, each of which looked like something else. The glass bottle of rose-coloured bath salts had the form of an elephant; a squat object which should have been a jar of cold cream masqueraded as an overblown pink rose. A long stick with a wide flat circle of powder puff at the end was painted with the face of a black-

and-pink, very exotic lady. The bases of a procession of bottles peeped from the wide-spread taffeta skirts of a row of dolls.

Peter's entranced gaze veered to a small stand near by on which rested a telephone book in a tapestry cover bound in gilt braid together with another and larger doll concealing the telephone instrument. The electric-light brackets by the dressing table were shaped like candles, with small pointed globes, and the reading lamp by the bed cast its rosy glow through the frosted petals of a cabbage-shaped flower.

Peter shifted his weight from one cramped leg to the other.

"Gosh!" he breathed. "What a way to live! No wonder somebody bumped her off!"

His change of position brought him within sight of the door, where stood a girl in maid's uniform. Her round flushed face was a study in alarm, pleased excitement, and admiring awe. It was a larger number of emotions than her ingenuous countenance was used to expressing at once, and the effort had widened her eyes to the roundness of very blue marbles. She stood fiddling with the doorknob, obviously seeking an excuse to remain in the room. The stolid set of Dr. Cavanaugh's shoulders and his relaxed attitude before the dressing table indicated bland and patient waiting.

In the darkness Peter grinned.

"She'd give her eye teeth to stay, and the doctor is calmly sitting her out," he opined. The window was closed and he could not hear what was said; but in another moment the maid, with a broad smile making her cheeks bulge rounder than ever and a lingering gaze of extreme respect toward the figure at the dressing table, withdrew, closing the door behind her.

Peter eased himself to his knees and reached for the upper ledge of the window. He had no intention of spying. He would open the window and tell the doctor he was there. Then, if he wasn't wanted, he'd depart along the thorny path by which he had come. Dr. Cavanaugh's eyes reflected in the wide mirror of the dressing table suddenly met his—met them without change of expression, but with an unmistakable glance of recognition. In another instant, the window was quietly opened from within.

"You might as well come in—you seem to be a fairly ubiquitous young man, by the way."

Peter felt exactly like a small boy caught in the farmer's apple orchard and required to make an ignominious descent from the tree. Stiffly he thrust his long legs over the window sill. His first words seemed to himself absurdly inadequate to the situation.

"But—but you couldn't possibly have seen me in that mirror!" he stammered. "I was behind a window at least fifteen feet away, and in the dark!"

The doctor gently closed the window before turning to the astonished and shamefaced Peter.

"You have a good mind," he said gravely. "You seized on the one factor that seemed inexplicable. As a matter of fact, I didn't see you. I merely looked encouragingly in the direction where you were most likely to be."

"Most likely——!" Peter flopped heavily on the lace-covered bed. In his astonishment he completely forgot that he might have been expected to make rather than to ask for explanations.

"There's no 'quick, Watson, the needle' about it." The doctor's heavy face was illumined by one of his rare and genial smiles. "I saw you start to follow me across the street, and then think better of it. Well, I've observed that you are a young man who never thinks better of getting things—only of the best means of getting them. You didn't follow me in at the front door; therefore you would follow me at the rear. I've known Don Ellsworth for years.

I've walked under that pergola—though I never tried your mode of progress along the top. From the looks of you, I don't think I ever shall."

"I'll go if you say so." Peter strove to keep his tone matter-of-fact, but there was no banishing the wistful eagerness from his shining, expectant eyes.

"It's housebreaking, you know. God and the police look with disfavour on it."

Peter leaped to his feet, his stiffness forgotten.

"God and the police may not like it, but Jimmy surely will!" he chortled. "Gee, what a tragic waste of talent it is that you're not on a newspaper, Dr. Cavanaugh! You'd be a wow as a reporter."

There was not a trace of irony in Dr. Cavanaugh's response to Peter's earnest tribute—the highest it was in his power to pay.

"We're both very lucky men," he said. "We're doing the thing of all things in the world that we'd choose to do. Most men are less single-minded—or less lucky. Which reminds me that you haven't asked what I'm doing at this moment in the boudoir of a lady with whom I am only slightly acquainted. Has it occurred to you that we may be just two housebreakers together?"

"At least I can be flattered to meet such a distinguished fellow-burglar," Peter said with cheerful impudence. "I'll bet a dollar you thought you'd come around before the police got to it, and take a look at those breach-of-promise papers!"

"I hope most of your investments are sounder than that one," said Dr. Cavanaugh, "because in this instance you'd lose at least fifty cents of your dollar."

"But what about the other fifty cents?" inquired the unchastened Peter.

Chapter XXV

"THE OTHER fifty cents," said Dr. Cavanaugh, "is safe. I did come, among other things, to look into the matter of those papers. But Captain Camberwell is responsible for my presence in this unconventional fashion. He didn't quite fancy leaving to the estimable detectives promoted from the traffic squad the survey of the last spot where, so far as we know, Mrs. Ellsworth was seen alive. And the rest of the department, in a rare burst of diplomacy, backed him up. It's rather a ticklish case, this, from their point of view. Mr. Ellsworth has not given them what you'd call cooperation. He was not at all cordial to the sergeant who came in response to Mrs. Kane's call. To be exact, he turned the policeman out of the house."

"Yes," Peter agreed with a reminiscent grin. "He's rather good at that. I'd like to have been present at the interview—it must have had its dramatic moments."

"Doubtless. At any rate, Ellsworth has them rather baffled. The department is shy about sending a couple of uniformed policemen flourishing a search warrant to batter in the door of a prominent millionaire unless they have something more definite to go on than they have with Ellsworth. He might make things too uncomfortable later, if they were on the wrong track. And yet it is obviously necessary that an investigation be made of the scene of Mrs. Ellsworth's disappearance. Camberwell is thoroughly competent to undertake the job himself, of course; but Ellsworth, I'm afraid, would not have greeted him with the respect his very high talents deserve."

"No," Peter grinned again. "Respect for people who come to interfere with what he regards as his private affairs isn't one of Mr. Ellsworth's outstanding traits. I've noticed that myself."

"Well, the upshot of it all was, that at Camberwell's request I was called upon to fill the breach. Camberwell has an all too flattering opinion of my abilities. But at least I have the advantage of personal acquaintance with Ellsworth. He'd hardly shut the door in my face—provided I arrived when he was here to shut it at all, which, in the circumstances, I thought would be hardly tactful. I'm armed with a deputy sheriff's badge and a search warrant to use as a last resort—but I rather think our police friends had faith that I'd manage to get along without what I believe are sometimes referred to as strong-arm methods. In return I stipulated that my services, such as they are, must be taken strictly as a favour. I prefer to have an entirely free hand; and the police accept that little idiosyncrasy, albeit with a certain reluctance."

"I'll bet they do!" Peter looked across at the doctor, who had resumed his somewhat precarious seat on the dressing-table chair, with a very boyish enthusiasm. "They're like the transcendental female who told Carlyle she 'accepted the universe'; and the old bird said, 'Egad, she'd better!' The police, if I know them, will take whatever you choose to give them, and be grateful. But what's your idea about Ellsworth, anyway? Does this—er, visit mean that we're getting the dope on him?"

"'We' haven't what you call the dope on anybody yet; and I

make it a point not to have too many ideas in advance of the evidence."

The faint emphasis on that "we" brought a quick embarrassed flush to Peter's cheeks.

"You know I didn't mean——" he faltered, feeling more than ever like a small boy.

"Quite. You wouldn't be here at this moment if the 'we' were disallowed. I did my own bit of housebreaking precisely because I haven't a fixed idea about our young friend. But I don't want him to run into more trouble than is strictly necessary, so I was willing to take the part assigned me in conducting this more or less official preliminary survey, at the same time following a little idea of my own. If he's left those papers alone, well and good. If he's taken them away, he may be a panicky fool or—something else. In either case, I can do more good by taking my time in looking about before the police wind the whole place up in yards of red tape and regulations. By the way, at the present moment you're not representing a newspaper. That's understood?"

"I'll take back to the office exactly what you give me permission to take," Peter assured him.

"We might as well begin, then. The safe won't be locked, so that part will be simple."

"But you haven't tried it yet!"

"No, but look at this." Dr. Cavanaugh turned to the dressing table and lifted the ornate roof from a box which was a replica of a French cathedral. Peter leaned over his shoulder. The chest was filled with a higgledy-piggledy assortment of jewels—a strand of pearls entangled in the points of a diamond-and-platinum brooch, bracelets, and rings piled in a helter-skelter mass.

"You see, she didn't even turn the key in her jewel case—the sort of person, I fancy, whose possessions were usually in a state of confusion. She had no fear of thieves, because the things that people are robbed of came easily to her. She could always get more. I'll put a nickel on the safe being unlocked—just a little private bet with my own judgment." Dr. Cavanaugh drew out the nickel and laid it on the smooth glass top of the dressing table.

"But mightn't Ellsworth have locked it?" Peter suggested.

"If he came here, he'd be in a hurry—and it would be his instinct to leave things as nearly as possible as he found them." Dr. Cavanaugh rose to his feet with a little sigh. "I suppose we might as well find out. It's always more interesting to work out a problem than to check it. But facts must have their day."

"There's another chance, you know," Peter suggested. "The dame with the trick teeth may have been lying all along. Perhaps there never were any papers, or any threat of a breach-of-promise suit. Perhaps Ellsworth married because he wanted to, like anybody else—though I will say"—Peter cast a scornful look upon the row of silk-flounced dolls on the dressing table—"I don't think much of his taste."

"It was a taste, at all events, which a good many people shared," Dr. Cavanaugh reminded him. "But you mustn't let Mrs. Kane's teeth prejudice you. Ellsworth's marriage differed, I am optimistic enough to believe, from most marriages that are still in the flush of their first year. If Mrs. Kane has not given us the right key to it, I still believe that a key of some sort is needed. She may be concealing something—a good deal, in fact—and she may be quite capable of lying. But on this one point, I'm inclined to think she was telling the truth—if only because it burst out of her unintentionally, when she had made up her mind to keep those teeth safely in place behind closed lips."

The wall safe was obvious enough, its front being merely

concealed for decorative purposes behind a square of tapestry through which the bulge of the knob was plainly visible. Dr. Cavanaugh motioned to Peter to hold up the corner of the tapestry, and confidently pulled at the handle. Peter found that he was holding his breath. The doctor reached behind him with his free hand and pocketed the nickel.

The door swung open.

The safe was empty.

Chapter XXVI

"WHEW!" PETER exhaled his pent breath in a long, whistling sigh. "So Ellsworth's made off with the evidence that his marriage wasn't precisely a love match. Not that I blame him for disliking the lady. I think I'd have disliked her considerably, myself."

"It looks that way." Dr. Cavanaugh stared gloomily into the empty cavity. "I'm sorry. It doesn't prove anything, of course."

"Well, it's rather an indication, isn't it? It shows that Ellsworth thought the information contained in those papers was dangerous—and it wouldn't be dangerous unless it led to something he wanted to hide. He wasn't aware that the Kane woman knew about it, of course."

"Precisely," Dr. Cavanaugh agreed wearily. His face with its deeply graven lines looked suddenly older. "I wish he'd thought of that. It's the mistake so many people make—the mistake of not realizing that concealment, whatever the motive, is bound to be taken as you've taken it. And it makes it impossible for me to help him. If he hadn't already taken these papers, I was going to warn him for heaven's sake to leave them alone. I've known him a long while, you know. I wanted to prevent his doing a foolish thing—if I could. But now it's out of my hands. I can't go to a man who's possibly guilty and tell him the way he ought to proceed to establish the appearance of innocence."

Peter, his hands thrust deep in his pockets, strode to the window and stared out into the darkness. Warning? The doctor had meant to warn Ellsworth. Had he been warned already—warned that the papers revealing his forced marriage still existed and were likely to be found unless he got them out of the way? Who could have warned him—except Barbara? Barbara, who fainted when she learned that Sheila O'Shay's body had been found; Barbara, who had once been, and perhaps still was, in love with Ellsworth; Barbara, whom Peter himself had told of the breach-of-promise threat; Barbara, with the candid brow and the shining eyes of a child; Barbara, with the wary, withdrawn look that defied interpretation.

Peter's shoulders drooped dejectedly. He felt an irrational indignation against Sheila O'Shay for getting herself murdered and dragging Barbara into it. The sharp sound of the safe door closing recalled him.

"We'd better see what else there is while we're here," the doctor said with a slight shrug of his shoulders, as if he were shaking off an invisible weight. "We'll leave Don out of it for the present, and concentrate on Mrs. Ellsworth. She seems a person who might have left considerable traces behind her."

"I don't like her," Peter announced with great definiteness. "Too much fussiness." He thought suddenly of a girl whose clothes were slim and straight in a room full of firelight and orange marigolds. "I wouldn't have married her if she'd bluffed me with a dozen breach-of-promise suits."

"Nevertheless, several men did."

"Did——?"

"Marry her. She was a woman of very devastating charm. And if she had no conspicuous force of intellect, she had unusual force of will. She always got what she wanted—until, poor lady, in the end someone rebelled and gave her what she wanted least of all. I did not know her very well, but you hardly needed to know her well to see that."

"But a woman who kept all that junk!" Peter's voice vibrated with youthful and uncompromising distaste. He waved a hand toward the dressing-table mirror whose edges were completely bordered with old invitation cards, dance favours, dinner place-cards, even the stubs of theatre tickets.

"Precisely," the doctor said drily. "Nothing beclouds the judgment like moral disapproval. If you're interested in finding out who murdered Sheila O'Shay, it's just possible that you ought to be grateful for her passion for hoarding souvenirs."

He bent forward across the dressing table, made a quick and thorough survey of the various bits of paper at the mirror's edge, then turned to the small ornate desk with a drop-leaf lid which stood against the wall. As he lowered the flap which, when opened, formed a shelf for writing, a veritable avalanche of letters, bills, envelopes, and programmes cascaded from the bulging interior.

"I rather thought she was like that," the doctor mused, with a glance at the crammed pigeonholes, "when Mrs. Kane mentioned that Mrs. Ellsworth had saved the breach-of-promise papers. That was a rather motiveless thing to do, except for the not uncommon type of person who has a sort of collectors' mania for preserving every memento of her past life. And in that case, there may be other significant mementos. I think we'll have to look them over. Rifling a lady's desk is not a very nice occupation; but then, we're investigating the lady's murder, and murder is not a very nice occupation, either. I hardly think we can afford to stand on etiquette."

Peter sat astride the dressing-table chair, his long legs twisted about the rungs, his folded arms resting across its low back, and watched the doctor's deft fingers rapidly unfold sheet after sheet of folded or crumpled paper and toss them in a mounting pile on the floor at his feet.

"By the way, where's Ellsworth?" he asked after an interval. "Or am I interrupting?"

"Not a bit. A glance is quite enough for all of this stuff, so far. I'll tell you if I find anything." Dr. Cavanaugh's hands did not hesitate in their task of extracting and casting aside the contents of the desk. "Don is engaged in a very quiet poker session in a private room at his club. I unofficially escorted him there myself, although he did not know it."

"With the whole countryside moving heaven and earth to find his wife's murderer? Well, I thought I was beyond being surprised at anything!" Peter's capacity for astonishment was obviously not entirely exhausted.

"Not the whole countryside, young man. Only a few policemen and reporters and people like that. And Don Ellsworth, when faced with a disagreeable situation, does not sit down and contemplate it, even when that is precisely what he needs to do. All his life he has sought distraction—escape. Always he has found it easily enough. You needn't be too hard on him. With his upbringing, it was almost inevitable. Probably Sheila O'Shay, in the beginning, was one of those distractions. He may not find his diversion so easily this time, but the impulse to seek it was the most natural thing in the world for him. You might be grateful for that, too. He won't be in until the small hours of the morning—which gives us this very opportune leisure."

"He didn't know you were coming, then?"

"No. He's an irascible young man, and I didn't want to upset him unnecessarily."

"Yes," Peter agreed with a grin, "I've noticed the irascibility."

"I told you I was a housebreaker, too, you know. I owe my presence in the house to Ethel. I'm rather elderly for pergolas—and perhaps just a shade too conventional."

"Ethel?" Peter rested his chin on the chairback and grinned an impudent question at the doctor's imperturbable back.

"The maid you saw in the door. I feel rather sorry for her—she'd have enjoyed this so immensely. She's a hero worshipper, and steeped in the traditions of Sherlock Holmes. Perhaps it's just as well she didn't stay to be disappointed. She rather fancies me as a sleuth. No power on earth could persuade her that I'm not, of course. Besides, she has a moth-and-star sort of devotion to Ellsworth. It is quite true that I thought my visit here might be of benefit to him. She relished the notion of the great investigator saving her master from unjust suspicion. In fact, she fairly gloated over the whole performance, and her own connection with it. Well, it looks as if everybody's hopes—yours and mine and Ethel's—are pretty well blighted. The net result of all this is nothing at all." As he spoke, Dr. Cavanaugh stooped, gathered the heap of papers into an armload, and thrust them back into the desk.

From the chair where Peter straddled came the sound of a low whistled tune, a lugubrious, wailing minor.

"By Jove!" he murmured. And again, "By Jove—I wonder now!"

He had been staring straight before him with his chin on his folded arms, his eyes fixed on vacancy. Suddenly he realized what he had been looking at all along. With a bound that overturned his chair behind him he sprang to the telephone table and seized the directory. For fifteen minutes he had been gazing absently at a narrow projection which marred the smooth line at the edge of the pages along the top; and then, in a flash, that little projection had taken on meaning. He fluttered the pages in fingers that trembled, and drew out a letter. Then, with the single sheet half removed from the envelope, he paused. It might be anything—it might be nothing. But the doctor had opened the window to him. Whatever it was, it belonged to the doctor.

"Here," he said in a rather faint voice, holding out the fluttering slip of paper to Dr. Cavanaugh, who had calmly picked up the chair. "What do you make of this?"

Chapter XXVII

Dr. Cavanaugh finished his righting of the overturned chair. Then he reached deliberately for the sheet of paper, holding it gingerly by the edges.

"No use gumming up the finger prints," he observed. "Camberwell's very fond of nice finger prints."

He laid the sheet of paper face upward on the dressing table, securing each corner with one of the toilet articles for a paperweight.

"It's your find, young man. Come and have a look."

Together the two men bent over the flattened page.

Dear Sheila [it read]:

I've found you out. You sentenced me to a sojourn in hell, such as you would neither understand nor care about. Did you ever in all your life, I wonder, care about anything but your own desires? You've attained them every time, those desires, riding roughshod over all who opposed you. You've used everything you have—your beauty, your terrible charm (yes, it is terrible, Sheila; even I, who know you well enough to hate you, feel it even yet)—for your own purposes, destroying others along the way. But you who have destroyed others may yet be destroyed by the very forces you have raised. There are things that not even you can manage. I have come to myself at last, and you have me to reckon with. You had better arrange to see me at the earliest opportunity.

DAVID ORME.

"Hm!" the doctor's deep bumblebee hum broke the silence as he straightened from his leaning position over the dressing table. "What do you think of that, Peter?"

"It's a brand-new angle—thank heaven!" Peter exclaimed.

"You needed a new angle?"

"I did," Peter agreed emphatically. A new angle—and one with which Barbara, at least, had nothing to do! "It's a threat, obviously. Who's David Orme?"

"Precisely. Who is David Orme? It's going to be somebody's business to find that out."

"It might be an alias, of course," Peter suggested.

"I hardly think so. The writer of that letter expected Sheila O'Shay to know who he was."

"Yes," Peter broke in eagerly, "and that handwriting doesn't look as if it were disguised, does it? It's a bit shaky, but quite natural and flowing."

"I'm not a handwriting expert, but I'm inclined to think you're right. Camberwell, of course, can tell. Taking it at face value, it's the writing of an educated man—the letters are very small, for one thing, and there's the Greek 'e' and the final 'd's.' While an educated man might try to imitate the handwriting of one who was almost illiterate, the reverse would hardly be feasible."

"There's the choice of words, too. 'Attained your desires.' Nothing rough-neck about that—and yet it's not exactly stilted, as if he were trying to talk big. Gee, this begins to look good!" Peter was rocking back and forth on his toes with suppressed excitement.

The doctor reached absent-mindedly for a cigar, and then regretfully thrust it back into his case.

"Too bad," he murmured, "but we can't leave a lot of smoke about. I'll have to tell you again, young man, that you've a good mind for seizing significant points. Perhaps you noticed also the choice of ideas. That is a threatening letter, yes; but it goes in for what are called glittering generalities. The writer was thinking more about his own feelings than about any definite plan of action. He's what we psychologists call an introvert. There's the double parenthesis, too—correctly punctuated, by the way. His mind wound in and out among his emotions. He couldn't resist that bit about her 'terrible charm.' Unfortunately, though we know all this about his insides, there's not much of a clue by which to pick him out on the street."

"What about the envelope?" Peter grovelled a moment on hands and knees and retrieved the envelope where it had fallen under the telephone stand. This time he was careful to touch it only at the edges. "It wasn't posted at all," he said disappointedly. "Delivered by hand. Still, this is sort of funny, isn't it?"

The envelope, which he laid on the table beside the letter, was addressed in a single line: "Sheila O'Shay (Ellsworth)."

"A regular demon for parentheses, that bird. Now what do you suppose he put those in for?"

"If I were being facetious, I'd say he was imitating the newspapers. You wouldn't say, now, that this letter was written by a newspaper reporter gone wrong?"

Peter looked as startled as if a gun had suddenly been pointed at him, barrel foremost.

"I certainly wouldn't," he said sharply.

"There! You see how careful we must be not to jump to conclusions. Even you, who have nothing whatever to do with it, looked momentarily guilty when confronted with a suggestion which seemed to come home to you. You are not David Orme, but you remembered that you had expressed a rather extreme dislike for the lady in the case."

"I never saw her in my life!" Peter protested.

"I know you didn't," Dr. Cavanaugh said soothingly. "But I wanted to warn you to be very cautious about theorizing. The race is not always to the swift—they sometimes race in the wrong direction. By the way, did you happen to notice the pages of the directory where the letter was thrust?"

"I'm afraid I didn't," Peter admitted. "I ought to have told you and let you take it out yourself. I just didn't think! It was somewhere near the front of the book—that's all I remember."

"Well, don't worry. It can't be helped. It just gives the police a chance to exercise their own wits instead of ours."

"I'm sure it wasn't as far back as the 'O's,' " Peter said dejectedly. "And yet it was stuck in with the edge just a little beyond the margin, as if to mark the place. I don't think she had any idea of hiding it there."

"No. She wasn't hiding it. Mr. Orme, whoever he may be, wouldn't be in the telephone book anyhow. If he were, he'd have telephoned probably instead of writing—and he wouldn't have 'found her out' at this late day if he were living in the same town with her. She was rather a public character, you know. But she might have known how to get in touch with him through someone else. They may have met since that letter was written, for all we know."

"I'm awfully sorry," said the crestfallen Peter. "I've made a perfect foozle of it."

"On the contrary, you found the letter, which may be important evidence, and is certainly well worth looking into. It is your—er, scoop."

"You mean I can have it for the office?" Peter beamed.

"Hardly that—you forget Mr. Camberwell's penchant for finger prints. Besides, your enterprise in getting it at all might not be appreciated by the police department. But I see no objection to your making a copy, if you think your editor would like it—you've certainly earned that much."

"Like it!" Peter was already scribbling frantically with a stubby black pencil on a sheet of copy paper snatched from his coat pocket. "I'll say he'll like it!"

"I shall tell Camberwell that you assisted me in my unofficial inquiry," the doctor said. "That will allay his curiosity—and there's no reason that I can see why we should try to keep the letter secret. If it was written by the criminal, he'll expect it to be found sooner or later. And when the police begin to look for him, he'll be a very poor criminal indeed if he isn't aware of their efforts. I'm beginning to take a personal interest in the news-gathering projects of the *Herald.*"

"It'll make the city edition," Peter sighed happily. Suddenly his pencil paused in midair. "Here's another thing," he said. "That letter was written on cheap paper—almost as poor as this stuff in my pocket. It would hardly take the ink. And yet it was written with a good smooth pen point. It must have been fountain pen ink, or it would have blurred more than it did. Unless the paper is a blind—and the only apparent blind about the whole business—this Orme person carries an excellent fountain pen but is reduced to the cheapest possible kind of paper. Gee, I'm beginning to find him interesting!"

"So am I," said Dr. Cavanaugh.

Chapter XXVIII

"WELL, LOOK what the cat brought in!"

Jimmy, who prided himself on being the first of the *Herald* editorial staff to arrive in the morning, had signalled the freight elevator as usual in the gray light of a six-o'clock dawn, swung around the jutting corner of the photographers' dark room—and was brought up short in his headlong progress across the local room by the sight of Peter, hunched over his typewriter, the light from a battered, green-shaded desk lamp outlining a harsh circle about his slouching shoulders. At the moment, Peter's fingers were poised silently over the typewriter keys, but simultaneously with Jimmy's greeting they resumed action in a clattering burst of sound.

"Don't fuss me," Peter growled, with a brief glance at the city editor. "Be with you in a minute."

The fanfare of the typewriter keys continued in irregular, rapid-fire staccato, then ceased with a rattling cadenza as the last sheet of copy paper was ripped from the carriage. Peter strolled with elaborate nonchalance between the empty desks, numbering the pages as he went, and thrust them with a flourish under Jimmy's nose.

"Read 'em and weep," he said.

Jimmy clawed the sheets of copy paper toward him, pushing his eye shade at a rakish angle above his left ear. Peter leaned across the desk in a pose of extreme casualness, listening to the faint slip-slip as each page was turned methodically face downward. At last Jimmy looked up.

"It's a pretty good yarn," he said solemnly; and that, Peter knew, was the supreme accolade bestowed rarely by the city editor on work well done. Jimmy marked the first of the sheets, "first run, hed to cum" and yelled for a copy boy. Then, for the first time, he looked closely at Peter.

"Hell's bells!" he exclaimed, "where have you been all night, anyhow?"

"Oh, just around." Peter waved his hand vaguely in a circle of the horizon.

"Well, you look as if you'd been around and over and through," Jimmy remarked caustically. "Say, there's no funny business about this, is there? It'll check, all right?"

"Cavanaugh's behind it," Peter assured him. "He gave me the letter to copy."

"And just where did the dog fight come in?"

Peter was indeed a disreputable object. His face and the backs of his hands were scored by red lines along which the blood had congealed. His coat was ripped under the arm, and several jagged three-cornered tears decorated each trouser leg. His chin showed the need of a morning shave, a black smudge across his forehead gave him a sinister, piratical expression, and his eyes were bloodshot from lack of sleep. Nevertheless, he faced the city editor with an incorrigible grin.

"Oh, there wasn't any trouble—no trouble at all. These are honourable wounds, received in the line of duty—before I got around to the doctor. I guess it's about time I got around to a cup of coffee, though. And if you don't mind, I'd like to buzz home long enough to get into a suit that hangs together a little better than this one."

Jimmy surveyed the hollow-eyed, smiling figure before him.

"Go home and go to bed," he growled. "I guess we can live without you for the rest of the day. If anything breaks, I can let you know."

Peter, however, continued to lean across the desk.

"I say, Jimmy," he pleaded, "I'd rather follow this up. I've got a hunch about the man who wrote that letter. D'you suppose there'd be any chance of giving me a few days, just to root around on my own? It may not come to anything, of course."

"When you're as old as I am," Jimmy said in his gruffest tones, "you'll have enough sense to take a day off when it's handed you on a silver platter. But there's no fool like a young fool. Go wherever you durn please. You can turn in an expense account for that suit; but I warn you, if you go getting another one slashed up as if you'd been the centre of a stiletto contest, it's your own lookout. And if you hang around here another minute trying to look bored, you're going to burst."

But Peter, with a final grin over his shoulder, was already halfway to the door.

It was a very different Peter who parked Bossy on a side street two hours later and made his way along the drive marked "Tradesmen's Entrance" to the back door of the Ellsworth house. He had donned a sweater in place of a coat, and buttoned its high collar close around his chin. A wide-visored cap was pulled far down over his eyebrows, casting his face into deep shadow. He had even discarded his cigarette in favour of a short curved pipe.

The picture thus presented before his mirror had delighted him hugely.

"If it ain't the spittin' image of Sherlock Holmes on a rampage!" he addressed his reflection enthusiastically. "It shouts 'disguise' to the very housetops. And of course the object of a disguise is to look as much like a disguise as possible. If not, why go to all the trouble?" Regretfully he abandoned the package of cigarettes on the dresser. "Ethel's favourite sleuths always smoke pipes—I know they do. And Ethel, my dear, you're going to have the biggest thrill of your young life. It's too bad I can't make it really good—wait till evening and then throw pebbles at your window. But I don't know which window, and I couldn't hit it anyhow. Besides, I can't wait. You'll just have to be satisfied with things as is."

As a finishing touch, he pinned his police "Press" badge under the rolled bottom of his sweater, and then devoted half an hour to the composition of a note which, after several scribbled drafts, he finally copied in laborious hand-printed capitals.

"Urgent and secret," it began. "If you would be of service to the cause of clearing the innocent and bringing the guilty to justice, come at once to the shrubbery at the second bend of the driveway to the left, and tell no one. I am the private assistant of C., whom you left in a certain room overlooking the back garden between ten and eleven o'clock last night. P. P., Investigator."

Peter surveyed this literary production with beaming pride.

"Won't she just love it, though?" he gloated. "And the funny part is that, reduced to plain English, it's true enough."

Having delivered his message to an astonished cook at the kitchen door, Peter retraced his steps along the driveway as far as the second bend, and half concealed himself in the thick shrubbery.

"If anybody with any sense comes along, I'm sunk," he murmured. "I'd send myself to the psychopathic ward for investigation, on sight."

The only footsteps, however, were light ones, tiptoeing along the gravel from the direction of the house. Peter waited until they were almost opposite, and then stepped forward from his place of concealment.

"Sh!" he hissed loudly and unnecessarily to the palpitating Ethel, who was far too impressed to open her mouth. "Come behind these bushes, where no one can see us. I have something of the utmost importance to communicate."

Chapter XXIX

"I'D HAVE known you for a detective anywhere!"

Ethel stood in the doorway of the vine-covered summerhouse at the garden end of the pergola, to which she had conducted Peter, and surveyed him with respectful ardour. Peter cast a disapproving eye at the rose tendrils thrusting their way here and there through the lattice of the walls; he had an idea that he would never cease to regard roses as the most vicious and hostile of floral specimens.

"That, of course, is because you know about detectives," he said. "Come in and sit down, where we won't be seen."

Ethel perched herself on the extreme edge of one of the small iron chairs which, with a little green-painted tea table, furnished the interior of the summerhouse.

"Oh, there's nobody now who uses this place," she assured him. "I've always adored detective stories, but I never thought—never in the world—that I'd ever have a chance to be part of a real one, not even after Mrs. Ellsworth disappeared. It didn't seem a bit like a story somehow. Everything went on just about as usual. I know Dr. Cavanaugh's awfully grand, but he doesn't act one bit like a real sleuth, does he?"

"He conceals his talents," Peter said solemnly.

"Do you work with the police?" Ethel's hands were clasped tightly in her lap and her face was a round beaming moon of excitement.

"I'm 'with' but not 'of' them." With an air of great caution Peter flashed the shield of his police press badge momentarily into view. "I'm a sort of special deputy private investigator," he said with dignity. "I picked you out to help me because your reading has given you a certain familiarity with detective methods. But first I must ask you to swear to absolute secrecy."

"What do you want me to swear on?" Ethel gasped.

"What have you got?" Peter inquired practically. The "swearing" was an inspiration of the moment, and he had quite forgotten that, to be properly ceremonious, it must be done "on" something.

"I don't know as I've rightly got anything on me——"

"Never mind. This will do." Peter unpinned the police badge from his sweater and held it, his thumb concealing the embossed word, "Press," in the palm of his hand. "This is a symbol of the majesty of the law," he announced sonorously. "Now, then—'the-truth-the-whole-truth-and-nothing-but-the-truth-so-help-you-God.' " He rattled off the formula as he had heard the bailiff deliver it a hundred times in court.

"I do," Ethel responded fervently.

"Well, then, let's get down to cases. Did a man, probably a fairly young man and not very well dressed, ever come around to see Mrs. Ellsworth?"

"No, sir; not that I remember."

Peter's face fell. Was it going to be no good, after all?

"Not a small, dark man, who insisted on seeing Mrs. Ellsworth personally?"

Ethel sat a moment in silent concentration.

"Oh!" Her face lighted with sudden recollection. "He wasn't very dark, though——"

"Never mind that. It was just a guess, to get you to thinking."

"But he didn't get to see Mrs. Ellsworth——"

"That's all right, too. Tell me everything you can remember about it. Take your time."

"I'd forgotten all about him. I thought he was just trying to sell something. Those canvassers will move heaven and earth to see the lady of the house. But come to think, he didn't have a bag or anything like that with him."

"How long ago was this?"

"It was—let me think—I remember I hated to stop to answer the door because it was the middle of the afternoon and I was trying to slip some time in to sew the flower on my dress for a dance I was going to with my sweetie. And the dance was on the sixteenth, because my boy friend gets paid twice a month and he said he'd have plenty of money to show me a real swell time——"

"The sixteenth. That was just two days before Mrs. Ellsworth disappeared."

"Why, so it was! I never thought of it from that moment to this."

"All right. Now think hard, and tell me exactly what happened. You're doing fine."

"Well, this man was at the door and asked for Mrs. Ellsworth and I said, 'What name, please?' and he said, 'You may take her this,' and handed me an envelope. I didn't think much about it, because they have all sorts of advertising dodges these days—sometimes it's charity, or magazine subscriptions, or buying tickets to draw an automobile, or things like that. But I took it up to her and she read it and threw it down on the desk without saying a word. Then she picked it up again and handed it to Mrs. Kane and said, 'I'll be damned if I do'—excuse the language."

"That's all right. Mrs. Ellsworth's language isn't your fault. Go right ahead."

"So then I thought it was tickets or something she was turning down. She told me to tell him there was no answer and for him not to call again. But I wasn't more than halfway down the stairs when Mrs. Kane came down after me and said she'd attend to it herself. Gracious, how it all comes back, now that I think of it!"

"Yes," Peter prodded. "And then?"

"Let me see. I didn't want Mrs. Kane to see me going right back to my room, because I never did like that woman and it would be just like her to tell me I wasn't minding my duties. So I stood back in the hall waiting for her to get through at the door and go back upstairs. I couldn't hear what they said."

"Not a thing?" Peter's voice was a groan of disappointment.

"Well, now, let me think. He had on kind of a dark suit, blue it was, and it was all wrinkled and pretty dusty. Dust shows up a lot on blue, you know. I noticed the dust because he said, 'I'm staying at the auto camp grounds for the present, and I'm not going away till I see her.' And I thought he must be travelling about the country, but he'd better brush up a little, even if he was camping out, if he expected to sell anything."

"You heard him say that?" Peter leaped to his feet so suddenly that Ethel shrank back, startled.

"Oh, sir, I——"

"Now don't get scared. You're doing splendidly. I couldn't do better myself. What sort of looking man was he?"

"He was just an ordinary kind of man. Not very big—not as tall as Mrs. Kane. He was kind of thin looking, as if he'd been sick or something."

Peter thought this over, chewing the stem of his pipe and longing with his whole soul for one of his familiar cigarettes. So far he had got exactly nowhere. He knew that David Orme had called at the Ellsworth house—which he had known already—with the additional information that he had stopped at the automobile camp grounds. But David Orme, so far as the description went, might be any one of thousands. Peter might pass him a dozen times, meet him face to face on the streets, without a chance of recognizing him.

"That's all there was to it," Ethel said with finality. "He went away then."

"And he never came back?"

"Not that I know of—not when I was on duty. I never saw him but the once——Why, yes, I did, too, the very night after the dance! It went clean out of my head, because that was the night my boy friend and I, we fixed it up to get married." A very pretty rose-coloured flush swept across Ethel's round face; her eyes, suffused and tender, stared into romantic distances.

"That's very nice," Peter said kindly. "I congratulate the young man."

"Oh, it's me that's to be congratulated," Ethel said earnestly. "He's the grandest fellow. He——"

"I'm sure he is." Peter reached forward and gave her hand a friendly pat. "Some day I want to hear all about him, but we'll have to put that off a bit. So you saw Orme—this auto camp person—that night? Are you absolutely sure it was he?"

"Oh, yes, I'm quite positive. You see, my friend—Dan, his name is, but I call him Danny; it's sort of a pet name. He's awfully cute. He said he was going to call me 'Gas' because my name's Ethel—ethyl gas, you know. But he doesn't, really; he just says things like that to be funny. He said——"

"I'm sure he's witty as Oscar Wilde," Peter interrupted. "But you saw——"

"I never saw Oscar Wilde. But I think Harold Lloyd's just killing."

"Yes," Peter agreed hastily. "And you saw this man——"

"Oh, yes. Danny came around for me to the back entrance, in his Ford. When we turned out of the driveway—it's a sharp curve, you know—this same man was standing close under a tree at the corner of the lawn. The headlights were on him only a minute, but I know it was him, because his hand was resting against the tree trunk, and the last two fingers were off at the first knuckle, just the way they were when he had his hand up against the jamb of the door the day he asked for Mrs. Ellsworth."

"Suffering cats!" breathed Peter. And again: "Suffering cats! Why in the name of all that's holy didn't you give me that description before?"

"It never entered my head. You see, Danny and I——"

Peter bounded across the intervening space, seized Ethel by the shoulders, and planted a resounding kiss on her astonished cheek.

"You and Danny are going to have the finest wedding present the little old pay envelope can afford!" he shouted. "Keep it under your hat, Ethel darling. And watch young Peter do some grand and lofty sleuthing!"

His long legs were twinkling in full retreat down the driveway before Ethel recovered her breath.

"Well, if that ain't the limit!" she exclaimed to the empty air. "Detectives sure are funny,"

Chapter XXX

"If he has any sense, he'll have beat it away from here into other spots, and left no forwarding address," Peter informed Bossy severely as he swung into the boulevard leading to the camp grounds. But despite his efforts to batten down his enthusiasm with stern common sense, excitement prickled up and down his spine and tightened his hands on the wheel. It did not so much as occur to him that he had set out, unarmed and alone, to pursue a possible murderer. He did not even wonder how he would induce Orme to give himself up, if he found him. Peter was a profound believer in the futility of crossing bridges before he came to them—the bridges were so very likely not to be where you expected them, or to be missing altogether.

Despite his lack of sleep, he was buoyed up beyond the reach of fatigue; his head felt a little light but uncommonly clear. Bossy seemed to dip and skim along the highway like a gull coasting down the lanes of air. His cap blew off and rolled hoop-wise to the side of the road, but he did not pause to retrieve it. There was no real need for hurry—if Orme had not left long since, he was unlikely to get away in the course of an hour—but speed gave him the illusion of pressing on in an obscure race with fate.

"Gee, if the luck only holds!" he murmured once, and for a moment his long face took on the look of one who has uttered a prayer.

If this man Orme was mixed up in it, Barbara wasn't. Perhaps she was trying to shield Ellsworth—"loyalty, the useless, difficult virtues." There were things about Ellsworth that certainly weren't clear; but Orme was another line altogether. There was no connection between the two men that Peter could see. It looked as if the mystery of Sheila O'Shay's death might be further complicated by the mystery of her life. If there were things that she herself had wanted to conceal, digging them out would not be so simple. Peter's eyes darkened as his mind veered from Sheila's picturesque and polychromatic career to Barbara, fighting her way so gallantly, so foolishly, through shadows.

"Gosh, I'll bet that woman had a past as checkered as a Scotch plaid," he told the wheeling landscape with a half grin. Then his wide mouth set in a grim line. "If I'd had the chance to marry a girl like Barbara, I'd have bumped off the old girl myself before I'd have let her bulldoze me into marrying her. Ellsworth is the fool of the world—unless it's Peter Piper."

For Peter was coldly, dismally conscious that if he got Orme, and if Orme cleared Ellsworth, he himself might be clearing the way for Ellsworth to marry Barbara.

"Well, it can't be helped," he muttered through clenched teeth. Barbara, in the numbing chill of her orphan-asylum childhood, had found the glory of life in the vision of another world, where honour gleamed above peril, where loyalty fluttered like a pointed banner at a spearhead, where men rode into death with the scarves of their ladies bound to the sleeves of their coats of mail.

There was nothing very knightly about the battered Bossy careering along an asphalt highway guided by a reporter in a torn sweater. And yet, in that world of Barbara's, if a knight set out to rescue a lady, he tied no strings to it. He did not barter for a reward, even in his mind. He simply did it. And whatever the nature of Barbara's folly, Peter knew that he must save her from it. For one split second Peter saw Barbara in that barred room smelling of whitewash in the city jail. Never! If it came to the worst, he would drive her himself to the Mexican border. He didn't know what he would do. But they should not get Barbara—never—no matter what she had done.

With a squeal of brakes and a dragging of wheels on the pavement, Peter brought Bossy to an abrupt halt. He had almost driven past the entrance to the automobile camp.

Bossy looked by no means out of place in the scattered company of derelict cars parked in a field worn to dusty smoothness by innumerable tires. A hot-dog stand on wheels filled one corner, and a strip of unpainted cabins at the rear offered shelter at twenty-five cents a night. But most of the campers were content with tent-like roofs stretched from the frames of their cars to stakes thrust into the ground. A number had only rolls of tattered bedding spread beside the running board. Thin lines of gray smoke wavered upward from rusted camp stoves squatting here and there about the enclosure.

Peter stretched his cramped legs and, tossing his pipe into a corner of the seat, lighted a cigarette.

"And the romance of gypsying has come to this!" he mused, his gaze drifting from a man stretched in stertorous slumber to a woman with draggled gray hair cutting thick slices of bread with a clasp knife; to a girl in grease-spattered khaki army breeches and high-heeled patent-leather pumps; to a group of quarrelling, dirt-smeared children.

Gypsying! Green dells and wandering tinkers, the singing

freedom of the countryside. Perhaps it had always been like this, really, just as Barbara's knights had ridden out of castles unblessed by plumbing. These were the modern vagabonds, the unemployed, the drifters, the petty thieves, the incompetents, who bundled their families and scant possessions into ramshackle Fords and roosted, rent free, at public camp grounds until they were periodically weeded out, to rattle on again as far as their gas would take them—without hope, without plan, without beauty, without even the clean crash of real disaster.

Like most buoyant persons, Peter drowned periodically in depths of motiveless depression. He was sure that he would not find Orme. He was sure that Jimmy would fire him, that he could not find another job, and that he would slide step by step downhill until he and the last fragments of the chugging Bossy would come to roost somewhere in a public camp ground. He was sure that in some crazy, heroic, inexplicable moment Barbara had herself killed Sheila O'Shay and that he would have to stand by, helpless, and watch that shining head betrayed to the gray turreted walls—not unlike a mediæval castle, in their way—of the state prison.

That final vision roused him to action.

"Not till I'm dead, anyway," he said aloud, and dragged his steps drearily, hopelessly across the field to a corner where a young man sat on the running board of a mud-spattered runabout, munching a hamburger sandwich.

Peter held out his package of cigarettes and forced his stiff lips to a companionable grin.

"What's the luck up this way, buddy?" he asked, as a conversational opening.

"Rotten," the young man answered laconically. "There ain't no work for nobody no more, seems like. I gotta get something before I can move on. And the next place, it'll be just the same."

This pessimistic view of the economic situation chimed with Peter's discouraged mood; but after all, he had not come to discuss generalities of unemployment.

"I'd sort of arranged to meet a pal of mine somewhere around here," he remarked. "You been here long?"

"'Bout a month. I got a week's work picking strawberries. But hell, it's enough to break your back in two. I quit before my week was up, and been hanging around ever since, looking for something to turn up."

"Maybe he ain't showed up yet. A kind of a sickly looking chap——"

The man on the running board shook his head.

"With part of the last two fingers gone off his hand."

"Oh, *that* feller! Sure, I seen him. He ought to be 'round somewheres now—he's been sticking pretty close to camp. Ain't that him, over in the middle with the woman and bunch of kids?"

But Peter, having tossed the remainder of the cigarettes into the lap of his astonished companion, was already crossing the field in long, loping strides.

Chapter XXXI

PETER SLOWED his rapid steps to an indifferent stroll, and paused behind the group to which the man had pointed. Several persons were gathered about a table formed of unpainted planks laid trestle-wise across supporting end boards. A fat middle-aged woman in a torn bungalow apron was making a futile pass at two children who were squabbling noisily over a slice of bread and butter. The man, whose back was turned toward Peter, finished buttering a second slice and, reaching across the table, thrust it into the grimy hand of one of the contestants.

Peter's lips pursed in an inaudible whistle. He had met too many criminals to be surprised that a man might commit murder and yet take a sympathetic interest in the feeding of two strange and by no means attractive children. There flashed across his mind the memory of a hold-up man who had lost his job in a meat market because he could not bring himself to kill a chicken—and who, six months later, had shot down in the street a newsboy whom he suspected of recognizing him as a fugitive from justice. The man who reached the bread and butter across the table had the ends of two fingers missing from his hand.

"I'd like a word with you, Orme," Peter said quietly.

The man's shoulders quivered, but he did not turn. Peter rather wished that he would lay down the bread knife. He pondered the advantage of getting the table between them against the disadvantage of giving Orme that much of a start in case he turned and ran. Then, with a lift of the eyebrow as his sole tribute to what he designated as "the bread-knife angle," he stepped forward and touched the man on the arm.

"Your name is David Orme, I believe," he remarked conversationally. "Mine's Piper." His voice was carefully unemphatic, but his eyes were warily fixed on the long, keen blade of the knife. There was butter on it, and crumbs. His surface attention was all for the man at the table, but with an irrelevant, darting side-thought he wondered whether anyone had ever been stabbed with a knife that had crumbs and butter on it.

Slowly the man turned and faced Peter. The hand holding the knife trembled, but his voice was quite steady.

"Glad to know you," he said, "but you're mistaken. My name's Osgood—Daniel Osgood."

Forgetting caution, Peter's gaze shifted, startled, from the man's hand to his face. It was a surprising voice to come from a ragged fugitive, hiding under an alias, with murder in the background. It was low, vibrant, modulated, giving to the simplest words a hint of music. Peter knew with instant, absolute assurance that a man with a voice like that might commit murder, but he would never stab an unarmed man with a dirty knife. He slid into a seat on the bench beside Orme and leaned his elbow on the table.

"It *would* be," he smiled companionably. "It's a funny thing about people who change their names always keeping the same initials. In fact, the tendency is so familiar that I should think by this time everyone would take pains to avoid it. By the way, why didn't you clear out?"

"I didn't have the money," the man said simply.

"Oh, Lord!" Peter groaned. There surged over him an irrational impulse to protect this man from the trap which he himself had laid and into which the victim had stepped with such blind, unhesitating promptness. It was too easy!

"You ought to have a guardian!" he exclaimed almost angrily; and then, more gently: "it's a good thing I found you."

Suppose this babe had been pounced upon by men from the homicide squad, with their sweating methods and strong-arm tactics—it would be like seeing a rabbit torn piecemeal by dogs. Peter quite forgot that the man beside him was sought as a dangerous character—a slayer.

"But you haven't told me yet why you wanted to find me." There was not a trace of fear in the low voice, nor any combativeness. Peter leaned forward and peered at the face before him with his bright, near-sighted gray eyes before answering. It was a worn and sensitive face, young and yet ravaged; a face with delicate, clearly modelled features and dark sunken eyes. The perfectly shaped head had the smiting beauty of a profile on a Greek coin. And this was the man whom Ethel had dismissed as a "sickly looking fellow"! If sickness was there, it was a sickness of the soul. The curved lips, drooping slightly at the corners, the dark, steady eyes with their depths of pain, did not suggest weakness so much as the helplessness of one who is an alien in the world where he must live. There was a permanent bewilderment in those eyes—the eyes of a baffled poet thrust into a world of ugly prose in which he could never be at home, bruised and broken and still wondering. A man like that, wounded beyond endurance, might strike to kill—and still not understand what it was all about.

"Surely you know," Peter said at last, speaking patiently as if to a child, "that you are under suspicion for the murder of Mrs. Ellsworth."

The curved lips tightened into a hard, straight line. The face before him became as still, as expressionless as if it were chiselled in stone.

"I don't know any Mrs. Ellsworth." The voice took on a remote metallic ring, as if each word were the dropping of a coin.

Peter stared a moment. Then he remembered something—something that had puzzled him.

"But you knew Sheila O'Shay?" he asked breathlessly.

"Yes—oh, yes—Sheila O'Shay." The words were hardly more than an audible sigh. "A great many people knew Sheila O'Shay!" His hands were suddenly flung outward on the table in a singularly defenceless gesture. The knife, unnoticed, slid across the boards and fell noiselessly to the ground. The fat woman and her tumultuous offspring had wandered away out of sight.

"Yes," Peter said sternly, "but you wrote Sheila O'Shay a threatening letter. I don't know why you didn't take any pains to disguise it, but you didn't. Then you hung around outside the house, lying in wait for her. Sheila O'Shay was found murdered—and you are out here, hiding under an assumed name. You're absolutely no good as a fugitive, I'll admit—I could have done a lot better myself—but that's no sign you didn't do it. You trembled all over when I spoke to you."

"Oh, but that was before I knew you!" Orme's face broke into a radiant, confiding smile of sheer delight. "You're so very likable, you know! By the way, I don't think you're a policeman, are you?"

"No, I'm not," Peter said harshly. "But I'm just as bad. I'm going to take you to jail." He wanted to seize this unaccountable young man by the shoulders and shake him—shake him into a realization of the seriousness of the situation. It was like seeing a child watch the house burn down and clap his hands at the pretty fire.

"Well, that can't be helped, I suppose," Orme acquiesced.

"You'd have done better to face the music in the first place, if you couldn't get away any better than this," Peter said crossly. "You've made an awful mess of things."

"Yes," the young man nodded his head gravely. "I know—I do that often. I'm always making a mess of things."

"But hardly with your life in the balance!"

"Does it matter? Not a great deal, I think." Orme's tone was not in the least bitter. He might have been commenting on the prospect of rain.

"I'm afraid you'll wake up too late and find that it does!" Peter stormed.

"Well, don't let it bother you. It's my—er, potential funeral, after all!" Again that winning, sunny smile, like a child watching the mounting flames. Against his will, Peter found himself smiling back.

"I won't say that whatever you say will be used against you, because you'll be just putty in the hands of the police, anyway. But would you mind telling me—did you really kill her?"

"Maybe so," the young man said. "But that will be for the police to find out."

And this, through all the long drive back to town, was the last word that Peter had from him.

Chapter XXXII

"DID YOU put up any money on me?"

Peter threw his hat into the nearest armchair and leaned forward to examine the top of the desk, but the familiar nickel was not in evidence.

"No," said Dr. Cavanaugh, "the sporting element would be lacking unless I elaborated a system of odds. I'd hate to have you on my trail, young man—or perhaps this is what you call being on my trail already?" The doctor's clear brown eyes smiled with warm friendliness into Peter's as he pulled forward a chair.

"Oh, no, I've just got into the habit of consulting you. I hope I'm not making a nuisance of myself."

"I've no doubt you hope it. But even if you were a nuisance, you would regretfully persist."

"I suppose I would," Peter admitted.

"Well, then, if it's any comfort to you, I'm really not particularly busy at the moment, and you may help yourself to the cigars. It's rather lucky for me that I've retired from active practice—you might not leave me much opportunity to collect from my patients."

"I'm glad I'm not bothering too awfully," Peter said cheerfully, ignoring the box of cigars which Dr. Cavanaugh extended and pulling forth his inevitable crushed package of cigarettes. "Because, you see, I do feel sort of responsible for this babe in the woods I turned over to the police."

Dr. Cavanaugh smiled ever so slightly.

"Do the police look on him as a babe in the woods?" he inquired.

"They do not," Peter said emphatically. "As a matter of fact, I'm surprised at him myself. Honestly, I felt as if I were throwing him to the wolves. It had to be done, of course, but I didn't think they'd need to be half as violent as they probably would be, on general principles, to get everything out of him. And yet there he sits and says absolutely nothing. They've questioned him in relays, twenty-four hours at a stretch. They've planted a man in the same cell with him to gain his confidence. They've done everything but light a bonfire under him, and they're getting annoyed."

"You seem rather pleased about it," the doctor observed noncommittally.

"I can't help being proud of his grit. It's a perfectly useless line to take, and it'll only make it harder for him in the end. The district attorney has got to the point where he's out for blood. Why, they even held before his eyes a copy of the *Herald* with headlines about Sheila's murder and made him stare at it for hours—'Butcher' Joe crumpled under that stunt two years ago, you remember—and he just sits there, looking as if he were somewhere else. It isn't as if he were an old hand—a twelve-year-old child could have done better at covering his tracks. He really needs a guardian, and since I found him, I sort of feel that I'm it. At least I want him to have a fair show. He isn't the ordinary criminal type at all."

"Among all the things we don't know about Sheila O'Shay's

murderer," Dr. Cavanaugh murmured between puffs of his cigar, "we do know this one thing—that he wasn't an ordinary criminal."

"Well, it's a funny thing," Peter said, his brow wrinkled in a puzzled frown. "I went ramping out after this man, on suspicion of his being the O'Shay woman's murderer. If he's guilty, I want him to be convicted. In fact, I shall be extremely relieved and grateful if he turns out to be the guilty party. He's the most promising suspect that's turned up so far. And yet—I had to hire a lawyer for him, out of my own pocket. He didn't even have the sense to ask for one. There's a sort of innocence about him—I don't mean innocence of this particular crime, but of the world and all its works. I couldn't see him or anybody drift straight down the rapids to the big crash without even grasping what it was about. My wires are all crossed, somehow," he concluded ruefully.

"The world is very full of people whose wires are tangled." Dr. Cavanaugh spoke meditatively. "That, we might say, is the normal state of humanity. Motives are not laid side by side and neatly balanced. They are more like a basketful of loose skeins of silk after the kitten has been playing with them. You pull a motive and instead of the thread's coming out smooth for its entire length, you run into a knotted snarl of other motives, blocking it. The very few who are not like that—who can pull their threads out to the end—are the great single-minded people, artists who starve themselves and their families, financiers who wreck their competitors, scientists who inoculate themselves with deadly bacilli, even arch criminals. It's lucky for them, and also fortunate for normal, tangled humanity, that they are in the minority. But I take it you did not come to listen to my views of the world in general?"

"Well, I hoped you might work up a view on one person in particular," Peter admitted. "You see, I managed to put it up to a lawyer friend of mine—at least he has pretty good reason to feel friendly toward the *Herald*—that it would be worth his while to take up Orme's case for the publicity there'd be in it. I f he puts on a good show, that's fair enough—and I had to get his services at bargain rates, salaries being what they are in the newspaper business. He wants to look into the chances of an insanity defence. And we'd like to engage you as defence alienist to examine Orme."

"I've no doubt you would," Dr. Cavanaugh said blandly, following with his eyes the floating procession of a series of smoke rings.

"Of course, publicity means nothing to you—you could get as much free publicity as a movie star by lifting your finger. And there isn't any money in it. After all," Peter exploded, "I can't be expected to go broke in order to pay for the defence or a man I never saw in my life until I grabbed him for the sheriff! And even if I did go broke," he added more calmly, "I couldn't raise enough to interest you."

"So far as I know," the doctor said placidly, "nobody expected anything at all from you—except yourself. And you seem to be devoting considerable energy to seeking bargain rates in professional services for the sake of a notion of abstract justice."

"Justice be blowed!" It was in Peter's code to snort with indignation when accused of lofty sentiments. "This chap rather interests me, that's all. And I hoped he'd interest you."

"He does," the doctor agreed with unruffled tranquillity. "He interests me very much. He also interests the district attorney, who had the idea that a plea of insanity might be in order. He even suspects that our peculiar Mr. Orme is laying the ground for it by his present attitude. It just so happens that the district attorney's office has already requested my services as alienist for the prosecution."

Chapter XXXIII

"My grief!" Peter's hands were flung out in a gesture of despair, strewing ashes from his half-burned cigarette heedlessly over the doctor's Pekin rug. "That jig's up then. The jury won't understand half of what you say, but they'll believe all of it because you say it. I wish you'd waited for me," he added reproachfully.

Dr. Cavanaugh wafted three smoke rings into space before he answered.

"I did," he said at last.

"You—did?"

"That is, I waited for everybody. I am quite willing to examine Orme—his case, from what I hear, presents some interesting features—but I am not willing to go into it with any more definite bias than I would have if he had come as a patient to my office. The district attorney was rather heated in his comments on the insanity dodge as the current fashion among criminals of the present day—but, after all, we are not sure that Orme is a criminal, any more than we are sure that he is insane. By the way, how did he take the transformation of his captor into a good Samaritan?"

Peter leaned back in his chair and lighted a fresh cigarette from the stub of its predecessor.

"The police weren't allowing any newspaper interviews. They didn't want to run the risk of having Orme start something with the reporters before he'd talked to *them*. But my position was what you might call strategic."

"You have a way of putting yourself in strategic positions," Dr. Cavanaugh commented with a briefly quizzical glance in Peter's direction.

"Oh, it was nothing to crow about," Peter hastened to assure him. "Only, you see, if I'd chosen to play myself up in the *Herald* as the intrepid amateur who discovered and caught the man who wrote that threat before the police even got rightly started to search for him, it would have made them look rather silly. It wasn't like that, of course, really; I just happened to light on a tip and followed it; and capturing Orme was about as heroic as picking up somebody's strayed kitten. But they couldn't help seeing the possibilities of the other treatment—when they were tactfully pointed out. I merely turned Orme over to the sheriff and beat it back to the office—giving the police due credit for the arrest in a story that was on the street before the other papers even knew that anybody'd been arrested. That little scoop was quite enough for me, in the way of glory. But, naturally, when I suggested that I'd like a word with my pet tame prisoner, rules or no rules—well, I got it."

"Naturally." Dr. Cavanaugh agreed so suavely that Peter looked up with sharp scrutiny; but the doctor was intent on extinguishing the burning end of his cigar against the side of the ash tray. "And what did he say?" he asked without looking up.

"I told him I'd see that he had a lawyer, and he said, 'That's very kind of you, but you oughtn't to bother,' just as if I'd offered to call a taxi. I honestly do think there's something queer about him—nobody has any call to be as philosophical as all that when he's about to be tried for murder."

"But then, you see, you've never been on trial for murder—perhaps you are not in a position to judge," Dr. Cavanaugh reminded him.

"Well, I think I'd at least manage to be interested." Orme's indifference to the fate of his own neck was becoming a point of acute grievance to Peter despite his part in bringing that neck within reach of danger. "He didn't look up at all until I told him we were going to try to get you to come and see him. Then he stared, like somebody that's just been shaken awake. But all he said was, 'Oh! I've heard of him.' Still, the idea seemed to impress him. Whatever you decide about him, I'm glad you're going. You haven't got any advance theory, I suppose—in other words, a hunch?"

"If I had, it wouldn't be worth expressing. I'm afraid you'll have to cultivate a little scientific patience. Still, your impressions are helpful: they give us a little background—a starting point. And I may be your witness, not the district attorney's, after all, you know."

"Whoopee! I'll bet two doughnuts you will!" Peter beamed. "By the way, I found out how he withstood all that grilling by the detectives. 'I simply withdraw my attention,' he said. 'I just turn my back mentally, and trace out the development of some theme in music—a Beethoven symphony, for instance.' Just 'withdraws his attention,' mind you, while they take turns trying to sweat a confession out of him! Can you beat it?"

"It's a good method," Dr. Cavanaugh said. "But it will never become widely popular because most criminals don't know enough about Beethoven symphonies. Do you realize that you've uncovered the very first objective fact we've been able to gather about David Orme? Anybody who can lose himself in mentally following an elaborate musical composition while being subjected to the third degree must take music with more than ordinary seriousness—must, in fact, be a real musician."

"Suffering cats!" ejaculated Peter. "That's so—and he's lost two fingers off his hand," he added in a tone of awed sympathy. "No wonder he looks as if he'd been thrown into a world where he can't find his way. Music was his own particular world, and he was pitched out of it, without money, deprived of the only way he knew of making any—cast into the society of auto-camp bums——"

"Still," Dr. Cavanaugh brought him down to earth, "that hardly explains why he should forthwith walk out and murder a rich and beautiful and rather famous lady of the stage."

"No," Peter assented glumly, "it doesn't."

"You have gifts, young man, but you're too easily disheartened—too mercurial. In the language of psychiatry, if you ever went off your balance, it would be the manic-depressive type of disorder."

"Great Scott!" Peter looked very blank indeed.

Dr. Cavanaugh leaned back and abandoned himself to one of his rare and hearty laughs. It seemed to shake itself upward from his toes, rumbled mightily in his diaphragm, and ended in a series of throaty chortles that left his eyes suffused with tears.

"You see how easy it is to terrify mere normal folk," he chuckled. "All insanity is only an intensification of normal impulses, so you needn't worry."

Peter still eyed the doctor with some discomfort.

"I shouldn't have teased you." Dr. Cavanaugh's face had resumed its customary gravity. "You must have noticed one thing:

though Orme was making every conscious effort not to give himself away in any particular, he did reveal something significant without knowing it. All of us are likely to do the same thing. He hasn't given us a motive for killing Sheila O'Shay, but we have at least the suggestion that he has come to regard the loss of life—his own or anybody else's—as a mere scratch compared with something else which he has already lost."

Chapter XXXIV

Peter closed Dr. Cavanaugh's office door behind him in a state of unaccustomed mental turbulence. He loafed along the hedge-bordered path which led from the separate side entrance of the office to the front driveway, chewing a twig which he had absent-mindedly plucked from the closely woven leaves of box.

There is something intimidating to ordinary folk about the detachment of science, the impersonal clarity of knowledge. Peter no longer thought of the doctor merely as an expert in a field which interested Peter only as a source of copy on occasion. The psychiatrist loomed before his distorted mental vision as a marionette master pulling a hundred invisible wires. There had been a disturbing quality in his laughter: something Olympian and aloof, as if he alone knew what hidden paths they were following, as if they were all acting out a plot with the involuntary jerks of puppets while he sat behind the screen and held the script that gave meaning to their actions—held it by the power that came from understanding the mysterious springs of human conduct.

Peter shook his head impatiently and tossed the twig away.

"I'd better go to bed and get about forty-eight hours of sleep," he muttered. "The pursuit of crime is beginning to tell on me."

Nevertheless, he continued to loiter by the side of the hedge. Were all the people in the world more or less cracked, needing only a push to knock them off the narrow wall of normality, like Humpty Dumpty? True, Orme might have killed Sheila O'Shay without being insane; and he might, on the other hand, be unbalanced without having killed Sheila O'Shay. They were no nearer to finding out why he had written that threatening letter, why he had changed his name and fled, why that flight had been so inconclusive, so easily abandoned, than they had been on the night when the letter was first found. And whatever Orme's relations with the dead woman might have been, they did not explain Ellsworth's unwillingness to have her disappearance made public, his purloining of the evidence of the contemplated breach-of-promise suit, nor Mrs. Kane's effort to prevent the identification of the body.

Despite weeks of headlines and front-page stories, thousands of words thrown into type and out again, investigations and suspicions, the tule marsh mystery was as much a mystery as on the day when Jimmy first dubbed it "the best murder of the year." Motive! The doctor was right. Without understanding what pulled the wires in people's heads, clues were nothing but a meaningless jumble. And motives themselves were a queer mixture—even Peter's own.

What these people did and why they did it was, strictly speaking, none of his business. A month ago he did not know any of them, unless Sheila O'Shay's frequently published photograph in rotogravure sections and news pages constituted acquaintance. Yet here he was, losing sleep, forgetting meals, working uncounted hours of overtime in the attempt to find out who had killed Sheila O'Shay, and why. It was partly sheer human curiosity and pride, and unwillingness to confess himself baffled; partly the desire, not only that a solution be found, but that the *Herald* have a hand in finding it—and partly the need of setting Barbara somewhere in clear sunlight, of brushing aside from her, always, anxiety and doubt and trouble and folly. It was because he cared so much for Barbara that Orme must have a fair show. There must be no lingering shadows, no thrusting of guilt upon a possibly innocent man. If there were any chance of that, Barbara, he knew as surely as if he had known her all her life, would throw caution to the winds, even to her own mortal hurt.

And she had need of caution—that much was abundantly clear. It flashed upon Peter with the force of complete conviction that though Barbara might conceivably have killed Mrs. Ellsworth—because anyone might conceivably do almost anything, perhaps by a fatal accident in circumstances that would not bear explanation—she could not have taken that body to the marsh and burned it. With a sigh of audible relief Peter seized firmly on the supposition that she was protecting someone else with her quixotic loyalty. She might even have known, or suspected, what was going to happen. But in either case, neither quixotism nor loyalty would wipe out the ugly, hard legality of the phrase, "accessory after the fact."

Peter's whirring thoughts stopped short, as suddenly as the cutting off of a motor. He had drifted to the corner where the side path joined the main driveway, and saw Barbara herself at the curb, getting out of her car. He stood and watched her with sheer, unthinking delight—delight in the sunshine that made of her hair a gleaming cap on her uncovered head; delight in the childlike unconsciousness and swift, agile grace of her movements. He smiled as he noted that she had evidently forgotten her handbag. She leaned far forward into the car, poised with one foot on the curb, and groped in the crevice between the seat cushion and the back upholstery.

Slowly she withdrew her hand and stood staring with bent head—not at a handbag, but at something that gleamed and flashed with a row of tiny green lights that caught the sun. It was a large amber comb of the Spanish type, flaring fan-shaped to the double row of emeralds that curved, fully six inches from end to end, across the top.

Peter thought that he had cried out, that he had run toward her; but there was only a slight choking sound in his throat. His hand reached out automatically and clutched the hedge for support. That comb was famous from a hundred descriptions, familiar from a hundred photographs. The story had been reprinted times without number—how a headstrong Balkan prince had stolen it from his family's royal collection for a woman's whim, and had been sequestered under guard for three years to keep him out of reach of his enchantress when the theft and its motive were discovered; how the woman had worn it triumphantly ever since in her tawny, unbobbed hair, declaring that if they wouldn't let her have the prince she'd at least have the emeralds, and leaving the royal relatives to sputter helplessly.

It was the emerald comb of Sheila O'Shay.

Barbara held the huge, glittering ornament in her hand for a moment, her head drooping lower and lower. Then her face lifted. Peter saw her gaze dart from side to side, up and down the deserted, sun-drenched street. He had never seen such utter, trapped terror on a human countenance. Her fingers wrenched frantically at the comb, breaking it tooth by tooth, jewel by jewel, into fragments. Some of them dropped to the pavement, but she stooped to pick them up. Then she ran, her two laden hands pressed tightly against her breast, to the sewer opening at the corner.

"Don't!" Peter cried out hoarsely, but she did not hear him. He could not himself have told whether he was protesting against her act or against the whole world in which such things could be—an instinctive, horrified denial of his senses.

He saw her kneel in the dry rubbish of the gutter and thrust her hands through the storm grating that covered the entrance to the sewer pipe. When she withdrew them, they were empty. She turned then, and ran back to the house as swiftly as she had come. Her skirt and her light-coloured stockings were streaked with grime from the gutter, but she made no effort to brush off the dust; she did not even look down. With that white tortured face, staring straight ahead, she fled up the driveway, passed within three feet of Peter without seeing him, and dashed into the house.

Chapter XXXV

Sheila O'Shay's body had been driven to the marsh in Barbara's car—the one thing Peter had held to be inconceivable had happened. He saw the jaunty little sport coupé nosing its way through the night with its burden of death, Barbara's white face of terror above the wheel. Had she searched with frenzied fingers for the missing comb, not daring to strike a light? Had she, in the horror of those dark hours, not even noticed that it had slipped from the gleaming copper of Sheila's hair—perhaps not even known that it had ever been there?

A groan broke from Peter's lips. He was dully aware that something was pressing sharply against his forehead. The pain brought him slowly from the clutch of that imagined scene to a consciousness of his surroundings, like one who has plunged into deep water and rises, by no effort of his own, to the surface. He found that he was leaning against the trunk of a tree, his face pressed close to its rough bark. His breath came in sobbing gasps, as if he had been running to the point of exhaustion.

And then, as suddenly as the turning on of a light in a dark room, he was roused from the numbness of nightmare by a flash of absolute certitude. Barbara's hand might have held a knife or jerked a trigger, but Barbara could not have flung the body of Sheila O'Shay into the marsh and set fire to the grass. She could not have done it, simply because she was Barbara. If he had seen with his own eyes her figure at the wheel with that other huddled figure beside it, he would still have known that she did not do it—because she was Barbara. He had believed without evidence that this one thing she could not do. The physically impossible—or what looked like it—was often enough accomplished, but there were impossibilities that struck deeper. He had the evidence now, and he defied it. Evidence was as nothing, because no outer facts could give the lie to the central fact that was Barbara.

With a deep, tremulous sigh Peter moved away from the tree and walked slowly up the driveway where Barbara had run a few minutes—or was it hours?—before. Barbara needed saving far more than he had dreamed. He had admitted, fleetingly, the idea that she herself was responsible for Sheila's death, but he knew now that he had never believed it. It had taken the flash of emeralds in the sun to bring that idea into the light where he must face it—face it with all its implications.

His mouth set in a hard, straight line. He knew exactly what he was doing. There was no ignorance of the law to blind him. He knew that he was going to suppress his knowledge of material evidence of a crime. If Barbara was guilty, no wrangling lawyers, no avid press, no stolid jury should tear that bright and gallant spirit to shreds. If she was a murderess, she was still Barbara! He forced himself to say the word with dry, stiff lips: "Murderess!" And he heard, as clearly as if he sat in the courtroom, as he had heard it many times from his seat in the press row, the voice of the judge solemnly intone, "And may God have mercy on your soul." Never that—never that—for Barbara! He fought his way back to self-control, his nails forcing tiny red drops of blood from the palms of his clenched hands. If Barbara was guilty, he would share her guilt. He squared his shoulders as if against the wind. He was accessory after the fact of murder.

This time there was no hesitation on the doorstep before he rang the bell. Peter's training stood him in good stead; the black-and-white automaton who answered the door saw only a tall and rather pale young man whose clothes were badly in need of brushing—several twigs and bits of leaf were clinging to them—but who showed no evidence of excitement. She looked up at him with a tentative half smile of recognition, but he had evidently forgotten her. He fished a *Herald* card from his pocket and scribbled a message on the back.

"Please let me see you at once—it is most important." He paused a moment, and then added: "I am counting on you—we are friends, remember."

He looked up, as if he had just become aware of the figure in the open door.

"Oh, it's you! I hope you found the two bits—though you didn't deserve them that time. Will you cake this to Miss Cavanaugh, and tell her I'll wait in the room with the marigolds?"

"There aren't any marigolds—the season's past, sir," the automaton explained meticulously.

"Never mind—we know what we mean. You just cut along."

The automaton obediently "cut," wondering as she mounted the stairs how Miss Barbara had ever discovered such a very nice young man who obviously did not belong in her own social circle.

"He can't have any money—his clothes are a sight—but he does have a way with him. And Miss Barbara can afford to like whoever she pleases," she reflected enviously.

Peter stood anxiously waiting in the small room where daffodils had replaced the marigolds, but where a little fire still twinkled in the grate. He wished he had warned her to take off that dust-streaked dress before she came down. She might meet any number of servants, and they'd be sure to notice it and wonder. He wished he had told her to destroy his card—but, then, the girl might already have read it on her way up. He had thought only of Barbara while he was writing it—he strove now to remember the wording. It was noncommittal enough; still, it was better out of the way. His brain felt paralyzed with the sense of his own incompetence. There were so many things to think of—so many things that he had never had to consider before. Peter found himself wishing that he had committed any number of crimes so that he would have been practised in technic, would know exactly what ought to be done. Suppose he made some horrible blunder. Suppose he could not save her. Suppose——

"You wanted to see me?" She was there, slim and straight and childlike between the folds of the curtains. Before advancing into the room she turned and slid the folding doors shut. She was immaculately dressed in a straight little blue frock, and she held Peter's card, twisted in a tube about her slim fingers.

"Thank God!" Peter cried.

Barbara summoned a wan little smile.

"You always do have most astonishing ways of opening a conversation!" she said.

"I was afraid you wouldn't change your dress," Peter explained. "And may I have that, please?" He took the card gently from her fingers and dropped it on the glowing coals.

She looked up at him, faintly surprised, as one who has just passed through an earthquake might be surprised at the unexpected falling of a leaf. Unresisting, she allowed him to lead her to a chair and place her in it. Peter towered over her, his elbow on the mantel.

"Barbara," he said, "God knows whether I've the wit to be much good to you, but I think the first step had better be for you to marry me."

Chapter XXXVI

"Oh, Peter!" Barbara cried. Her voice was the thin, small voice of a terrified child at the touch of a reassuring hand in the dark. "If I only could!" She leaned forward, her hands clasped tightly between her knees, her pinched white face irradiated with a flood of rosy colour. Her eyes, seeking Peter's, were wells of glory.

Peter forgot that Sheila O'Shay had been murdered, forgot that she had ever existed. His world was narrowed to one consuming blaze of divine astonishment.

"But, Barbara! You can't mean——" he stammered.

"Of course." Barbara nodded her head twice, with slow emphasis. "I mean just that. I should think you'd have seen it from the beginning."

Peter, still with that look of awed wonder, leaned down to kiss the bright bowed head. But before he reached her, he forced himself back, holding to the mantelpiece as if he feared to trust his own unaided will.

"But listen, you amazing child, you *can't* mean it!" he said. "You don't know a thing about me, really. I'm just a hard-boiled newspaper reporter." (It was a fixed delusion with Peter that he was hard boiled.) "I earn fifty dollars a week, and the only car

I own or am ever likely to own is one you'd be ashamed even to collide with. I never thought of it before, but for all you know I might be nothing but a fortune hunter."

"I know quite enough." A shadow of the old gamin smile hovered at the corners of Barbara's lips. "Are you trying to persuade me to marry you or trying to persuade me not to—which?"

"If things weren't as they are, I'd try to have too much sense to ask you. But I've got to have the right to help you—to stand by, to the last ditch. Of course I'll do that anyhow, but it'll make things simpler. That's why I want you to marry me."

"Oh, no, it isn't!" Barbara's shining gaze was still fixed on Peter's face. "It's because you love me."

"Oh, that!" Peter's scorn was the most sublime assurance. "That goes without saying. Who wouldn't?"

"Still," said Barbara, "I'm glad you said it, even though I knew. I ought to be sorry, but I'm not. I'm glad—glad that I shall have it to remember, always. Because I'm not going to marry you, Peter."

"Don't be absurd!" Peter said angrily. "Please, Barbara, get this straight. Even if you hadn't looked at me like that, you glorious child—I don't know how it ever happened, but somehow it has—I'd have wanted you to marry me anyhow. Then, if we got things straightened out and you wanted your freedom, you could have it. Nothing, nothing at all, could possibly make any difference to me, except as it gave me something to do for you. That's the way I feel about it. Now, will you marry me?"

"Don't!" Barbara buried her face in her hands. "You make it so hard." Then she looked up, her small chin very stubborn, her eyes very steady. "I can't marry you, Peter—not ever."

"Why not?" Peter glared down at her belligerently.

"Because——" Barbara took a deep breath, then went on

steadily: "I'm going to tell you something I have never hinted to another soul. I told you how Dr. Cavanaugh adopted me out of the orphanage. I rather think that I am really his daughter."

It was so far from what Peter had expected her to say that he could only stare at her in blank amazement.

"But, darling child," he said, when he had caught his breath, "can you think for one moment that that would make any difference to me?"

"It would to me," Barbara said, so low that he had to bend toward her to catch the words.

"But it mustn't. I don't care a fig whether your parents had a marriage license or not. As the lawyers say, it's incompetent, immaterial, and irrelevant. Dr. Cavanaugh is a very great man—you might well be proud to get some of your heredity from a brain like that. Even if he did your mother and you a social injury by not marrying her, he's done his best to make it up to you."

"Yes," Barbara said gravely, "he is a great man, and he has been good to me. But oh——" Sobs rose in her throat, but she fought them down. "You don't understand—you never can understand—I can never tell you!"

"Listen to me," Peter said sternly. "We're talking at cross purposes. You're not being frank with me. I saw you find that comb behind the seat of your car, and destroy it."

Her hands reached out in a gesture of frantic protest, but he disregarded them.

"I said I didn't care what you've done. I mean it. As a matter of fact, I think that you probably killed Sheila O'Shay and that we may have the deuce of a time getting you out of it. Now, will you marry me?"

"You think that of me," Barbara said wonderingly. "You think that I killed her—I, with these hands, committed murder?" She held out her hands, palm upward, and looked at them curiously. "You think I am a murderess, and that I may be hanged for it, and still—still you want to marry me?"

Peter did not know that he had moved until he reached her and lifted her from the chair and held her close, his cheek against her hair.

"They shan't hurt you, Barbara. Nobody shall hurt you. I won't let them." Staring into the distance above her bowed head, Peter defied the world.

"I think," murmured Barbara, "that it might be worth dying for, to know that somebody felt like that." Then, very gently, she slipped out of those encircling arms. "But I won't do it, Peter. No power on earth—not the power of love itself—can make me marry you. That is the ultimate truth, and you will have to believe it."

Peter looked long and steadily into her eyes lifted bravely to his, but they did not waver.

"It only makes things a little harder, darling," he said at last. "You know that I'll do whatever I can, anyway. And we mustn't be frightened. I was standing in the driveway when you got out of your car; I'm sure that no one else saw you. Perhaps, when all this is over and forgotten, you'll be willing to decide differently."

"I can't. Please, unless you want to pain me terribly, don't ask me again."

"But you don't want me not to love you, do you, Barbara?"

Once again Barbara's face was lighted by its elfin smile.

"I don't think there's anything can prevent—either of us," she said.

Chapter XXXVII

PUBLIC INTEREST in a murder trial is as unpredictable as the success of a theatrical production; but the trial of David Orme was sure fire from the beginning.

"It's got everything," Jimmy asserted with enthusiasm. "Sex appeal, mystery, big money. It's a wow of a story!"

Peter glared dourly at his fellow human beings as he fought his way through the crowd in front of the courthouse. It was a quiet, even a contented crowd, content to stand and stare all day at the familiar outlines of the building—familiar and yet subtly dramatic now because of the drama of life and death opening behind its walls. There was absolutely nothing for them to see, Peter reflected crossly, and yet they thought nothing of waiting there, hour after hour. There were women with small children jammed against their skirts, men carrying their lunches in paper bags. Ropes guarded by policemen cleared a lane to the door; but inside, the crowd poured itself down the corridors from wall to wall. They showed no disposition to make way for Peter.

"I'm sorry, you'll have to let me through," he reiterated mechanically, displaying his press badge and reënforcing it with the sharp prodding of elbows.

"There's too many of these here press fellows, that's what, keeping everybody else out. Where do they get all their pull, anyhow?"

Peter shouldered the speaker aside, forcing his way forward, yard by yard.

"Say, young man, how do you get in to see this boy that's killed somebody? I've been here since six o'clock this morning and I ain't no nearer than when I started." Peter felt the pressure of a hand on his arm and turned to look down into the face of a neat little old lady garbed in her best of faded black.

"You don't get in," he snapped. "And you wouldn't understand a word of it if you did. You'll learn a whole lot more if you go home and read the *Herald.*"

"Well, I never did see the inside of a courtroom," the old lady persisted plaintively. "I thought it would be kind of nice to see it once."

That was what it was to them—a show. It would be equally a show if it were Barbara inside instead of Orme.

A hastily erected fence of unpainted laths walled off the entrance to Department 24. Peter ran the gamut of six policemen, holding fast to his card of admittance: "Press Pass. Admit J. A. Piper representing *Herald* to all Court Sessions of Orme Trial. Attest A. W. Moore, clerk; Charles Harvey, judge. Seat number 53." It was his ticket to the arena, where the gladiators would lunge at one another with their word lances, where the judge would loll in his chair—"thumbs up, thumbs down." And outside, the blindly patient crowd waiting hungrily for its crumbs of vicarious excitement.

Peter flung himself, worn and dishevelled, into seat 53. Inside the courtroom it was very quiet. In one corner a muted telegraph instrument ticked sharply, like the chirp of an industrious cricket. Behind the railing which divided the courtroom in half, Peter recognized the roll of fat on the back of the neck of the district attorney; the scrubbed blondness, like a small boy just out of the tub, of the young defence lawyer; the stalwart, motionless shoulders of Dr. Cavanaugh. Orme himself was overshadowed by the huge figure of the deputy sheriff from the homicide squad who sat beside him. Twelve men and women ranged in two rows along the side wall contrived to look at the same time blank and self-conscious. One of them wore a green hat perched high above her sallow face. Peter decided that a hat like that deserved a peremptory challenge.

"The case of the People against David Orme . . . as alleged in the indictment . . . That he did wilfully and feloniously murder one Sheila Ellsworth . . ." intoned the district attorney.

The judge, with a face all sharp angles, like a cubist drawing, topped by hair that glistened like spun sugar, rapped out questions.

"Conscientious scruples against the death penalty in a proper case . . . Any prejudice for or against the defence of insanity . . . The criterion of accountability is this."

Questions. Questions. Questions.

"The people will excuse Mr. Warren . . . The challenge is with the defence . . . The defence will excuse Mrs. Barnes." That was the woman in the green hat. Thank heaven he would not have to face that hat in the jury box day after day!

The personnel in the twelve chairs shifted. The bailiff pulled slips of paper out of a revolving tin box and boomed new names one by one. Orme—Peter could see him now, over the shoulder of the sheriff—sat with folded arms, staring dreamily into space, his profile motionless in relief against the plaster of the wall. Not once did he glance toward the jury box. The questions and challenges floated unnoticed over his head. Not once did he start at the words, "murder," "Sheila Ellsworth," "hanged"—words reiterated and hammered on Peter's consciousness until he wanted to strike out against them in unreasoning fury.

The very worst feature of being tried for murder, Peter decided, was the torturing, abysmal boredom of it. If they would only get on with it! The press correspondents slumped in their chairs, jotting down the names and addresses of jurors and crossing them out again when they were challenged. A sketch artist in the row ahead amused himself by drawing a libellous caricature of the court reporter. With one accord the men and women in the jury box denied that they ever read anything in the newspapers or had ever heard of the murder of Sheila O'Shay. The faint slip-slip of pencils on copy paper, the chirping of the telegraph cricket sounded as a constant faint overtone to the droning of questions and answers.

There was an indefinable stir, like a wind sweeping through a forest.

"Court adjourned until two o'clock."

"Order in the courtroom, *please!* Keep your seats!"

"First juror chosen in Orme Murder Trial"—it would be shouted in extras on every corner within the hour. Stumbling and pushing, the reporters crowded the aisle, breaking for the telephones in the witness room outside.

"Bet you two bits they don't get a jury in a week!"

"Not with Judge Harvey—he'll speed 'em. Say, do you remember in the Cogswell case he told 'em he was going to begin trying it by Monday noon, jury or no jury?"

Peter grimaced over his shoulder at the "Q and A" twins of the *Herald* staff. They sat in adjacent seats, one of them taking down in shorthand the questions and the other the answers of the witnesses. Betweenwhiles, they invariably engaged in a spirited conflict over the expected progress of the case in hand. As he turned, Peter for the first time had an unobstructed view of the chairs set back from the table, within the enclosure.

"Here, Harry!" He thrust his pages of notes into the hand of the nearest of the Q and A twins. "Take care of this for me, will you? Phone it in to the office and tell Jimmy I'll be around to write the rest of the story in half an hour. And if he tells you to remind me there's a one o'clock deadline, you tell him if I miss it he can fire me, and to go to—anywhere you like."

Peter nudged his way up the aisle and vaulted the low railing to the enclosed area, his eyes fixed on a small black hat just visible above the back of a chair.

"Barbara!" he exclaimed. "Why did you come? How did you get in?"

The little figure in the big chair faced him calmly.

"Father got a pass for me," she announced. "He's to be an expert witness, you know, and I've never seen him in action. I told him I thought it might be interesting." Peter wondered if he would ever in the world get over being astonished at Barbara. Except for the tired lines about her eyes, she was as nonchalant as if they had met in the lobby of a theatre instead of a courtroom.

"But you can't stay. You mustn't," Peter said in a low tone. "It's too much for you to stand. And it won't do anybody a particle of good."

"Won't you sometime ask me something that I don't have to say 'No' to, Peter?" For one moment her upturned face was full of appealing wistfulness; the next, it had hardened into a look of weary fortitude. "How can I possibly know what will do any good unless I stay to find out?" she said.

Chapter XXXVIII

Peter's impressions of the succeeding days of the Orme trial were like a series of island mountain tops emerging out of the sea. There were waste stretches which he did not remember at all, although at the dose of each court session he hammered out in the *Herald* local room that series of courtroom stories which laid the foundation for his reputation as one of the most brilliant special writers in the country.

If Orme was not guilty, Barbara must be. If Orme was found guilty, Barbara would walk with firm, light steps into the arena and let her body and soul be torn while the newsboys shouted "Extra" and the crowd licked its lips outside, rather than allow him to suffer unjustly. Peter, slumped in seat 53, his eyes fixed on the small black hat, just visible above the chairback where Barbara sat beside Dr. Cavanaugh, felt his brain clamped in a tight, inescapable circle of thought. And yet some other portion of his mind functioned independently, automatically recording names, addresses, incidents, pictures.

He seemed to have spent an endless lifetime alternating between the courthouse and the *Herald* office. He could scarcely recall a time before the trial began; he could not look forward to the time when it should be ended. He sat through the droning hours with half-shut eyes which yet saw with minute detail every aspect of the courtroom. And out of the welter certain scenes were stamped, bright and clear, in his memory.

The first of these was Don Ellsworth on the witness stand—Don Ellsworth facing with dilated, desperate eyes row upon row of press correspondents, each scribbling intently on pads of copy paper. He no longer had the look of a sullen, violent boy. The thing that he had fought and hated more than anything else in the world had happened, and he faced it with tense composure. He stared before him like a man in front of a firing squad, standing rigidly erect until he had twice been told to be seated in the witness chair.

"Will you just relate in your own way, Mr. Ellsworth, the circumstances of your wife's disappearance from your home?"

"I was first aware that she had gone on the morning of March 19th." Ellsworth spoke in a hard, mechanical voice, as if he were reciting a lesson by rote. "My wife's maid came and told me that——"

"Never mind what anyone told you. Just relate what you did."

Ellsworth's eyes flashed briefly from the rows of reporters to the lawyers' table. Peter was suddenly reminded of a bull being pricked by the lance tip of the toreador. Don opened his lips to retort, but thought better of it.

"I went up to my wife's boudoir. I found that the lights had been left burning. So far as I could tell, none of her clothes were missing except an evening cloak and the dress which she had worn at dinner the night before."

"And what did you do then?"

"Nothing. I waited, thinking that some natural explanation of her disappearance would be forthcoming. When she had not returned after several days, the police were notified. That is all I can say of my direct knowledge."

"Have you ever seen the defendant, David Orme, before?"

"I think not."

"I will ask you to read this letter, introduced in evidence as People's exhibit A. What is your interpretation of this letter?"

"I object, your honour. What the witness thinks the letter means is incompetent, irrelevant, and immaterial."

"If the witness knows any circumstances which will explain the letter, he has the right to state them. You may answer the question," the judge rapped out with metronomic precision.

"I had some reason to suppose that Mrs. Ellsworth had done Orme—or he thought she had done him—some injury."

"What reason?"

"She had also done me what I consider a grave injury and I imagine I am by no means the only one to suffer at her hands."

"Your honour, I object. I move the answer be stricken from the record as unresponsive."

"It may be stricken out."

"I withdraw the question. Did your wife ever speak of Orme to you?"

"She did."

The bent heads of the correspondents rose like a field of flowers turned upward by the wind. There was a faint rustling sound of suppressed excitement.

"Will you kindly relate the substance of such conversation or conversations?"

"My wife told me that David Orme was the name of the latest of her husbands—previous to myself!" The dry bitterness of the voice smote the courtroom like a blade of ice.

"Had you any reason to suppose that your wife might have left the house voluntarily with her former husband?"

"I object!" Graham, the defence lawyer, his round boyish face crimson, popped to his feet as if sprung out of a box. "What the witness supposes his wife might have done is incompetent, irrelevant, and immaterial, and calling for the conclusion of the witness." The words were like the splatter of a shotgun.

"Your honour," the district attorney boomed reproachfully, "surely the witness may relate any conduct on the part of his wife directly bearing on the circumstances of her leaving the house!"

"Reframe your question."

"Did your wife do or say anything to indicate that she was in communication with Orme?"

"My wife's former husbands were not a common topic of conversation between us." Again the air was cut by that sword of ice.

A gust of laughter ran through the courtroom—the nervous, explosive laughter that is release from intolerable tension.

"Silence in the courtroom, *please!*"

"Your honour, I move that the answer be stricken from the record as unresponsive.' "

"It may be stricken from the record. Answer the question, Yes or No," the judge said with bored severity.

"She did not."

"That is all, Mr. Orme."

"You may cross-examine."

"I understood you to say," Graham began cheerfully, "that you looked through your wife's clothes on the morning when she was first missing. Doesn't that indicate that you thought she might have packed her clothes before leaving?"

"I object," rumbled the district attorney, "on the ground that the question is leading."

"Objection overruled. The witness may answer," the judge said with his usual curt weariness.

"I was taking the possibility into account."

"And yet you did nothing—nothing whatever—to discover your missing wife's whereabouts for three days. Weren't you, to say the least, somewhat anxious to know what had become of her?"

The forced control of the man on the witness stand was suddenly shattered. His hands gripped the arms of the chair as if he would tear them from their supports.

Chapter XXXIX

"IF YOU want to know what I thought, I'll tell you," Ellsworth said in a loud rapid voice. "At first I thought it quite likely that she had run away with someone. If I had known that Orme was about I might have suspected him, but as a matter of fact, I did not speculate. I did nothing about it because if that was the case it released me from a situation that I regretted with all my soul. But when I thought it over, I knew positively that that was one thing she wouldn't do. My wife was a very emotional woman, but she would never have deliberately given up sure money for the sake of any emotion. She might have relished the excitement of meeting Orme again, but she would never have given up her financial position as my wife to go back to him."

Graham and the district attorney were both frantically striving to make themselves heard above the storm. The gavel of the bailiff thumped like a tomtom.

"Silence, gentlemen!" The voice of the judge ripped across the turmoil. "The last remarks may be stricken from the record. Mr. Ellsworth, kindly confine yourself to answering the questions."

"I thought your idea was to find out the truth." Ellsworth

turned furiously upon the judge, as if confronting a new assailant from an unexpected quarter.

"So it is," the judge said firmly. "Nevertheless, you must submit yourself to the rulings of the court. The defence may proceed with the next question."

"You say that you did nothing for several days after your wife disappeared. Did it not occur to you, regardless of your personal feelings toward Mrs. Ellsworth, that the police should be notified?"

"It did. But I had already sacrificed a great deal in the effort to keep my personal affairs from being made public. It appears that I was to be unsuccessful. But I would have given anything under heaven to avoid—this!" Ellsworth's arm flailed out in a wide gesture, sweeping the press rows, the jury, the bailiffs, and lawyers in an inclusive circle.

"Is it not a fact that you deliberately took and concealed certain papers belonging to Mrs. Ellsworth and having a bearing upon the circumstances of your marriage?"

"I object. The circumstances of Mrs. Ellsworth's marriage have nothing whatever to do with the case——"

"Objection sustained."

"Let me answer, please. I demand the chance to explain. I've done my utmost, all my life, to keep out of the papers. Now I want my side to be heard. These insinuations—they will be made public—they already have been. Let them at least have the truth!"

"Calm yourself, Mr. Ellsworth. This case is not being tried in the papers—officially," the judge said sardonically. "If you desire to make a statement, you may do so."

"The papers which I took from Mrs. Ellsworth's safe were the documents in a breach-of-promise suit which she threatened to institute prior to our marriage. I took them because I feared that they would be considered suspicious evidence against me—give me an apparent motive for—for doing away with her. A psychiatrist tells me that this fear was due to a genuine wish that she should pass out of my life—that I was afraid because I really did have such a motive, although it never was a conscious one. It was a sort of panic. I wanted to keep out of it as far as possible. I might have known it couldn't be done—that the crash had come. But if I had really wanted to kill Sheila, I'd have done it before I married her. And if I had killed her, I'd at least have had the sense not to try to cover her disappearance. It's horrible that I can't, even now, be sorry she's dead. But I'm punished for that, punished by having to endure all that I've most dreaded and loathed, punished by—this!" Again the rigid arm swept outward. Then Ellsworth's head dropped forward on his arms, flung across the railing before him. "That's all," he mumbled, almost inaudibly. The fierce repression of years had broken down, loosing the torrents in one mighty outburst. Having lost all that he had guarded, he flung the remnants of his wrecked life to them, with a strange relief in the abandonment.

"We will take a recess for ten minutes," said the judge.

The reporters hurled themselves at the doors.

"Great stuff!"

"Too late for the home. The morning papers'll get it, durn 'em."

"Never mind, they'll run an extra on this—see if they don't."

"New lead—add Orme trial"—this over the telephone.

"Copy boy! Rush this to the office, and step on it!" This from the Q and A twins in chorus.

Peter, having telephoned his flash, left the smoke-filled witness room with its clangour of telephones and stood leaning against the wall at the back of the almost empty courtroom. He started at the touch of a hand on his arm and turned with surprise to find Don Ellsworth standing, white and spent, beside him.

"I want to tell you something," Don said in a low, tremulous voice.

"Take it easy." Peter forgot his own fatigue in the lapse from intense excitement. His gray eyes beamed upon Ellsworth with friendly reassurance and sympathy.

"But I want you to know this," Don rushed on, glancing about to make sure that they were not overheard. "I hoped to marry Barbara Cavanaugh—maybe you already knew that, or guessed it. Well, that's over. She has told me that you are the man she cares for. And it's true. I thought she cared for me once, but even if I hadn't lost my chance, she never looked at me as she looked when she spoke your name. I wanted to let you know that—personally. And to tell you before I go that I was a fool for blazing out at you when you came to the house."

"Oh, that's all right. All in the day's work," Peter said inadequately. He felt very much as if he wanted to cry, but his gray eyes only shone a little more warmly on the man beside him.

"What I really wanted to say, though, was this," Don went on. "The other is only between ourselves. But I thought you might like to know that as soon as this is over I'm going to Africa to hunt big game. I don't know a thing about big-game hunting, but I guess it can be learned. I don't know a thing about Africa, either—only I have an idea it's a country where there aren't many newspapers." A wan smile flickered across Don's face. "I thought you might like to have that as a scoop for—the *Herald,* isn't it?"

"Thanks," said Peter briefly. He dared not trust his voice beyond the single word.

The two hands met in a grip that left both sets of fingers aching.

Chapter XL

THE APPEARANCE of Mrs. Kane as a witness for the people caused a ripple of uncontrollable delight to sweep across the rows of press seats.

She stalked up the narrow aisle, her voluminous skirts almost brushing the chairs on either side. With the unswerving directness of an ocean liner, she had already stepped to the platform before the astonished clerk could check her progress.

"Mumble-mumble-mumble—nothing-but-the-truth-so-help-you-God," chanted the clerk.

Mrs. Kane fixed him with severity in her eye.

"That's what I'm here for," she announced succinctly.

The judge blew his nose behind his handkerchief. The bailiff, with rigid, contorted countenance, banged his gavel. The sketch artists seized their pencils with furious haste.

"It ain't possible." One of the Q and A twins nudged the other.

"As the farmer said when he saw a giraffe, 'There's no such animal!' " murmured his companion.

"Silence in the courtroom, *please!*" admonished the bailiff, with the harassed air of a teacher trying to maintain discipline over a class of unruly youngsters.

Mrs. Kane surveyed the room with a disapproving stare which said as plainly as words, "What have all these people got to do with it, anyhow? They'd better go home and mind their own business."

"Mrs. Kane," began the district attorney with wary courtesy, "do you know the defendant, David Orme?"

"Well, I ought to," clicked Mrs. Kane, viewing the questioner with manifest scorn of his stupidity.

The roll of fat across the back of the district attorney's neck reddened.

"I didn't ask you whether you ought to; I asked you whether you did. Answer the question, Yes or No," he said sharply.

"I already said so."

The district attorney cast an imploring glance at the judge, who was sedulously staring out of the window.

"What were the relations between Mr. Orme and Mrs. Ellsworth at the time when you first knew him?"

"Just what they are now. He was and is Miss O'Shay's husband."

"*What?*"

A rustle of astonishment passed over the courtroom. The lounging reporters straightened and leaned forward as if pulled by invisible wires.

"You heard me," Mrs. Kane remarked caustically. "He left, and Miss O'Shay let him go. She never got a divorce from him."

"Your honour, I object!" Graham leaped to his feet as if galvanized by an electric shock. "The witness cannot possibly know this of her own knowledge."

"I certainly do. There's precious little about Miss O'Shay that I don't know of my own knowledge."

"Objection sustained. You may reframe your question."

"Will the reporter please read the question? I—I seem to be a little confused as to what the witness was answering."

The court reporter bent over his notes.

"The last question of the district attorney was, 'What?'" he announced in matter-of-fact tones.

The angular face of the judge became a deep mahogany colour. He glared out the window for a moment, then gave it up and seized his handkerchief. From the bench came a series of choking sounds interspersed with snorts. The men in the press rows rocked back and forth, throwing decorum to the winds. The bailiff drummed an unheeded tattoo with the hand holding the gavel while with the other he wiped his eyes.

"The court will please come to order," said the judge, emerging from cover. "Proceed with your next question, Mr. District Attorney."

"What, if any, evidence have you as to the relations existing between the deceased and the defendant?" The district attorney was decidedly jumpy. He looked as if he were handling a firecracker which might go off unexpectedly.

"If you mean Miss O'Shay and Mr. Orme, Miss O'Shay told me herself. Orme simply disappeared. She was afraid if she started divorce proceedings he might turn up. Besides, she didn't want to wait. She was afraid she might lose her chance of landing Mr. Ellsworth."

"Just a moment. She told you all this?"

"Of course she told it to me!" Mrs. Kane's teeth wobbled dangerously but clicked into place. "Did you think I made it up?"

"The witness is admonished to confine herself to answering the questions."

"You knew Mr. Orme by sight at the time of this marriage?"

"Yes," snapped Mrs. Kane, glaring balefully at the judge who had presumed to clip her utterances.

"Can you fix the date of the separation?"

"It was year ago come April."

"And when did you next see Mr. Orme?"

"He came to Mr. Ellsworth's house and brought this letter they've all been talking about. I told him that Miss O'Shay wanted him to go away.' "

"And then?"

"I saw him hanging around the house. I spoke to him and told him it was no good waiting, but he said he would not leave till he had talked with her."

"And what was the last time that you saw him, prior to this trial?"

"On the evening of March 18th—the last night I ever saw Miss O'Shay alive—she answered a telephone call from the extension in her boudoir at about half-past eight o'clock. I remember the time, because she had only just come upstairs, directly after dinner. She threw a cloak over her evening dress, and went out immediately, without telling me where she was going. I went to the hall window at the front of the house to see what she was up to. When I looked out, I saw Miss O'Shay and Mr. Orme walking down the driveway toward the street together. That was the last I saw of her—she never came back."

Chapter XLI

THIS TIME there was no need of the bailiff's gavel. In the amazed silence that filled the room the telegraph instrument sounded suddenly loud. The breaking of a pencil point by one of the Q and A twins came as a tiny, sharp explosion of sound.

The district attorney mopped his brow and leaned back with a sigh of relief.

"That is all, Mrs. Kane."

"You may cross-examine."

The young defence attorney eyed the figure in the witness chair as if he were a lion tamer entering the cage of an unknown and highly temperamental beast of prey. His ruddy face had grown perceptibly paler. But he scraped his chair back from the table and advanced to the attack.

"Mrs. Kane," he said, "is it not somewhat unusual for a lady to confide her intimate personal affairs to her maid?"

"I've nothing to do with whether it is unusual or not. Miss O'Shay did it."

"Will the witness kindly answer the question?"

"Your honour, I object. The question is purely rhetorical. The witness cannot be expected to testify as to what is or is not usual."

"Objection sustained."

"Mrs. Kane, can you explain how Mrs. Ellsworth came to confide her marital and other affairs to you?"

"Yes. It was because I loved her." The face with its slipping teeth and its sausage roll of polished black hair was no longer funny. It was grim, and in a strange way majestic. "Miss O'Shay was a foolish, headstrong woman, but I loved her like my own daughter, and she knew it. I was the one person in the world who never flattered her, to whom she could always turn in the scrapes she was forever getting into. God knows I did my best to keep her out of trouble. She didn't take my advice, not very often she didn't. She was always wild—always took what she wanted, and never mind the consequences. And then I'd do my best to keep the consequences from hurting her—too much. Always she got what she wanted, and always it hurt her in the end—till the very end of all——" The sunken mouth twisted, the sharp eyes squinted shut, holding back the tears. One of them splashed down on the back of her cotton glove, and she wiped it off with the other hand. "She was nothing but a wayward girl, all those years—a wayward girl, spoiled by all the attention she got, playing with fire and thinking it wouldn't burn. Why wouldn't I know?—I, who took care of her from the time when I kept a boarding house and she was hardly more than a child, half starved, tramping the agencies hunting a job in the chorus!"

Graham gripped the table before him with both hands.

"Your honour, I ask that the last remarks of the witness be stricken from the record as unresponsive. The character of Mrs. Ellsworth as interpreted by Mrs. Kane is beside the point."

"The witness answered your question. She has a right to explain her answer. The remarks may stand."

"Why, if you were so devoted to Mrs. Ellsworth, did you withhold this vital information? Why did you refuse to cooperate with Dr. Cavanaugh in his efforts to identify the body?" Graham pounced.

"Your honour!" The district attorney was pained and reproachful. "I object! The question is complex."

"I will reframe the question." Graham had himself in hand now. He faced the old woman in the chair with an air of solemn triumph. "Mrs. Kane, why did you refuse to give Dr. Cavanaugh a hair of Mrs. Ellsworth to compare with the hair of the body found in the marsh?"

The district attorney leaped to his feet.

"Your honour, I object! Is it the intention of the defence to impeach this witness?"

"It is," Graham said sturdily. "I am laying the foundation for that, your honour."

"The witness may answer."

"Of course I may answer. Why shouldn't I—now that it can't be helped?" The black eyes were open now, wrathfully fixed upon Graham. "You needn't think you're worrying me a bit, young man. I'd have you know I've talked down a lot smarter men than you are in my day—or than the judge, either, if it comes to that!"

The judge's mouth twitched.

"I must admonish you that if you do not confine yourself to answering the questions put to you you lay yourself open to contempt of court."

But Mrs. Kane was not to be intimidated.

"I guess I've been laid open to lots worse things," she muttered. Then, having disposed of the majesty of the law, she faced the courtroom, patently ignoring with a bony shoulder the end of the table where the defence attorney sat.

"I wouldn't help them to find her murderer," she said, "because it was the last scandal I could protect her from. All her life I tried to do that for her. Many and many's the time I've failed. But for all the things that got out about her, there were plenty of others that didn't get out. She was a bad, lovely woman, was Miss O'Shay. But I didn't want something bad to be the last thing people remembered about her. She was so terrified of growing old—of losing the power of her beauty that had brought her everything she wanted. She was terrified of that when she married Mr. Ellsworth for his money and committed bigamy to get it. Why should I care what happened to him—to Orme, or Ellsworth, or any of them? Why should I want her name to be hawked about again, a scandal in her very death? Do you think I cared about getting somebody hung for her death? One of her beautiful hairs was worth more than Orme's neck. I didn't want anybody to know that she had ever been afraid. If she wasn't dead, it was her own business and I'd know it soon enough, because she'd tell me, without bringing the police into it to bother her. But if she was dead, then—then I wanted people just to remember—not that she was bad, but only that she was lovely."

The tall, spare figure, wrapped in its bizarre draperies, topped by an absurd purple hat, stood erect. The black eyes, glowing with the fire of a fanatical, protecting angel, looked straight before her, beyond the courtroom walls.

Graham sank back in his chair.

"That is all," he said dispiritedly.

"Your honour, the People rest," said the district attorney.

Chapter XLII

"Don't take it so hard." Peter tilted his chair back against the wall at an acute angle which left his long legs dangling in space. "God knows I don't want you to get him off if he's guilty. You're putting on a good show, and that's all that's to be expected."

Graham stabbed the desk blotter before him with the point of an unused pen, as if he found some satisfaction in impaling a series of minute invisible objects.

"The heck of it is," he said, "I don't believe he is guilty."

Dr. Cavanaugh, who had eased his large bulk into a comfortable chair by the window, turned a serene gaze upon the worried lawyer.

"That gives you a certain rather impressive sincerity," he said blandly, "but it may not weigh very heavily with the jury. Juries are likely to have a general idea that lawyers are an unscrupulous lot. It's partly, of course, because legal procedure seems to them a very elaborate game whose rules are too complicated for them to understand—and human nature has a way of being suspicious of what is beyond its comprehension. Whatever makes people ill at ease is likely to make them hostile. The average man would assume you to be an honest person, my dear Graham. You have an open countenance, if I may say so—not at all the sort of person who would misrepresent the value of a stock, for example, or cheat at a bridge game. And yet, because you are a lawyer, they will suspect you of working a magic hocus-pocus to try to throw dust in their eyes, even if you know your client to be guilty."

The three men were gathered for an evening conference in the office of the defence attorney, at Graham's request. The young lawyer's round cherubic face seemed to have lost some of its roseate chubbiness. There were puffy circles of fatigue under his eyes, and his mouth sagged in a discouraged droop. Peter's long face looked even longer than usual, and his cheek bones stood out sharply. His brows were drawn together in an anxious frown; that frown had become so habitual of late that it had etched two lines in parallel grooves above his eyes.

Since the adjournment of court at half-past five, Peter had gone back to the office and written his lead for the next morning's city edition. He had stopped only for a cup of coffee on his way to the lawyer's office. Graham had come directly from the courthouse; the calf-bound books marked with slips of blue paper which strewed the desk and the pyramid of ashes in the brass bowl at his elbow indicated that he had taken no time for dinner. Dr. Cavanaugh had stopped downtown for an early and leisurely repast. Of the three, he alone showed no sign of perturbation.

"You know," Peter brought the front legs of his chair to the floor with a thump, "I believe Ellsworth and the Kane woman were telling the absolute truth, queer as their stories were."

"Their testimony was a good deal worse than queer," Graham said gloomily; "it was devastating. And yet, when you go over it in cold blood, dislike of publicity and fear of scandal—especially somebody else's scandal—sound like mighty feeble motives for trying to cover up the facts in a murder."

"That's the trouble with motives." The doctor examined his cigar with calm detachment before lighting it. "The strongest of them so often do seem feeble—to the other fellow. There's the familiar notion, for instance, that all murders are committed from jealousy, anger, fear, or greed. And yet there was the woman who took a hammer to her husband because he did not want her to go to a bridge party. A patient not long ago came to me suffering from what we call a compulsion neurosis. He was obsessed by the homicidal impulse to kill his wife because for twenty years she had sipped her coffee audibly from a spoon. Perhaps if one of us had had to listen to that sound for twenty years we'd be inclined to call it justifiable homicide."

"At any rate," Graham interrupted irritably, "to-day's testimony brought out a perfectly good, recognizable motive—two of them, in fact—for Orme to kill Mrs. Ellsworth. It might have been jealousy, and it might have been revenge. You may call him a psychopathic case, Doctor, but those are going to look like mighty sane human motives to the jury."

"Psychopathic or not," Dr. Cavanaugh asserted, "Orme is not the type of personality to be moved powerfully by either of those two particular emotions. If he did kill her, it was for some other reason."

"Well, just try to convince the jury that regardless of motive and opportunity he simply hasn't the right kind of face for it!" Graham snorted.

"I will, my lad, I will," Dr. Cavanaugh said cheerfully. "I've convinced juries of much queerer things than that. They've almost got into the habit of believing me."

"You've examined him, Doctor. What did you get out of him?" Peter's chair was once again poised at its precarious angle.

"As to actual events, no more than you already know. You are in as good a position to judge as I am. What do you think?"

"I honestly don't know," Peter said slowly. "I've seen a good many murderers, but I've never seen one like him. The evidence is all circumstantial, of course. But he did write the threatening letter, and he was the last person seen with Sheila O'Shay before her death. Our best hope is persuading the jury there's a 'reasonable doubt.' Circumstantially, it's a strong case; but circumstances take funny quirks sometimes."

"Well, I don't believe he did it!" Graham stabbed at the blotter so viciously that the pen stood erect and quivering. "A guilty man would either try to get out of it or throw up the game. But that's not evidence. If it weren't for that belief, I'd never have kept on with the case, not even for you, Peter. He's absolutely no help. He's adopted an attitude of—of passive noncooperation. And if you'd ever had a client like that, I guess you'd get a few homicidal impulses yourself!"

"You're wearing yourself out to no purpose." Dr. Cavanaugh's calm authority had its effect. Graham plucked the pen out of the blotter and leaned back in his chair. "You leave the evidence to me. That's what I'm here for."

"Is Orme going to take the stand?" Peter inquired.

"He says he is, and I can't very well stop him. But I haven't a ghost of an idea what he's going to say. That's a pleasant position for a man's lawyer to be in, isn't it? I suppose if he's as cracked as Dr. Cavanaugh says he is, he might say almost anything."

"I didn't say he was as 'cracked' as all that," Dr. Cavanaugh corrected mildly. "I haven't a notion in the world but that he'll tell the exact truth. Perhaps that's what he's afraid you'll argue him out of if he lets you know about it beforehand."

"Look here, Doctor!" Graham half rose, his face flushing angrily.

"Just a moment." The doctor waved him back with a placating gesture. "Orme may have the idea that the truth will not sound convincing. And since it is your job to be convincing, you might not look very favourably upon that particular brand of truth. It might need a good deal of varnishing. It is just possible that Orme is holding with all his strength of will to his purpose of telling exactly what he knows—and that he is afraid he might weaken under our combined persuasion if he gave us the chance to argue with him. Mind you, I know no more about it than you do! But there is nothing more stubborn than an unstable personality set on combating its own instability."

"Well, I've done my best to keep him off the stand," Graham said wearily. "You remain our one white hope, Doctor. I was afraid even you would slide out from under, after to-day's testimony."

"Neither Ellsworth nor Mrs. Kane could possibly alter the facts relative to David Orme," Dr. Cavanaugh said. "I am willing to stake my professional reputation on that. In fact, I am hereby wagering a nickel"—he produced the coin and balanced it on the tip of his finger—"that I shall acquit David Orme. And it won't affect the verdict one particle if you two come out now and have the dinner you should have eaten two or three hours ago."

Chapter XLIII

THE HAGGARD beauty of David Orme as he walked firmly to the witness chair had its immediate effect on the courtroom. Despite the commonplace of modern dress and surroundings his face might have served as model for the painting of a tortured god—Orpheus torn by the nymphs, or Prometheus chained to the rock. The carved immobility with which he had sat day after day beside the sheriff had given place to a controlled but vibrating tension. That face, with its hollowed temples and sunken eyes, somehow relegated the jurors, the group of court officials in their railed enclosure, and the rows of newspaper men in their numbered seats to inconsequence, even tawdriness. Whatever else he might be, David Orme was not a sordid criminal.

Before he had opened his lips except to murmur an almost inaudible response to the oath, the room was attuned to strangeness. A shiver of excitement—something not heard, not seen, but felt like the blowing of a wind—rippled across the press rows. The men and women in the jury box uncrossed their legs, ceased fiddling with things in their hands, and leaned slightly forward.

If Graham viewed his witness with some trepidation, he concealed his uneasiness under a manner of firm and confident friendliness.

"Will you just tell the jury in your own way the circumstances in which you first became acquainted with the lady known as Sheila O'Shay?"

"I was a member of the orchestra in the theatre where Sheila was dancing." There was not the slightest concession to the formality of a court proceeding in Orme's manner. His voice was not raised in the consciousness of addressing an audience, neither did it sink to the embarrassed mumble of stage fright. It was low, but carried with perfect clearness to the farthest corner of the courtroom. "I played"—his lips twisted sardonically as if forced to admit the point of a rather cruel practical joke—"I played the sandpaper. Rubbed sheets of sandpaper together, you know. It was what is called a jazz orchestra. Perhaps I may be allowed to explain that I was trained to be a concert violinist. I was what is sometimes called an infant prodigy——"

"Your honour," the district attorney blurted, "I fail to see what bearing the witness's musical abilities with sandpaper or otherwise have on the issue being tried before this court. Surely the present testimony is irrelevant and immaterial, to say the least of it!"

The hurt indignation in the prosecutor's voice failed to win any response from the angular, unmoved face of the judge.

"This man has taken the stand in his own defence, charged with the most serious offence in the criminal code." He might have been waving aside the importunities of a troublesome child. "I am inclined to give the witness considerable latitude. You may proceed, Mr. Orme."

Orme had awaited the end of the interruption with apparent indifference.

"I was studying with Ysaye in Belgium, and was to make my formal début the following year, when a bicycle accident resulted in the amputation of two of my fingers." He glanced down curiously at his hand, as if, even yet, the tragic finality of that accident were hard for him to grasp. "Naturally, that ended my career. But as I had lived nothing but music all my life, it did not occur to me that any other occupation was open to me. Friends interested themselves in my behalf and secured me the post of sandpaper artist in a jazz band." Again the exquisitely carved lips writhed in that sardonic smile. "I am trying to be brief, but these things have really a great deal to do with what happened afterward." Orme glanced upward with a look of apologetic inquiry at the judge.

In some subtle fashion the angles of the judge's face had lost some of their sharpness.

"Take your time, Mr. Orme. The court is willing to hear whatever you have to say."

"Good boy!" whispered the Q twin to his mate—and received a warning glare from the bailiff.

"When I saw Miss O'Shay on the stage," Orme went on, twisting his hands together in his lap, "I thought she was the most glorious person I had ever seen. She was like a movement from Tartini's 'Devil's Trill' sonata. She restored music to me—the music I could no longer bear to hear. I had not the faintest notion of seeking her acquaintance—there really would have been no way for me to do so if I had wanted to, and the idea did not enter my head. But—for some reason she noticed me, sitting there below her night after night in the orchestra pit. She learned my name, sent me a note, and asked me to call one night after the performance. She was like that. She could always take what she wanted, hold it—and throw it away. I know this will sound almost incredible, but she really did love me, poor and unknown as I was, a failure with no possible prospect of success." There was a mute apology in Orme's smile, and yet no one in the courtroom found it hard to believe that the facilely emotional, impulsive Sheila O'Shay had been stirred by the man with the face of a Greek statue whose worshipping eyes followed her every movement from the orchestra pit.

"She did love me then!" Orme's voice rang out, suddenly loud, in passionate affirmation. "It was as if somebody had stepped down out of heaven and lifted me up." There was a long pause; then he went on with forced calmness: "We were married. And then, of course, she got over it—in what seemed a very little while. She—there were other men. I—found it very hard. You see, I——" The face of the man in the witness chair became so ghastly white that the bailiff hastily handed him a glass of water. He looked down at it as if he hardly knew what it was. Then he gulped the entire contents of the glass, handed it back with a murmured "Thank you, I'm all right now," and continued:

"She told me that I had no right to dictate her conduct, that she earned more in a week than I did in a year, that she had—bought me, like any other bauble that caught her fancy, and that, the fancy having spent itself, she was through with me. And yet, I struggled on. I could not believe it would end like that. I couldn't see love as an easy thing, easily relinquished. It wasn't like that with me, you see."

There was another long pause. The judge stared out of the window. Graham prodded a sheet of paper before him with the point of a pencil. The district attorney referred to some documents in a cardboard file at his elbow. The faint swish of pencils racing across copy paper, catching up, was audible from the press rows. The jury regarded Orme with strained attention. He seemed to be calling upon some inner reserve of strength, gathering together his resources. At last he moved slightly, sitting up very straight in the witness chair.

"One night," he said in a low, penetrating voice, "she told me that she did not believe I had ever been a real musician. She said I had never been good for anything but to rub sheets of sandpaper together, She cast slurs on my music—on music! I lifted my fist"—Orme glanced down at his clenched hand as if it belonged to someone else—"and struck her down. Then I left."

Suddenly he slumped back in the chair, his head falling forward on his lifted hand.

"We will take a recess for ten minutes. The jury will bear in mind the admonition of the court not to discuss this case with others or among themselves——"

With a clatter of hinged seats, the reporters stampeded for the door.

Chapter XLIV

WHEN ORME resumed his place on the witness stand, a splotch of colour on each cheek had replaced his deadly pallor. If he was aware of an approaching crisis, this was his only tribute to it.

"On the fifteenth of March of this year I discovered that my wife had entered into a bigamous marriage with Mr. Ellsworth." His tone was studiously detached, as if the statement referred to nothing more disturbing than a mortgage or a bill of sale. "I wrote her a letter—a hurt and angry letter. I will admit that I even had the strange idea that if I could talk with her she would come back to me. On the evening of March 18th I did see her."

A sigh of excitement, of many breaths exhaled at once, rustled through the courtroom.

"We walked along the street, talking. It was soon made absolutely clear to me that whatever feeling for me Sheila had once had was as lost, as forgotten, as one of her last year's costumes. I don't know just why, but the idea of this bigamous marriage was more revolting to me than anything that had gone before—a queer kind of pride, of self-respect, perhaps. It seemed utterly humiliating to throw our marriage into the garbage can, as if it were of no significance whatever. I offered to allow her a divorce, but she did not want Mr. Ellsworth to know that legally she was still married to me. I don't recall clearly what we said. It is all rather confused in my mind. I remember that we stood on a street corner. And then I left her and went out to the auto camp where I had been staying. That is all." The expression on Graham's naturally sunny countenance was almost comically disconsolate. He looked as acutely uncomfortable as a dog who finds a tin can tied to its tail and sits tight with the realization that the slightest movement will let loose a hideous concatenation of sound. His reproachful gaze flickered for a moment across the inscrutable face of the judge. Very evidently the defence attorney considered that a punishment was being inflicted upon him which he didn't deserve; but he wisely decided to let bad enough alone. He forced his voice to a tone of jaunty indifference.

"No questions," he said.

"You may cross-examine."

The district attorney softened his habitual roar to a dulcet reasonableness.

"There are a few points in your recital, Mr. Orme, which the People would like to have further elucidated. I will ask you to look at this letter, entered in evidence as People's exhibit A."

"The defence stipulates that the letter in question was written by Mr. Orme," Graham said wearily.

"Well, then, I will ask you, Mr. Orme, is the wording of this letter that of a man actuated by affection for the recipient?"

"I'll say it wasn't," the A twin commented in a sibilant whisper.

"No talking in the courtroom, *please!*" barked the disciplinary bailiff.

"I told you I was angry when I wrote it. And 'affection' is hardly the term I should use for my feelings toward Sheila O'Shay. I loved her—terribly." Orme spoke with tremulous intensity.

"Quite so. And this lady whom you 'loved terribly,' " the district attorney sneered, "you first knocked down, then abandoned, and then disregarded so completely that you did not learn of her subsequent marriage until almost a year after it had taken place." Although he merely leaned forward across the table, the district attorney seemed fairly to spring upon the man before him. "And what, may I ask, were you doing in the meantime?"

"I don't know," Orme said dully. "I seem to have been just wandering around."

"Oh, yes, wandering around. And your wanderings, I take it, were conducted by automobile?"

"I have never had a car."

"Yet you made the public automobile camp your headquarters. Can you explain that discrepancy?"

"Someone must have given me a lift on the highway as far as the auto camp. Then, when I was there, I stayed. I had no money, you see."

"Quite so, no money. And having thus belatedly discovered your wife's marriage to a rich man, you doubtless saw an opportunity to recoup your finances by threatening to make the illegality of her marriage known."

"I would not have taken a cent from Sheila if I had been dying!" Orme's face, which had paled to the gray-white of dead ashes at the opening of the cross-examination, suddenly flamed.

"Of course not! And yet your earnings as a sandpaper artist could scarcely have supported your menage during the period of your married life."

Graham half rose to object, thought better of it, and relapsed into his seat.

"I did not think of money then one way or the other. I did not dream that she thought of it, either. I loved her."

"So you have told us. And yet you made no effort to keep in touch with her affairs—affairs which were rather widely published—until three days before her death?"

"I have told you that I did not know of her marriage to Ellsworth."

"And can you explain this singular ignorance?"

"I have no explanation to make. I have already stated the fact."

"And having had your little chat with the lady, you left her on a street corner—having made no attempt to follow up the threats conveyed in your letter to her—and fled back to the auto camp, where you concealed yourself under the assumed name of Daniel Osgood?"

"It was the name by which I was known there. I adopted it after I left Sheila."

"Oh! And just why did you find it necessary to adopt an alias at all?"

"I—don't know."

The district attorney dropped his air of elaborate sarcasm. He half rose from his chair, pointing his finger menacingly at the man in the witness chair. His voice boomed through the courtroom.

"David Orme," he roared, "I suggest that you deliberately waited until Sheila O'Shay was in a position which you could threaten. I suggest that you used threats of exposure in order to wring money from her, and that, when she refused to submit to blackmail, you struck her down in a rage—you had done just that before, I believe you said—and killed her. I suggest that you were in possession of an automobile in which you drove the body to the marsh and which you afterward junked or ran into the bay; that you then very astutely thought to lose yourself in the floating population of the auto camp, hiding under an assumed name, in order not to arouse suspicion by attempting to flee from the scene without funds. I suggest, David Orme, that you did wilfully and feloniously murder Sheila O'Shay!"

Orme rose to his feet, his eyes fixed in a fascinated stare on the face of the prosecutor. He was trembling violently from head to foot, but he steadied himself with both hands on the arms of the chair behind him. Graham's protesting hand, lifted to signal an objection, was unheeded.

"Before God, I don't know whether I killed her or not!" he screamed in the high shrill voice of hysteria. "But I don't see how I could have done it—because I loved her more than my music, more than anything else on earth!"

Chapter XLV

After the emotional stress of the morning session, the quiet urbanity of Dr. Cavanaugh, as he settled himself comfortably in the witness chair, restored an atmosphere of normality to the tense courtroom. Dr. Cavanaugh was very much at ease and completely at home, and he showed it. He distinctly conveyed the impression that murder trials were no treat to him. He took the oath with the careless nonchalance of a caller presenting himself to a familiar hostess, and awaited developments with a manner that subtly combined a willingness to be helpful with a patient acceptance of inconvenience to himself in thus being summoned.

Graham had regained something of his former optimism.

"Will you tell the jury, Doctor, something of your professional career?"

"I was graduated from the Harvard Medical School, and after my interneship was for several years on the staff of Graham Hospital for Nervous and Mental Diseases. I then spent four years in study abroad. I was a member of the Viennese Psychoanalytic Society, which met with Dr. Sigmund Freud of Vienna in the first study of psychoanalysis. I also spent a year with Dr. Jung in

Zurich. I may say that I am not an adherent of any one school of psychoanalysis—in fact, I think I may be said to have made my own original contributions in the field. On my return to this country, I established my own psychiatric hospital and clinic. For the last six or seven years, I have retired from active practice, although I am still sometimes called into consultation and have taken such cases as have interested me from the point of view of research."

"You are a specialist in nervous and mental diseases?"

"Psychopathology is my particular field—yes."

"And have you written anything for publication on the subject?"

"I have contributed articles too numerous to mention to the medical journals of America, France, England, Austria, and Germany. I am the author of several books: *Abnormal Aspects of Genius*, *Abnormal Behaviour in Relation to Medical Jurisprudence*, *The Criminal Mind*, and *Autistic Thinking in Normal Life* are probably those best known to the layman."

"And you have, I think, served as alienist in a number of criminal cases?"

"As alienist, or sometimes rather as a psychological investigator—yes. I was expert witness for the prosecution in the case of the People *versus* James Kelly, the case of the People *versus* Edwards and Edwards, the case of the People *versus* Mary Emerson, the case of the People *versus* Watson and Eaves. Kelly was condemned to death; Edwards was condemned to death and his sister to life imprisonment; Mary Emerson was convicted but died before the date set for execution; Eaves was too young to receive the death sentence, and Watson, after conviction, was killed in an attempted jail break. I was witness for the defence in the trials of Edna Raleigh, Hubert Smith, Everett and Laura Connelly, and John Potts. Raleigh, Smith, the Connellys, and Potts were acquitted. I may add that in-numerous instances my services have been requested to conduct a preliminary investigation which in some cases prevented the accused from coming to trial and in others identified the criminal who was being sought. Many of these investigations were such as not to require my presence in court, but I believe they have been more or less a matter of public knowledge."

The jury was obviously impressed. The cases mentioned by Dr. Cavanaugh included a group of the most spectacular trials of the last decade. His name had gone forth in magazines and newspaper stories as a wizard who pulled amazing white rabbits of truth out of the black hat of mysterious circumstance, and his books were written in a strikingly vivid though by no means sensational style which had brought them readers far beyond the circle of his professional confreres. It was quite true that so far as was known he had never been engaged to investigate a case which he had failed to solve, and that the side which secured his services in a trial had invariably received a favourable verdict.

"I believe, Doctor, that you have been popularly referred to as 'The Man Who Makes No Mistakes'?"

"Oh, my dear Mr. Graham," Dr. Cavanaugh protested amiably, "we must concede a good deal to popular exaggeration. Perhaps"—he took the jury into his confidence with a deprecating smile—"it is only that my mistakes have never found me out!"

Graham, beaming like an impresario whose star performer is capturing the audience, waved the point aside.

"You are acquainted with the defendant, David Orme?"

"I am."

"You have examined him professionally?"

"I have."

"Will you kindly explain to the ladies and gentlemen of the jury the circumstances and results of that examination?"

"I have seen the defendant more than once."

Graham looked slightly surprised, but recovered himself promptly.

"Very well; go right ahead, Doctor."

"I will be as brief and as nontechnical as possible. If your honour and the jury will bear with me"—Dr. Cavanaugh glanced upward at the judge's bench—"I will go over the entire circumstances of my dealings with the defendant."

"You have all the time at your disposal that you need, Doctor." Even the judge treated this witness with marked and courteous respect. He no longer stared out of the window or gave his bored attention to the wranglings of Graham and the district attorney. It happened that this was the first case he had tried in which the great Dr. Cavanaugh appeared as expert witness, and he obviously looked upon it as an opportunity full of interest.

"Thank you," Dr. Cavanaugh nodded affably. "I will begin, then, with the early afternoon of a day last month, when I returned to my house from a morning round of golf and found a man whom I now know to be David Orme sitting on the doorstep of my office, blocking my entrance."

Graham's head jerked back, his startled gaze seeking the doctor's face. The district attorney's chair made a scraping sound as he pushed himself back from the table with both hands. But Dr. Cavanaugh, apparently oblivious of the sensation his statement had caused, was turned toward the jury box, his eyes studiously regarding the toe of his shoe as he crossed one knee over the other and leaned back at ease in the witness chair.

"Behold the Ethiopian emerging from the woodpile!" Harry chortled to his twin in gleeful excitement.

"Just cast your eyes on Graham—he's getting something he didn't bargain for," the other twin urged, digging an elbow into his mate's ribs for emphasis.

"No talking in the courtroom, *please!*"

Abandoning his futile attempt to catch Dr. Cavanaugh's eye, Graham, with an obvious effort, schooled his voice to noncommittal formality.

"And on what date, Doctor, did this—this meeting occur"

"On the fourth of March of the current year."

The district attorney's chair scraped sharply again—forward, this time.

"I beg your pardon? I—I think I must have misunderstood." Graham was clutching the edge of the table before him with both hands. "Will you repeat that date, please?"

Dr. Cavanaugh turned and surveyed his agitated questioner with mild amusement.

"I said"—he raised his voice, as if he had just discovered that Graham was slightly deaf—"March 4th, of this year."

"But that—that was before Mrs. Ellsworth disappeared!" Graham seemed hardly able to credit the testimony of his senses.

"The inference," Dr. Cavanaugh assented smoothly, "is quite correct."

Chapter XLVI

"PROCEED." IN that one word Graham gave it up and abandoned himself and David Orme to Dr. Cavanaugh. He was no longer directing the examination—he was merely a part of the audience. He glanced briefly at the district attorney, hoping that the prosecutor was too absorbed in his own astonishment to notice that his surprise was shared by his opponent.

"Mr. Orme was at that time in a state of extreme agitation. He told me that in passing the house he had recognized my name on the door plate. The maid told him that I was out, and saw patients only by appointment. Nevertheless, he settled himself on the doorstep to wait. He told me at once that he was without funds, but begged me to help him in what he described as a 'terrible extremity.' I admitted him to my office, gave him a mild sedative, and, when he was somewhat quieter, asked him the nature of his trouble.

"I will summarize his statement as succinctly as possible, in order not to weary you." Dr. Cavanaugh paused and glanced at the jury with his smile of courteous apology. Every face was turned toward him with strained interest. Even the judge leaned forward.

"Mr. Orme told me at that time that he had been, for almost a year, suffering from a complete loss of memory for preceding events. His memory, that is, was clear for the period between last April and the present. For events preceding that time his mind was a total blank. As perhaps you know, this state of amnesia is technically called a 'fugue.' "

The jury didn't know, but they appreciated the implied flattery, and tried to look as if they did.

"I went back rather carefully over the patient's personal history for the last eleven months. If I may be allowed to use an imperfect analogy, it was as if the strip of continuity, of the stream of memories which makes us conscious of ourselves as unbroken personalities, had been cut off at a particular point, with no way of uniting the severed edges. He had found himself walking along a country road, hatless and without luggage. If he had had a wallet containing money and a means of identification, he had lost it or it had been stolen from him. The only clue to his identity which he could discover was a fountain pen in his pocket, with the initials 'D. O.' engraved on a gold band around the barrel. From that time on, for a period of eleven months, he had worked as a casual ranch hand, using the name of Daniel Osgood, which was suggested to him by the initials on the pen. He had kept moving, in the hope that eventually some scene or circumstance would recall his past life to him. On the day when I saw him, he had received his first hint—the first stimulus which seemed to have aroused a response connected with his past life. I hope I am not being too detailed—taking up too much of your time with all this?"

Harry laid down his pencil and stretched his cramped fingers.

"Gee," he whispered to the Q twin. "Spell me on this, will you? It's all answer and no questions. Do you think you're getting paid just to sit and loaf in a ringside seat at this trial?"

"All right, hand it over. But say, do you notice what a sense of the dramatic the old bird has? He always asks if he's boring them at the most crucial moments."

"I haven't had time to notice anything but keeping up with my pothooks."

For once, even the bailiff was too absorbed to chastise the offenders against courtroom etiquette.

"Go on, please, Doctor. The court will be glad to listen to all you have to say."

"The circumstance to which I refer was a moving picture. Orme, or Osgood as I called him then, had dropped into a moving-picture house, more for a place to sit down and rest than for anything else. But an incident in the picture had roused in him an intense, though indefinite, emotional disturbance. It was a scene in which an angry man knocked a woman down. He was unable to stay for the conclusion of the story, and rushed out into the street, in a state of acute excitement. His first clear recognition out of the past was the sight of my name on the door plate when he passed my house—he recognized it, that is, as belonging to a more or less well-known psychiatrist."

"'More or less'—get that?" nudged Harry.

"It would be unnecessary to take you step by step through the analysis by which, in the course of the next two weeks, I finally knitted together the severed portions of Orme's consciousness. Working backward, I discovered that in his childhood he had received a powerful shock when his father, in a drunken rage, had struck his mother and knocked her down. The woman had hit her head in falling and was stunned; and the child, left alone with her when his father had stormed out of the house, had believed her to be dead. The incident was buried in his subconscious and apparently forgotten. It was only a short time afterward that a musician became interested in Orme's remarkable talent and undertook his education, separating him from his family associations. But the horror of the scene, intensified by his helplessness, nevertheless made an ineffaceable and powerful impression. When, as he has told you, he in a moment of anger struck his wife Sheila O'Shay and saw her fall as his mother had fallen, he found himself reproducing the scene which had given him so profound a shock in his childhood. He in his own person was reenacting the rôle of his hated father. The reproduction of a similar scene on the screen naturally caused a resurgence of the emotional storm, and gave us a starting point for reconstruction. The amnesia from which he was suffering explains the fact that Orme was unaware of his wife's subsequent marriage until so long after it had taken place.

"There are other items, of course, which require explanation. Not everyone would have responded to the same set of circumstances as David Orme responded to them. We must remember that he was and always has been an unstable personality—an instability recognized by the laity in references to the high-strung sensitiveness, the 'temperament' of certain geniuses. In such a personality, a rift in the stream of memory technically called a fugue is invariably a means of escape from an unbearable reality. When Orme found himself performing the same act which had so horrified him in his father, he reacted by a complete denial of the intolerable fact—by, in short, forgetting the painful situation and becoming, in effect, someone else. I have no doubt whatever that the emotional strain of seeing his wife again on the night of March 18th caused a slight recurrence of retroactive amnesia, which explains his confusion as to the details of the interview and his inability to remember his parting from Sheila O'Shay and his return to the automobile camp grounds where he was staying."

"Just a moment, your honour," the district attorney boomed. "I ask that that last statement be stricken from the record as incompetent and calling for the conclusion of the witness."

"But, your honour," Graham interposed, "Dr. Cavanaugh has been called to the stand as an expert witness. The statement was a part of his diagnosis of the defendant's mental condition."

"The statement may stand. Proceed, Doctor."

"That is all, I think."

Graham looked inquiringly toward Dr. Cavanaugh, but except for an almost imperceptible curve of amusement at the corners of his mouth, the doctor's face was inscrutable.

"No questions. You may cross-examine."

"Now, Doctor," the district attorney began with heavy reasonableness, "if the defendant's actions are fully explained by all this fugue and retroactive amnesia business, how do you account for his failure to make any mention of these occurrences on the witness stand?"

Chapter XLVII

"I OBJECT!" Graham exploded. "A moment ago my learned friend across the table was very meticulous about statements calling for the conclusion of the witness."

"If your honour please, I should like to answer the question."

"I withdraw the objection." Graham subsided meekly.

"The most significant factor in Orme's life of recent years"—Dr. Cavanaugh turned from the district attorney and addressed the jury conversationally—"has been the loss of two of his fingers. From a squalid childhood he had been lifted by his talent into a world of music—a world where he met some of the greatest names of Europe on a plane of congeniality and equality. At one stroke he was hurled out of that environment, hurled back into a poverty and a limitation far worse than that in which he started because it was now complicated by thwarted ambition. The result, in a man of his temperament, was a sense of inferiority—an inferiority actual and yet undeserved—which conditioned his entire life. It was for that reason that Mrs. Orme's skepticism regarding his musical ability moved him even more powerfully than the cooling of her love and her attentions to other men.

"He transferred to the loss of his memory the same intense feeling of inferiority which had goaded him ever since the loss of his fingers. It was a further lopping off, you see—another blow of fate stamping him as incomplete, as unable to hold his own with normal men. You must remember that we are here dealing all along with exaggerated reactions. In the short time at my disposal for treatment, I was unable to eradicate from David Orme's mind the idea that his flight from reality in the form of a fugue was an act of personal and moral cowardice. It was not that, of course—it was absolutely beyond his control. But remember the tortured pride with which he endured the humiliation of rubbing sandpaper in a jazz orchestra when he had expected to take his place among the world's great violinists. He had dragged himself back from the temptation of suicide because he thought it cowardly to run away from life. And yet, after enduring that depth of bitterness, he found that after all he had run away. Rather than admit that flight, with the moral stigma which he placed upon it, he was willing to let things take their course, even if his silence resulted in his conviction. Life, you see, was already a prison to him, and a sentence of death would offer him honourable escape, his final release."

For a moment, silence hung over the courtroom. Every mind was contemplating the vision of a tormented soul called up by the doctor's quiet and yet compellingly earnest utterance. The district attorney was the first to shake himself free of the spell.

He shuffled his notes, coughed, and changed his position.

"May I ask, Doctor," he said, concealing his uneasiness under an air of ponderous assurance, "whether it is your custom to take your patients off the streets and give them a course of treatment at their mere request, with no assurance of their ability to pay for your services?"

"Your honour"—Graham sprang to his feet, finding relief in action—"do I understand that the district attorney is attempting to impeach this witness?"

"What Mr. Graham understands is beyond my power to fathom, as I make no pretence of being a mind reader—or a psychiatrist." The district attorney turned with vicious joy to an antagonist whose weapons he could parry with his own. "I think the question is proper to cross-examination, your honour."

"The question is allowed."

Dr. Cavanaugh looked down at the district attorney with an invulnerable placidity from which the intended thrust glanced harmlessly aside.

"Of late years it has been my custom to take only such patients as interested me—and to take them wherever I found them. Fortunately I am no longer dependent on an income from my practice, as I believe I stated on direct examination, and am able to devote my time for the most part to special research. For some years I have been working on the problem of the relation of fugue states to genuine dissociation of personality. From that point of view I found Mr. Orme interesting."

"Oh, so you were very much interested in Mr. Orme's case!"

"Very much, yes."

"Well, Doctor"—the district attorney's bludgeoning voice went on—"isn't it a fact the scientific mind, like the musical mind, is subject to 'temperament'? In the enthusiasm of research, is it not frequently found that facts are interpreted to meet the hypothesis which the investigator is trying to prove?"

"That is sometimes true of some investigators, yes."

"Well, then," the district attorney panted a little in his approach to his goal, "what was to prevent David Orme, knowing the intense interest you took in his case, from making up the whole story which you have told us, and using it as a cloak of defence?"

"The main thing that prevented him was that he couldn't do it." So far as the doctor was concerned, the district attorney had evidently reached his goal, only to find that nothing was there.

"You have heard of malingering, Doctor?"

For the first time, Dr. Cavanaugh permitted his smile to broaden.

"Yes, I have heard of malingering."

"How can you be sure that Orme was not malingering—deliberately concocting a story and imitating the symptoms of this fugue you speak of?"

"Again, if I may, I will resort to an analogy. Suppose you were to ask me to imitate the playing of Fritz Kreisler. If I made the attempt, the imitation, I venture to say, would deceive no one. Even if I deliberately prepared for the test and had a certain degree of skill, the result, while it might pass before hearers without musical training, would certainly be detected without difficulty by musicians. The imitation of a mental disorder, contrary to popular belief, is infinitely more difficult than the imitation of a master's playing. In fact, not even a student of the subject could possibly maintain the fiction for any length of time without giving himself away. The amateur who thinks that by grimacing and tearing his hair he is giving a convincing clinical picture of insanity is doomed to instant disappointment. Functional and organic derangements of the mind are as numerous and as complex in their differences as physical disorders, and their symptoms are as definite. You might as well ask the physician whether a patient down with typhoid fever or tuberculosis was not making a vague general pretence of being ill. I may add that my own experience has been fairly extensive, and that it has not been devoid of the malingerers of whom you speak. Their efforts were quite readily detected."

The district attorney glanced covertly at the jury. They were obviously impressed. He wished he had left that particular line of questioning unopened. Graham was leaning back, taking things as they came. He could set Dr. Cavanaugh up there and turn him loose! The district attorney inquired of the universe, not without silent profanity, why the devil they hadn't been able to hook Dr. Cavanaugh for the prosecution—then he would be sitting back, and Graham would be doing the worrying. He passed his handkerchief across the back of his neck, where the roll of fat stood out in a thick ridge. Then he leaned forward, moving to a new line of attack.

"Granting that all you say is true, Doctor—and I am without the advantage of the technical learning necessary to argue the point with you" (the district attorney hoped that would have its effect on the jury—that they would see themselves and him together as allies, as plain men pitting their robust common sense against the hairsplittings of the academic expert) "there still remains no reason why Orme should not have had another impulse to knock Sheila O'Shay down. And why, having killed her with the blow, he should not have concealed and destroyed her body, as he thought—and then have conveniently suffered another loss of memory. Or let us say that the emotional crisis put him into that state of fugue again."

"I take it you mean to put that suggestion in the form of a question." Dr. Cavanaugh spoke before Graham could do more than grunt the beginning of a protest. "At any rate, I will answer it. It might have been physically possible for Orme to have left the Ellsworth grounds with his wife at half-past eight, in accordance with Mrs. Kane's testimony, have quarrelled with her and killed her, then have left her body lying casually somewhere while he wandered about, and finally have returned for it and taken it to the marsh in a very clever and almost successful attempt to conceal his crime. That would be physically possible, but it would not be psychologically possible. No one in a state of mind capable of elaborating the plan for concealing the body in the marsh and setting fire to the grass in order to destroy it would have failed to carry through the plan at once."

"But there is no evidence that he didn't carry it through at once! No one knows what time he arrived at the auto camp. Why assume an interval of aimless wandering?" The district attorney was startled out of all caution.

"Because," said Dr. Cavanaugh, "he hadn't had time to go to the marsh and get back when I saw him."

"When you saw him?" The district attorney clutched at the torn shreds of formality. "I withdraw that. When did you see him, Doctor?"

"At half-past nine o'clock on the night of March 18th I chanced to look out of my office window and saw David Orme sitting on the curb. I did not know at the time, of course, that he had reverted to his abnormal state—that he was then suffering from a recurrence of amnesia, although on this occasion a slight and temporary recurrence. I was busy with a caller at the time, and I intended, as soon as the caller left, to go out and speak to him and ask him what he wanted. He was very shy of interrupting me, and I took it for granted that he had seen the caller enter, and was waiting outside until I should be at liberty. At a quarter past ten I opened the door to let my visitor out—just in time to see Orme rise from the curb and walk away down the street. As it was late, I did not bother to call after him, thinking that he had tired of waiting and would come again. Sheila O'Shay's murderer did not leave her body unguarded while he spent three quarters of an hour sitting on a curbstone before he went back and drove that body to the marsh for concealment. His presence outside my house is an alibi for David Orme. Incidentally, I think we may safely say that he is the only man on record who, in defending himself against the accusation of a crime, was all the while in possession of an alibi which he had completely forgotten!"

Chapter XLVIII

"Cavanaugh clears Orme! Doctor gives Orme alibi!"

Already the cries of the newsboys were wafted faintly upward to the courtroom of Department 24.

"Jury out at—make it 11:40, Jimmy." Peter slammed the telephone receiver on the hook and threaded his way through the chattering group of reporters in the little witness room. They swung their legs from the table or leaned against the wall, smoking with the furious zest of men who had been deprived of cigarettes during the long hours in the courtroom.

"Two to one they'll be out less than an hour!"

"They might hang—that old bird with the goat's beard in the second row wasn't taking in much of the doctor's fireworks."

"Not a chance. I'll bet a dollar they'll acquit on the first ballot."

"Done! They'll stay out long enough to get one more dinner on the taxpayers, anyway."

"All the same, Orme might have done it."

"Purely circumstantial evidence. Juries don't like that. They can remember too many circumstances of their own that might take a deal of explaining."

"It was the doctor that did it. He handed it out like Jehovah on Sinai. If he told them to render a verdict that the moon was made of green cheese, they'd do it. Clever of Graham, bringing that in about 'The Man Who Makes No Mistakes'—they got it firmly fixed in their minds that the great Cavanaugh just couldn't be wrong."

"He certainly made the D. A. wish he was some place else."

"Hello, Peter! You look as if you needed a drink."

"I do," Peter agreed morosely, and slid through the door.

The rows of chairs in the courtroom were deserted. With stray sheets of copy paper and stubs of pencils strewing the floor, it had the dishevelled look of a room after a party—that indefinable atmosphere of a place where things have recently happened and are no longer happening. Half a dozen correspondents sat on the rail of the jury box, like a line of birds teetering on a fence, chatting with each other, the photographers, and the now humanized bailiff. The chairs behind the lawyers' table were pushed back, empty. Above the back of a chair next to the railing which divided the room in half, Peter caught sight of the top of a small black hat.

He swung open the gate and dropped into the chair beside Barbara.

"Well," he said with weary relief, "that's over!"

Barbara turned to him a brooding face.

"Oh!" she breathed, "do you really think it is?"

Peter turned sidewise, resting his elbows on the arm of the chair. By leaning forward just three inches, he could kiss the tip of her ear. He glanced over his shoulder at the group on the rail of the jury box. Better not risk it. He relinquished the opportunity with a regretful sigh.

"There's not a doubt in the world!" he said confidently. "I wish you'd take off your glove, Barbara. I think I could grab your hand without anybody noticing."

Obediently, almost absent-mindedly, Barbara took off her glove; but she smiled up at him with tremulous gratitude as her cold fingers relaxed under the reassuring pressure of Peter's clasp.

"But that speech of the district attorney's—it sounded horribly convincing, with all that talk of motive and opportunity, and the way he kept emphasizing the threatening letter and the attempt to escape."

"Yes, it was a better argument than Graham's—for people like you and me, but not for the jury. The jury will think the D. A. is a bit of a bully, and Graham a nice honest kid, desperately in earnest and at a disadvantage. Which is just about right, both ways. But Graham has brains as well as a pink-and-white complexion. He knew he didn't have to argue the case. What he had to do was to cut everything else away and hammer that jury with Dr. Cavanaugh's testimony and nothing else. They've got to remember that testimony as the one important issue—and that Dr. Cavanaugh is a man who can't be mistaken. Orme is acquitted beyond a shadow of a doubt—and it was your father that did it with his little hatchet."

"Yes." Barbara was staring straight before her at the state seal on the wall behind the judge's bench. "He was—very clever—wasn't he!"

"He was the whole works!" Peter began enthusiastically. Then he saw that her lips were trembling, trembling so that she could hardly control them for speech. He glanced again over his shoulder at the chatting reporters. "To hell with them!" he grunted with low-voiced violence, and, raising his hand to Barbara's chin, turned her head gently toward him. Her eyes shone unnaturally large in her small thin face—pitifully smaller and thinner than when he had first seen it.

"You poor—little—girl." Peter's crooning voice had a tone

which no one had ever heard in it before. "I know what you want to do. You want to put your head on my shoulder, and cry and cry and cry. And God knows how much I want you to do just that! Barbara, whenever you want a shoulder to cry on, promise me that you'll cry on mine. That's what I'm for. It's the one best thing on earth I'm good for, Barbara!"

"Yes," Barbara said faintly, "I'd like that." The tears welled slowly in her eyes and slipped down her cheeks. The tip of a pink tongue emerged, like a kitten's, to lick them from the corners of her mouth. Something in that childlike, wholly unconscious movement wrenched Peter almost unbearably.

"Damn these people," he murmured fervently. "Damn everything!" He squared his shoulders, blocking the view of the men by the jury box. Then he pulled out a crumpled handkerchief and awkwardly but efficiently mopped Barbara's wet face. A shred of tobacco clung to her chin.

"At least I'm sure you—you don't do this very often," Barbara smiled through her tears. "You haven't what I'd call a fatal facility!"

"Listen to me," Peter said urgently. "This can't go on. You can't wear yourself out like this—you'll go all to pieces."

"Oh, no, I won't"—Barbara's voice was steady now—"I can't afford to."

"But now that Orme has got off—and your father did get him off, sure as shooting—don't you think you'd feel better if you sometime told me all about it? Wouldn't it be a help to share it with someone—someone who would love you, no matter what happened?"

"No, Peter, I couldn't." Barbara spoke with a desolate, wistful finality. "I can't tell anyone—ever. But I'll say this much, though it's more than I thought I would, more than I ought. Only, somehow, I want you to know. You say it wouldn't make any difference, but I do want you to know, Peter—even though maybe you won't believe it."

"I'll believe anything on God's earth that you say to me, Barbara."

"It's only this: that I—I didn't kill Sheila O'Shay!"

The sound of shuffling feet from behind the door through which the jury had filed out; the sound of trampling feet as the courtroom doors were thrown open; a voice, the composite of many voices, saying, "Here they come!"—all came to Peter as a rushing confusion in which he was somehow propelled to seat 53 as the judge took his place on the bench and the bailiff banged for order.

"Ladies and gentlemen of the jury, have you considered your verdict?"

"We have."

Down the murmurous lines of an interminable rigmarole droned a voice:

"The case of the People against David Orme. . . . Do you find the defendant guilty or not guilty?"

"Not guilty."

"So say you all?"

"So say we all."

Somebody was trying to scramble over Peter's outstretched legs. Somebody leaped over a chairback to reach the aisle.

"My God, Peter, have you gone to sleep?"

Peter stared blankly at Harry, the Q twin, who was shaking him by the elbow.

"I believe you and I are working on a rag called the *Herald*. It's supposed to be a daily newspaper. Its city editor is one Jimmy Sears, who at this moment is shouting himself hoarse and tearing out handfuls of red hair. Suppose you postpone your little dream and come along!"

The dazed look receded from Peter's eyes.

"Call a taxi, Harry, while I phone in. With luck, we'll make the one-o'clock deadline!"

Love and sorrow and joy and life must wait. Peter Piper of the *Herald* was on the job.

Chapter XLIX

PETER KNEW that he should feel flattered by Professor Gambion's invitation to dinner. Besides, he had always liked the old professor; and he knew that, despite the difference in their ages, the liking was reciprocal. He smiled a little at the transparent craftiness which had led Gambion, on this particular occasion, to invite him to meet the distinguished Judge Hood, visitor from another state. Gambion had seized upon Peter as one of the most promising of his students, and Peter suspected that in the professor's eyes he had fallen from grace in becoming a reporter instead of concentrating on the finishing of his law course—with an income of nothing a week. Judge Hood would be set forth as a shining example: "There, if you stick to the straight and narrow paths of jurisprudence, goes Peter Piper at fifty!"

Yet Peter did not want to go to Professor Gambion's house for dinner. He wanted to do nothing but think—even though thinking followed the course of a single reiterated circle. His thoughts padded on, round and round and round again, wearing ever deeper a track that led nowhere save back to its own beginning.

He believed Barbara. He believed Ellsworth. He believed Mrs.

Kane. He believed Orme. Not one of those four had killed Sheila O'Shay. They were simply not the right people for it. It did not hitch on to them. That murder was committed by someone who knew exactly what he was doing. The case had not progressed one inch nearer to solution than in the beginning. It was deep—far deeper than anyone had yet penetrated. There was a mind behind it—a mind far superior to Orme's or Mrs. Kane's or Ellsworth's. As for Barbara, her bare word was better than a thousand proofs. She had intellect, but she also had character. She had the temperament for truth. She was crystalline. It wasn't a code of moral teachings with her, something imposed from without, to be sloughed off when the demands of self-interest became too strong. It was herself.

Peter sat back in the shadow just beyond the firelight, smoking one cigarette after another and now and then sipping at the glass of sherry that stood on the arm of his chair. The old professor had saved a small cellar from the pre-Volstead era, and one of his precious bottles had been brought out in honour of his old friend, the judge. Now and then Peter roused himself to listen to their desultory talk.

"You're on a newspaper, I believe Gambion said?" Judge Hood turned to Peter, courteously including him in the topic of conversation. They had been discussing, as everyone was discussing, the Ellsworth case, and from that had drifted to famous unsolved crimes of the past.

"Guilty, your honour," Peter admitted smilingly.

"Then I'm sure you'll bear me out against the professor that many of the great unsolved crimes were not really unsolved at all. A group of selected editors and newspaper men, in the mood and with their tongues loosened, could reveal what I believe you youngsters call the 'low down' on many of them. The solution is merely 'not for publication,' for various reasons—influence sometimes, or lack of evidence sufficiently conclusive for a court of law. The Elwell and the Hall-Mills murders in New York, the Taylor and the Ferguson cases in California, are supposed by many people to fall into that class."

"Still," the professor maintained, tilting his glass against the light and squinting through it, "the only reason that the criminals who undertake to perpetrate the 'perfect crime' seem such utter asses is because they were asses. Their jelly wouldn't jell; but that's no reason to deny that there is such a thing as jelly. Of course we don't know about any successful 'perfect crimes'! If they were successful, we shouldn't know about them. But that's no ground for saying that they don't happen. The normal criminal is stupid, because the normal intelligent man knows that he can go farther, and with less risk, by sticking to the paths of rectitude. But there is such a thing as the abnormal criminal mind—the man of sufficient intelligence to fool the police and the public and make his way unscathed through the whole elaborate machinery we have constructed for the protection of society, but a man whose intelligence has a fatal flaw in it somewhere, a limitation which allows him to disregard the rights of his fellows and become a criminal."

"Yes," the judge agreed, "there are men like that—though they don't always turn to crime. There was Dawson, for instance. Remember him?"

"Dawson? Let me see. Oh, yes, the queer fellow with delusions of grandeur whenever he got drunk, in our class at law school! What made you think of him?"

"I happened to run across him not long ago."

"Committing the perfect crime?" Peter suggested.

"Nothing quite so dramatic. But the only reason that Dawson

has not committed a perfect crime is because he has had no occasion to. You may be surprised to know, Gambion, that Dawson has made a name for himself as one of the most brilliant prosecuting attorneys in the history of my state."

"You don't say so!" Gambion blinked. "Why, in our young days, Dawson was avoided even by the fellows whom most of the other fellows avoided! He was a complete and perfect rotter."

"He still is. Among the few who know, there is no more unsavoury reputation in the city than Dawson's. But you forget those delusions of grandeur that used to disgust us, the tales of the great things he was going to do that he told when he was drunk."

"Yes?"

"Well, he's done just those things. And he's done them because he combines uncommon ability with consuming egoism. That's why I said he would be a great criminal if he wanted to—and he'd want to, right enough, if it were necessary to his progress. Morality, after all, despite its complications, pretty well boils down to one thing—the faculty of taking the other fellow's point of view. You know that somebody else would dislike being robbed or killed or cheated just as you would dislike it. You put yourself in his place, feel his situation as your own. Call it imagination, sympathy, the faculty of getting out of your own skin. Now and then somebody lacks that faculty. And if he does, the moral code to him is merely a convenient artifice, like etiquette. He eats with his fork because in general it's the easiest thing to do. But if eating with his fork became inconvenient to him, he'd throw the fork away without hesitation. The egoist is the single-minded person. Because he is single minded, given native ability, he will go far in his chosen direction. But if he meets with an obstacle which cannot be circumvented, he will destroy it, without regard to the rights of the obstacle. In other words, he will commit a crime dictated by his egoism, and will conceal it by his intellectual astuteness."

"Yes," Peter said, "I've heard something like that before, in another connection." The words of Dr. Cavanaugh came back to him as clearly as if he heard them again in the doctor's quiet, authoritative tones. "The few who can pull their threads out to the end are the great single-minded people: artists, financiers, scientists, even arch criminals."

Then something crashed in his brain. A light, like the dozen fiery globules of a bursting rocket, each separate against the sky, but all emerging from a single source, flamed in the darkness of his mind. He leaped to his feet, knocking the wine glass from the chair arm. The gleaming fragments of glass caught the firelight, and a thin trickle of fluid darkened the hearthrug.

"My God!" he said wildly; and again, in a low, awed voice, "My God!"

Hood and Gambion were both staring at him, startled into immobility.

"What's the matter? Are you ill?" the judge exclaimed.

Mechanically Gambion stooped to pick up the fragments of the shattered glass.

"I may be crazy, but I don't think so. I believe I've got it! I think I've solved the Ellsworth case!"

Bareheaded, banging the door behind him, Peter rushed from the house.

Chapter L

PETER IGNORED Bossy, waiting at the curb, and swung down the street with long, uneven strides. He felt an imperative need of physical action to bring some sort of coherence to the wild idea which had flashed across his mind in Professor Gambion's library. His pace lagged, at times stopping altogether. It was incredible—incredible even to himself! Then he pushed on rapidly, as if the whole amazing scheme would escape unless he could pursue and overtake it.

Barbara was protecting someone—someone whose claim upon her was strong enough to bring that thin whiteness to her cheeks, that desperate purpose to her eyes; a claim that not even murder could break. Her silence was not self-protection; he was sure of that. Barbara had told him that she had not killed Sheila O'Shay—and Barbara could not lie. And she was not protecting Ellsworth. She did not love Ellsworth. Her sentiment for Ellsworth had never been love—not love as Peter knew it, not the love that was a steady flame in Barbara's eyes when he had held her in his arms in the little room with the firelight, nor when he sat beside her in the courtroom. Besides, Ellsworth had not the temperament of a cool, calculating murderer.

"Among all the things we don't know about Sheila O'Shay's murderer, we know that he is not an ordinary criminal." Cavanaugh had said that. "How easy it is to fool mere normal people." He had said that, too.

Peter went back, step by step, over the scenes in the courtroom. Cavanaugh had acquitted Orme—there was no doubt of it. But why had he given no hint to Graham, nor to Peter, himself, that he had known Orme prior to the murder? Peter, who was acute enough, had not had the slightest suspicion of those earlier meetings. Perhaps Cavanaugh had the right to withhold the knowledge from Peter, but Graham was Orme's lawyer. Graham should have been told. And even though he had merely allowed Peter to deceive himself, it was nevertheless a deliberate deception—a deception with a motive. Motives! "The strongest motive is likely to seem feeble to the other fellow." Yes, Cavanaugh had said that.

And yet—if he were wrong! He must be wrong—it was too bizarre. It was beyond belief, almost beyond imagination. If he were wrong, he would show himself the world's most utter fool. If he were wrong, he stood to lose Barbara—she would never forgive him. And yet, deep down below the seething chaos in Peter's mind, that flash of light burned on. Reason, common sense, credibility were all against it. But it burned on. And there was only one way to find out. Peter felt suddenly helpless. Who was he to pit his wits against the subtle, calculating mind that had framed this murder? It was David against Goliath. He had only his little stone of truth to throw—if it was the truth! But it was truth. Wild as it was, it had clicked somehow—the click of absolute certainty, of a reason beyond reasonableness. David against Goliath, but David, with his little stone of truth, had won!

Dr. Cavanaugh opened the door to Peter's ring, his big frame silhouetted against the light. For the first time Peter noted that the square shoulders had acquired a slight stoop. The flesh hung upon the doctor's cheeks in folds, deepening the lines of his face as if they had been marked with a heavy pencil. It was not surprising that he should feel the effects of fatigue and overwork in a difficult and exacting case; but Peter's association with him had been so close that he had hitherto failed to observe the change. He felt now that every sense was sharpened, that his nerves reached out like antennae, responding to almost imperceptible stimuli. He was like a man feeling his way through the jungle, listening for the danger that lurked in the rubbing of blades of grass, watching for the shifting of a shadow.

Dr. Cavanaugh leaned forward to recognize the young man standing hatless in the gloom. Peter saw his fingers tighten on the doorknob. But his voice was genial. He greeted Peter as an unaccountable but always welcome friend.

"The ubiquitous Peter! I thought your labours were over by this time."

The sincere heartiness of his tone rocked Peter back to sanity. But with that new alertness which nothing escaped, he saw that the doctor's eyes were hard and impenetrable, like agates.

"I've come to mull over the aftermath of our current mystery." To his surprise, Peter heard his own voice speaking in easy and natural tones. He knew that his hands were steady, that his face betrayed nothing of the tumult in his mind. He lighted a cigarette, testing himself by holding the match until it almost burned his fingers. The tiny flame did not so much as quiver.

"Is there an aftermath?" Dr. Cavanaugh settled himself in the chair behind the desk, waving Peter to an armchair drawn close beside the student lamp. He glanced obliquely at Peter as he selected a cigar from the box beside him. Deliberately he struck a match and held it, watching the point of flame creep closer until it almost burned his fingers. The flame did not waver.

"You saved Orme—single-handed. The papers are full of it. Yours is the honour and the power and the glory. In theatrical parlance, you ran away with the show, and landed another triumph for the man who makes no mistakes. Graham was simply nowhere. And yet, I wonder—isn't it barely possible that that star performance was itself a mistake?"

"Your account really flatters me unduly." The doctor lifted a deprecating hand.

"Not at all. I've noticed your impeccable modesty, Doctor. You never boast—you have no need to. It is an admirable attitude. But I'm still left wondering."

"Surely you don't think Orme was guilty?"

"No," Peter said meditatively. "I don't think Orme was guilty."

"And you are kind enough to say that it was I who got him off?"

"Yes, you got him off. And yet it must be rather hard on you to realize that, for the first time, you have met your match. You set out to solve this case—and you have not solved it. You have made your first failure. The public has not caught that angle of it yet—but it will. The man of no mistakes is fallible, after all. The tule marsh murderer was too clever for him. And presently it will occur to them that the great man is not quite so great as they thought him. 'He did some clever work,' they will say, 'but perhaps he played in luck. It may not have been so hard as it looked. He couldn't find the man that killed Sheila O'Shay. And if that man could beat him, there are others who can beat him, too.' You have been a legend, Dr. Cavanaugh. And a legend must be perfect, or it is nothing."

"And do you imagine," Dr. Cavanaugh said gravely, "that I have not thought of that?"

"Yes," Peter nodded, "I believe you have thought of it."

"And suppose——" Dr. Cavanaugh paused, pursed his lips, and sent a perfect smoke ring into the air. He watched it until it wavered and broke. "Suppose I have not really failed? Suppose I could solve the mystery—if I would."

Peter leaned forward. In the shadow he had the illusion that the face of the doctor was carved in gray rock—heavy, sinister, brooding. And then he knew that it was only the face of a man who was very tired.

"Dr. Cavanaugh," he said in a voice thin and taut with the intensity of his emotion, "I believe that you have the answer. I came here to fight it out with you. But I am not going to fight you. When all's said and done, you are a very great man—and you have been good to me. I leave it to you. I leave it to you—absolutely."

"Yes," the doctor agreed gravely. "It is left to me. If I do not tell you the answer, you will never know it. There is not a shadow of proof. And remember, my failure is in my own hands. If I choose to fail——"

"Do you think you can bear to fail, Doctor? Other men, of course—but you?"

Silence was in the room, silence that vibrated like a bell.

Suddenly the doctor smiled—a smile of strange, remote tenderness.

"Peter," he said softly, "we are none of us immune from the weaknesses of humanity. None of us quite immune. None. Just two people in my life have touched me deeply. I am far greater than either of them. They are bound by all that I have cast aside. They are straws in my hands. And yet—— Those two, Peter, are you—and Barbara. I am going to tell you the answer."

Chapter LI

Dr. Cavanaugh leaned back in his chair. The lines in his face were deep corrugations, like crevasses worn in stone; but the face itself was somehow changed, smoothed by the relief that comes with the end of conflict, the victory of a final decision.

"I always said you were a bright young man, Peter," he said, as casually as if the story he had promised to tell were of no more personal import than a smoking-room anecdote. "How did you come to guess?"

"Partly because there was no one else whom Barbara would guard, not only with her life, but with her honour. That is what her silence meant. It is the only thing it could mean. It seemed wildly absurd, of course, to imagine you a criminal. You had the intellect to carry it through, to make it a perfect crime. But that wasn't enough. You must not only have the wit to conceal a crime, but the character to commit it. A chance conversation to-night made me understand the thing that has puzzled me in the way you handled Orme's trial. It was your ambition that took no account of the little question of playing fair with Graham when you sprang your previous meetings with Orme for the first time on the witness stand.

"You wanted to tower—to make us all pygmies. You didn't even see that it wasn't cricket to keep Graham in the dark. And you had me fooled, too. You had me fooled perfectly. That worried me, because you shouldn't have wanted to fool me. You were not only clever enough to do it—but you could want to do it. You told me the truth about yourself when you spoke of the single-minded people, the people who go their own way, the supreme egoists. You did not call them that, but that is what it amounts to, doesn't it? They are outside morality. They are not held by all those tangling threads that bind us to others. You didn't mind letting Graham down, you didn't mind letting me down, so that you could have the glory.

"I remembered things that you said. And the way you laughed when you told me once that we are all more or less insane. Your laugh troubled me at the time, though I didn't know why. I know now. It was because that laugh was the only time you ever came out from behind the wall you had built around your real self. You came out for a moment then. You laughed because you alone were secure in a terrible sanity—a sanity in which you could rule us, entangle us, play upon us. You alone were free and unhampered. And to-night it all came to me. It made everything clear. You said once that clues were negligible compared with motives. Well, you were right. I haven't a clue to go upon. I haven't a shred of evidence. The only thing I can see clearly in the whole dark business is a motive. Not even that—just the insight into the sort of man you are. You could conceal your acts—but you could not quite conceal your character. And even yet I don't understand how you dared to do it—how you dared to take this case and follow it through, discover all that you did about it, uncover everything—and stop just short of uncovering yourself."

The doctor smiled.

"Yes," he said, "that presented its problems. I may say, in fact, that this was my most difficult case. Perhaps it will be remembered as my greatest triumph. You ask how I dared. But I dared do nothing else! The only safety lay in the path of danger. There was Camberwell. I could not leave Camberwell to work alone, perhaps to stumble on the truth. I must keep the threads in my hands. And I dared not do less than my best. Camberwell is too good a man to be deceived by a fake. It must be the real thing. And it was the real thing, every step of it! It is not easy to go about solving a problem, step by step, exactly as if you did not know the answer—to remember every moment the precise limits of your supposed knowledge. But I did it. I did it so well that sometimes I almost forgot that it was only a game I was playing. It had its fascination, too. The most dangerous game, played with superlative skill."

"It was you who killed her?" Peter asked quietly.

"Oh, yes, it was I who killed her. I could not do otherwise. I always knew, of course, that I should not hesitate if the need arose."

Peter looked curiously at the face before him. Cavanaugh bore his gaze without flinching.

"And yet you don't look like a murderer," Peter said.

"Why should I? Only a fool would be a professional criminal. Crime is the response to an emergency. Naturally I did not court emergencies. Words! Most of humanity is ruled by words, pretty words, ugly words. Honour, loyalty, crime—what are these but coloured words? Stripped of their colour, they are nothing. But only the minority is ready to pass beyond playing with those coloured words. I very early found that out. One must pretend to play the game that the other children are playing. Only so can one be free to play one's own game unmolested. So I treated their words with the utmost seriousness—only I knew, as they did not, that the words meant nothing. I learned to be very careful. I put on the mask of their conventional morality—only I knew it to be nothing but a foolish mask. There used to be rumours—before I learned that I must never let the mask slip. That is the reason I came out here to live. That is the reason I adopted Barbara. Barbara took the words seriously—oh, very seriously indeed! A household with a grown daughter to preside over it was by just so much more entrenched in conventionality than even the most discreet of bachelor establishments."

"Is she really your daughter?" Peter broke in. "She thinks she is. That's why she won't marry me."

"I encouraged her to think it. Knowing Barbara's code, I thought it would hold her to me. You see, Barbara knows that I killed Sheila. But I didn't expect this. I—see," the doctor said slowly. "She believes that she is my daughter, and having found out what kind of man I am, she fears that she has inherited some of my criminal aptitudes. It is not convention that has shocked her, but biology!"

"How little you understand us, after all!" Peter's eyes shone with a strange pride. "Barbara did not need that added bond. You could have been sure of her loyalty. You won it without lies. You won it by what you did for her. No lie could strengthen it. It is a part of her. You only hurt her—filled her with terror of herself!"

"But, my dear man"—Dr. Cavanaugh spoke in mild protest—"I could not possibly foresee that I would be obliged to kill anyone, still less that Barbara would find out about it! It was merely a general precaution. You may tell her the truth, of course. You may even tell her that I loved her. I have seen her suffer, and for the first time in my life I found that the suffering of others had power to hurt me. With all my strength, I had that weakness. You may tell her that I loved her. I wish she could have been glad to be my daughter. But since she feels differently——" The doctor's shoulders straightened. He also had his moment of pride. "Since she wishes to be free of any taint from me, you may tell her that I can pass on to her no physical inheritance."

"I'd like to tell you," Peter said, "that I don't feel like that myself. I wanted to marry her anyway. I still do."

"Thanks. It's a queer thing, Peter. Perhaps it is just as well that this is the end. For I have discovered my weakness. I wanted Barbara's love, and I want your respect—the only things in life I have wanted that I couldn't go out and wrest from the folly of humanity. The only things——"

"Maybe it's a flaw in me, too," said Peter. "At least I never thought I could feel that way about a man who has done what you have done. But I—so far as I'm concerned, you have what you wanted. You are a man with a great mind, and you are a brave man—and you have been good to me. I—I shall always be rather proud of saying that you were my friend."

The simple truth of his statement shone from Peter's eyes. But he saw that the doctor did not believe him.

"Words—words," he muttered. "Soft, pretty words, to cover the sting of reality."

"Would you mind telling me—why you killed her?" Peter asked.

Chapter LII

Dr. Cavanaugh drew a prescription pad from under the desk blotter, scribbled upon it briefly, and passed it across to Peter.

"There!" he said. "That is a signed indorsement of what I am going to tell you. You may want to have it to give to your editor."

"To—Jimmy?"

"Oh, I know that you are not going to turn me over to the police! You are going to give me my own way out. That is one of the foolish little words you are bound by."

Peter's jaw jutted forward.

"Yes," he said, "you're damn right it is."

"The solution of the Ellsworth mystery—the last case of Dr. Cavanaugh—is my little legacy to you for your paper. I think it is what you would call an important exclusive."

Peter tried to smile back, but the cords in his throat hurt him.

"I—I won't use it!" he blurted.

"Oh, but you must! I don't want to be remembered as a failure. My last case must be a success. I shan't know it, of course, where I am going—but I know it now. And your editor will like it. You ought to be pleased at that."

"Damn the paper!" Peter choked, uttering the worst blasphemy of which he was capable. “Damn everything! But if you'd rather have it so, I'll take it.”

“The man of no mistakes,” the doctor said, with musing irony. “Well, I made just one. I did not, after all, understand myself. I accounted for everything—and I did not know that the one thing I could not face was failure. I have scorned the world's judgments, but I am bound by them, after all. I could not have the world say that I had met one case which I could not solve. There was one other thing. I did not foresee that Barbara would find out. Barbara could not understand that crime was merely the logical response to an emergency. The burden of my guilt was too heavy for her. Her suffering was altogether irrational; but I couldn't let her go through life with that hurt. I had made her life beautiful, and I couldn't ruin the beauty I had given her. You see, when all's said and done, I couldn't pull out my thread quite to the end. That is my weakness.” The doctor paused and lighted a cigar. He smiled, a rare, quizzical smile at Peter. The match in his hand was trembling. He shook it impatiently, extinguishing the flame.

“You see?” He shrugged his massive shoulders. “But that's not your story. That, if you please, is the part you will leave out when you write it. It begins with the day I found Orme on the doorstep. That part is quite true. All that I said was true. I was far too clever to lie. Facts can be concealed, but they cannot be obliterated. Orme came to see me daily. When he talked with Mrs. Kane he told her that Sheila could reach him through me—there was no telephone at the auto camp, of course. And she did telephone me to arrange a meeting. You remember that I asked you whether you noticed where, in the telephone directory, Sheila had placed Orme's letter?”

Peter nodded.

"Yes, it was near the front of the book. Of course! The 'C's'!"

"Even there everything played into my hands. I was safe from even the remote chance that, finding that letter between the 'C' pages, you would connect it with the name of Cavanaugh. You missed your only clue. Well, I always said that clues were relatively unimportant. When Orme and Sheila left the Ellsworth house on the night of March 18th, they came to my office for a conference. Orme really did suffer a retroactive amnesia for that interview. I was not sure of that until I examined him in jail. It did not matter to me greatly—my plan was complete without it—but I could readily adjust my arrangements to this new circumstance.

"Orme insisted that Sheila should acknowledge their marriage. He was willing to give her a divorce—but that wasn't what she wanted. She knew that if Ellsworth were subjected to the publicity of a divorce, her hold on him would be loosened. He would never remarry her. And she wanted the status of his wife; she wanted his millions. She was approaching forty, you know. She was through with adventure, and wanted security. She told me that I would have to get Orme out of her way—if necessary, by having him committed to an asylum.

"You remember that I have never denied my previous acquaintance with Sheila O'Shay in the days when she was on the stage. That was a number of years ago—before I had learned that the world cannot bear to face honesty, that its pretty words must be taken with mock seriousness. Sheila had a roommate then—a dancer just rising to fame. Her name was quickly forgotten—you would not remember it. I had never pretended that my passing attachment to her was more than—what it was. I certainly could not afford to have my name linked with hers; a doctor must avoid scandal. When she lost her job because she was going to have a baby and could no longer dance, it was strictly her own business.

But she let her emotions run away with her. In a fit of depression, she jumped into the Seine. But she left a letter behind her for Sheila, telling the whole story. Why do suicides always want to explain themselves, I wonder? That would be a good subject for a monograph. I'm doing it myself, when it comes to that! I may even be quoted as a case in point. But the monograph won't be as good as if I had written it."

Dr. Cavanaugh neatly deposited an unbroken inch of cigar ash in the tray. Peter noticed for the first time that he had been puffing strenuously for a long time at a dead cigarette. He flung it aside and lighted another.

"Of course Sheila had kept that letter. She would! She was the kind of fool that keeps everything. But not quite a fool. For once in my life I had met a person like myself—one who let nothing stand in the way of what she wanted. Though with her, what she wanted was determined by her emotions instead of her intelligence. She threatened me with exposure if I didn't dispose of Orme. And I knew what the silly world would think of that story. My carefully constructed mask, my studied adjustment to the world's foolish hypocrisy, would slip with a vengeance! The world cannot look on the face of reality, and live. Honesty is the one thing it cannot bear. And, once started on the track, it would find other incidents of the past to dig up. No, I couldn't afford to let Sheila O'Shay keep that weapon in her hands. It would always be there, giving her power over me. If she did not use it then, she might later. I said very little—I was considering the problem, and how to meet it.

"Then Orme unexpectedly met it for me. That threat of railroading him to the asylum set him wild. She was contemptuous, as if he were a rag to be thrown into the gutter. It was her contempt more than her ruthlessness that made him see red. She was standing up, looking at me, presenting her ultimatum. Suddenly Orme seized the metal elephant from my desk and struck her with all his force on the point of her chin—a perfect upper cut, though he did not know it. She fell backward, striking her head against the corner of the desk. He stood looking at her for a moment.

"'I've killed her,' he said.

"I bent over her, and when I looked up, he was gone.

"She was not dead, only stunned; but there was the answer to my problem. I could finish the job and remove the danger of Sheila permanently from my path. I could conceal the body. In case Orme were found and connected with the case, he would believe that he was the murderer. He would either think that he himself had disposed of the body in a daze, or that I had tried to protect him. Either way, he insured my own safety. If necessary, I could get him off on a plea of insanity. I thought of all that at the time, but of course, as things turned out, it was even simpler, for Orme did not even know that he and Sheila had been present in my office. The repetition of the act which was of such profound emotional significance to him set him temporarily off balance again.

"So I put Sheila out of my way. I saw to it that the police should suggest that I search her boudoir. I found the dancer's letter in her desk, when I was rummaging through her papers, and slipped it into my pocket. Later I destroyed it. I took the body to the marsh in Barbara's car instead of my own, to avoid any chance of being recognized. The one thing I hadn't counted on was that I should meet Barbara in the hall when I was carrying out the body. She had been aroused by the sound of our voices, and had heard the crash of Sheila's fall. She stood there on the steps, her hand on her throat, and looked at me. She said absolutely nothing. But she knew. And she couldn't see it as I saw it, as merely the necessary adjustment to a problem. I saw the horror in her eyes. And yet, she said nothing. She would have gone through life in the shadow of that horror. I knew that I could trust Barbara. The words that I had cast aside meant too much to her."

"Yes," said Peter. "You could trust Barbara."

"Of course, the horror in her eyes should have meant nothing to me. Her loyalty should have been merely one of those useful weaknesses of humanity which I had learned to count upon. Pretty playthings!"

"Yes," Peter said again, "the useless, impractical virtues—incorruptible beauty. Barbara is like that."

"But I discovered my own weakness. It was hard to live with that horror in Barbara's eyes. I hope you can make it clear to Barbara that I loved her."

"Yes," said Peter, "I will make it clear."

"It won't matter to me, of course. I shall not know. And yet, somehow, it does seem to matter."

"I think it matters. You can count on me."

"I know I can count on you. You live by words—they mean something to you. Queer, isn't it? Honour, loyalty, trust—just words. And yet you live by them. They are your reality. And in the end, I have to count on them. And yet, I was the master of them all. I could save myself. Only, if I carried it through, if I saved myself, I should be branded as a failure. I should have to admit that for the first time I had taken a case which I could not solve. You were right when you taunted me with that."

"I'm sorry," Peter said painfully. "I'm sorry I put it to you like that."

"Oh, but I had already put it to myself! And if I let myself fail—there would always be the horror in Barbara's eyes."

"You see!" Peter exclaimed eagerly. "You were not the complete egoist, after all! There was a flaw in your crystal. Or perhaps the flaw was the other thing—the thing that enslaved your intelligence to one narrow personal ambition. I don't know——"

"It's rather an academic point, isn't it?" The doctor smiled.

"Don't!" Peter cried. "I can't bear it!"

"But it's nothing to make such a fuss about! And I rather fancy I've written a thing or two which will be remembered when all this has dropped into the limbo of forgotten news. After all, I've done some good work, Peter." Dr. Cavanaugh methodically stamped out the stub of his cigar against the side of the ash tray and half drew another from his pocket. Then he slipped it back again. "No," he murmured, "there isn't time. I don't suppose, Peter, you'd care to shake hands with me, for good-bye? Silly of me to care about a thing like that!"

Peter rose stiffly from his chair. His lips were pressed tightly together, and his throat ached unbearably. Dr. Cavanaugh opened the drawer of his desk. Peter's eye caught the gleam of a shining cylinder. Peter set his jaw, but it was too late. The tears were on his cheeks as he held out his hand.

"Good-bye, my friend," he said. Then it came to him to add the words the doctor would most wish to take with him. "The world will remember you as a great man."

The pressure of the doctor's hand was firm and warm.

"Good-bye, Peter," he said cheerfully. "You'd better go and find Barbara. I think she's in the little sitting room. I don't want her to be startled by the shot."

Chapter LIII

BARBARA WAS drowsing in the big chair by the fire. Peter came gently behind her, and held both hands over her ears. She looked up at him dreamily, only half awake. A muffled report came from the doctor's office.

"What is that!" Barbara struggled to her feet, but Peter's arms were warm and close around her.

"It's all right, darling. It's all right," he crooned.

She put up her hand to his face, and looked wonderingly at her wet fingers.

Peter sat down in the big chair and held her close, as if she were a child.

"It's all over now, dear. After all, it was the only way, the best way. There is nothing more to hide. Just remember that your father was a great man—and that he was good to you."

"You—know?"

"I know everything. He has told me all about it. And he chose to go out—this way. After all, you wouldn't have wanted it otherwise. Do you realize, Barbara, that there wasn't a shadow of proof against him—that he never could have been brought to trial? And yet he chose to wipe the page clean. He cleared up his last case, Barbara. He didn't save himself."

Barbara sat up suddenly straight, lifting her head from Peter's shoulder. Her eyes were like brown depths of water in the sun. For the first time they were clear of horror. Her hands were clasped tight against her breast.

"Do you know, Peter," she said, "I think I am rather proud of my father. I think I will marry you, Peter."

"Yes," Peter said. He wished Cavanaugh could have known that; but it was too late now. It flashed across his mind that Barbara was really Cavanaugh's daughter, that he had lied at the last to give her peace of mind. Perhaps. Well, let it go. Cavanaugh would have been glad to know that Barbara was no longer ashamed or afraid of her inheritance. Let that one tribute remain his.

"Will it have to come out? Will they have to know that he—did it? Couldn't it end—like this?"

"But he wanted them to know! He wanted them to know that he hadn't really failed to solve the case. He gave me a note to Jimmy. He gave it to the *Herald*."

"Peter, you couldn't!" Barbara pushed herself away from his arms, and rose to her feet in horrified protest. "You couldn't do a thing like that! All his great reputation, all those years of fine work, the record of his powerful intellect—crashed, smirched! You mustn't do it, Peter. You couldn't do that for the sake of a story in your paper."

"It is a great story, Barbara, there's no doubt about that. But you'll have to believe me when I say that I'd have suppressed it. I'd have let my paper down. You don't know quite what that means, I think. But I'd have done it. Only your father wanted me to have it. He didn't want his last case to be chalked up against him as his first failure."

"But he didn't see! He never saw things quite like ordinary people. For all his greatness, in that sense he wasn't quite sane. He didn't see that his confession would show that his whole life, his whole personality was a colossal failure—that he wasn't in reality the man of high integrity that everyone believed him to be. I couldn't bear that, Peter! We must protect him, protect his name, even against himself."

Peter's mouth twitched with the monstrous irony of it. Cavanaugh was to be denied his last triumph, after all. And yet it was the proof that Barbara had loved him. Would he have sacrificed his terrific ambition for the proof of that love? He had tried to live beyond good and evil, beyond emotion. He had laughed at the standards painfully reared by humanity. And yet, in the end, those standards had triumphed in his soul. "I'd like her to know that I loved her, Peter—that is my weakness." His weakness—or another and saner strength?

"I believe he would let you have it your way, Barbara. I believe he would give you that—but he would smile when he did it."

Peter reached out his hand with the sheet from the prescription pad which Dr. Cavanaugh had given him. He held it over the coals that twinkled redly in the grate until the corners turned brown. Then as the paper burst into flames, he dropped it into the fire and watched it flare for a moment and then subside in a little heap of white ash.

"There goes the biggest scoop the *Herald* ever had," he murmured. "God help me if Jimmy ever finds it out!"

A little clock on the mantelpiece tinkled out twelve strokes. The sound brought Peter to himself. Once again he was on the job—Peter Piper of the *Herald.* He lifted Barbara gently, and gently deposited her in the big chair.

"Listen to me, dear," he said. "I've got to telephone this to the office first. Then I shall have to call the—the other people who must be notified. You shall hear just what I say. But I want you to sit quite still in that chair."

He vanished briefly into the doctor's office. Dr. Cavanaugh had done his job cleanly and expertly, as he did everything. There was nothing there that would horrify Barbara when the time came for her to look. Peter touched the dead hand gently. On the corner of the desk lay a nickel—Dr. Cavanaugh's last bet with his own judgment. Peter wondered what that bet had been. Then he took the nickel, wrapped it in a piece of paper, and slipped it into his pocket.

"I don't think you'll mind my keeping this—in memory of a great man," he said aloud, to the dead, upturned face.

When he came back to the little sitting room, he walked at once to the telephone in the corner. He did not want Barbara to see that his eyes were wet. She was sitting in the big chair where he had left her, her head lifted bravely, her face calm with a great serenity. There were lines of pain about her mouth, but in her eyes was peace.

"Keep on ringing till they do answer," Peter said harshly into the telephone. "Jimmy? Well, you'll have to wake up for this. Dr. Cavanaugh has just committed suicide—a sudden breakdown due to overwork on the Ellsworth case. I was present. No, nobody else. Yes, it's exclusive, absolutely."

"I'll be right down." Jimmy's raucous voice over the wire was audible in the quiet room. "Meet you at the office in half an hour. Get all the dope."

"I've got it," said Peter.

"Now that Dr. Cavanaugh's dead, I suppose we never shall get the rights of the tule marsh murder." Jimmy's voice was hoarse with disappointment. "Lord, what a chance he missed! He's the only man that stood a chance of solving it."

"No," Peter admitted. "With Dr. Cavanaugh dead, I doubt if the case will ever be solved. But, Jimmy, that's not all. I've another piece of front page news for you. I'm going to be married."

"The deuce you are! And I suppose, as usual, you want it known that she's the eighth wonder of the world? Well, that can wait. You leg it down to the office."

"It's not going to wait very long," Peter assured him. "It's the real dope that I'm going to marry the loveliest girl in the world!"

"Hell!" said Jimmy. "That's not news."

THE END

DISCUSSION QUESTIONS

- Did any aspects of the plot date the story? If so, which?
- Would the story be different if it were set in the present day? If so, how?
- Did the social context of the time play a role in the narrative? If so, how?
- If you were one of the main characters, would you have acted differently at any point in the story?
- Did you identify with any of the characters? If so, which?
- What skills or qualities make Peter Piper an effective sleuth?
- Did this book remind you of any present day authors? If so, which?

John Dickson Carr, ***The Plague Court Murders.*** When a spiritual medium employed to rid a haunted house of a malevolent spirit is found stabbed to death in a locked stone hut on the grounds, Sir Henry Merrivale seeks a logical solution to a ghostly crime. **Introduction by Michael Dirda.**

John Dickson Carr, ***The Red Widow Murders.*** In a "haunted" town house, the room known as the Red Widow's Chamber has a deadly reputation. Eight people investigate and the one who draws the ace of spades must sleep in it while the door is watched all night by the others. In the morning, the inmate has been poisoned. Enter Sir Henry Merrivale to solve the crime. **Introduction by Tom Mead.**

Frances Crane, ***The Turquoise Shop.*** In an arty little New Mexico town, Mona Brandon has arrived from the East and becomes the subject of gossip about her money, her influence, and the corpse in the nearby desert who may be her husband. Pat Holly, who runs the local gift shop, is as interested as anyone in the goings on—but even more in Pat Abbott, the detective investigating the possible murder. **Introduction by Anne Hillerman.**

Todd Downing, ***Vultures in the Sky.*** There is no end to the series of terrifying events that befall a luxury train bound for Mexico. First, a man dies when the train passes through a dark tunnel, then it comes to an abrupt stop in the middle of the desert. More deaths occur when night falls and the passengers panic when they realize they are trapped with a murderer on the loose. **Introduction by James Sallis.**

Mignon G. Eberhart, ***Murder by an Aristocrat.*** Nurse Keate is called to help a man who has been "accidentally" shot in the shoulder, but then he is murdered while convalescing, and it becomes clear that there was no accident. *The New Yorker* wrote than "Eberhart can weave an almost flawless mystery." **Introduction by Nancy Pickard.**

Erle Stanley Gardner, ***The Case of the Baited Hook.*** The promise of thousands of dollars leads Perry Mason to take on a mysterious case, only to learn that he will not be defending the male caller but a beautiful woman whose identity is hidden behind a mask. **Introduction by Otto Penzler.**

Erle Stanley Gardner, ***The Case of the Borrowed Brunette.*** A mysterious man named Mr. Hines has advertised a job for a woman who has to fulfill very specific physical requirements. Eva Martell, pretty but struggling in her career as a model, takes the job but her aunt smells a rat and hires Perry Mason to investigate. Her fears are realized when Hines turns up in the apartment with a bullet hole in his head. **Introduction by Otto Penzler.**

Erle Stanley Gardner, ***The Case of the Careless Kitten.*** Helen Kendal receives a mysterious phone call from her vanished uncle Franklin, long presumed dead, who urges her to contact Perry Mason. Soon, she finds herself the main suspect in the murder of an unfamiliar man. Her kitten has just survived a poisoning attempt—as has her aunt Matilda. What is the connection between Franklin's return and the murder attempts? **Introduction by Otto Penzler.**

Erle Stanley Gardner, ***The Case of the Rolling Bones.*** One of Gardner's most successful Perry Mason novels opens with a clear case of blackmail, though the person being blackmailed claims he isn't. It is not long before the police are searching for someone wanted for killing the same man in two different states—thirty-three years apart. The confounding puzzle of what happened to the dead man's toes is a challenge. **Introduction by Otto Penzler.**

Erle Stanley Gardner, ***The Case of the Shoplifter's Shoe.*** Most cases for Perry Mason involve murder but here he is hired because a young woman fears her aunt is a kleptomaniac. Sarah may not have been precisely the best guardian for a collection of valuable diamonds and, sure enough, they go missing. When the jeweler is found shot dead, Sarah is spotted leaving the murder scene with a bundle of gems stuffed in her purse. **Introduction by Otto Penzler.**

Erle Stanley Gardner, ***The Bigger They Come.*** Gardner's first novel using the pseudonym A.A. Fair starts off a series featuring the large and loud Bertha Cool and her employee, the small and meek Donald Lam. Given the job of delivering divorce papers to an evident crook, Lam can't find him—but neither can the police. **Introduction by Otto Penzler.**

Frances Noyes Hart, ***The Bellamy Trial.*** Inspired by the real-life Hall-Mills case, the most sensational trial of its day, this is the story of Stephen Bellamy and Susan Ives, accused of murdering Bellamy's wife Madeleine. Eight days of dynamic testimony, some true, some not, make headlines for an enthralled public. **Introduction by Hank Phillippi Ryan.**

H.F. Heard, ***A Taste for Honey.*** The elderly Mr. Mycroft quietly keeps bees in Sussex, where he is approached by the reclusive and somewhat misanthropic Mr. Silchester, whose honey supplier was found dead, stung to death by her bees. Mycroft, who shares many traits with Sherlock Holmes, sets out to find the vicious killer. **Introduction by Otto Penzler.**

Dolores Hitchens, ***The Alarm of the Black Cat.*** Detective fiction aficionado Rachel Murdock has a peculiar meeting with a little girl and a dead toad, sparking her curiosity about a love triangle that has sparked anger. When the girl's great grandmother is found dead, Rachel and her cat Samantha work with a friend in the Los Angeles Police Department to get to the bottom of things. **Introduction by David Handler.**

Dolores Hitchens, ***The Cat Saw Murder.*** Miss Rachel Murdock, the highly intelligent 70-year-old amateur sleuth, is not entirely heartbroken when her bridge-cheating niece is murdered. Miss Rachel is happy to help the socially maladroit and somewhat bumbling Detective Lieutenant Stephen Mayhew, retaining her composure when a second brutal murder occurs. **Introduction by Joyce Carol Oates.**

Dorothy B. Hughes, ***Dread Journey.*** A big-shot Hollywood producer has worked on his magnum opus for years, hiring and firing one beautiful starlet after another. But Kitten Agnew's contract won't allow her to be fired, so she fears she might be terminated more permanently. Together with the producer on a train journey from Hollywood to Chicago, Kitten becomes more terrified with each passing mile. **Introduction by Sarah Weinman.**

Dorothy B. Hughes, ***Ride the Pink Horse.*** When Sailor met Willis Douglass, he was just a poor kid who Douglass groomed to work as a confidential secretary. As the senator became increasingly corrupt, he knew he could count on Sailor to clean up his messes. No longer a senator, Douglass flees Chicago for Santa Fe, leaving behind a murder rap and Sailor as the prime suspect. Seeking vengeance, Sailor follows. **Introduction by Sara Paretsky.**

Dorothy B. Hughes, ***The So Blue Marble.*** Set in the glamorous world of New York high society, this novel became a suspense classic as twins from Europe try to steal a rare and beautiful gem owned by an aristocrat whose sister is an even more menacing presence. **Introduction by Otto Penzler.**

W. Bolingbroke Johnson, ***The Widening Stain.*** After a cocktail party, the attractive Lucie Coindreau, a "black-eyed, black-haired Frenchwoman" visits the rare books wing of the library and apparently takes a head-first fall from an upper gallery. Dismissed as a horrible accident, it seems dubious when Professor Hyett is strangled while reading a priceless 12th-century manuscript, which has gone missing. **Introduction by Nicholas A. Basbanes**

Baynard Kendrick, ***Blind Man's Bluff.*** Blinded in World War II, Duncan Maclain forms a successful private detective agency, aided by his two dogs. Here, he is called on to solve the case of a blind man who plummets from the top of an eight-story building, apparently with no one present except his dead-drunk son. **Introduction by Otto Penzler.**

Baynard Kendrick, ***The Odor of Violets.*** Duncan Maclain, a blind former intelligence officer, is asked to investigate the murder of an actor in his Greenwich Village apartment. This would cause a stir at any time but, when the actor possesses secret government plans that then go missing, it's enough to interest the local police as well as the American government and Maclain, who suspects a German spy plot. **Introduction by Otto Penzler.**

C. Daly King, *Obelists at Sea.* On a cruise ship traveling from New York to Paris, the lights of the smoking room briefly go out, a gunshot crashes through the night, and a man is dead. Two detectives are on board but so are four psychiatrists who believe their professional knowledge can solve the case by understanding the psyche of the killer—each with a different theory. **Introduction by Martin Edwards.**

Jonathan Latimer, ***Headed for a Hearse.*** Featuring Bill Crane, the booze-soaked Chicago private detective, this humorous hard-boiled novel was filmed as *The Westland Case* in 1937 starring Preston Foster. Robert Westland has been framed for the grisly murder of his wife in a room with doors and windows locked from the inside. As the day of his execution nears, he relies on Crane to find the real murderer. **Introduction by Max Allan Collins**

Lange Lewis, ***The Birthday Murder.*** Victoria is a successful novelist and screenwriter and her husband is a movie director so their marriage seems almost too good to be true. Then, on her birthday, her happy new life comes crashing down when her husband is murdered using a method of poisoning that was described in one of her books. She quickly becomes the leading suspect. **Introduction by Randal S. Brandt.**

Frances and Richard Lockridge, ***Death on the Aisle.*** In one of the most beloved books to feature Mr. and Mrs. North, the body of a wealthy backer of a play is found dead in a seat of the 45th Street Theater. Pam is thrilled to engage in her favorite pastime—playing amateur sleuth—much to the annoyance of Jerry, her publisher husband. **Introduction by Otto Penzler.**

John P. Marquand, ***Your Turn, Mr. Moto.*** The first novel about Mr. Moto, originally titled *No Hero,* is the story of a World War I hero pilot who finds himself jobless during the Depression. In Tokyo for a big opportunity that falls apart, he meets a Japanese agent and his Russian colleague and the pilot suddenly finds himself caught in a web of intrigue. **Introduction by Lawrence Block.**

Stuart Palmer, ***The Penguin Pool Murder.*** The first adventure of schoolteacher and dedicated amateur sleuth Hildegarde Withers occurs at the New York Aquarium when she and her young students notice a corpse in one of the tanks. It was published in 1931 and filmed the next year, starring Edna May Oliver as the American Miss Marple. **Introduction by Otto Penzler.**

Stuart Palmer, ***The Puzzle of the Happy Hooligan.*** New York City schoolteacher Hildegarde Withers cannot resist "assisting" homicide detective Oliver Piper. In this novel, she is on vacation in Hollywood and on the set of a movie about Lizzie Borden when the screenwriter is found dead. Six comic films about Withers appeared in the 1930s, most successfully starring Edna May Oliver. **Introduction by Otto Penzler.**

Otto Penzler, ed., ***Golden Age Bibliomysteries.***Stories of murder, theft, and suspense occur with alarming regularity in the unlikely world of books and bibliophiles, including bookshops, libraries, and private rare book collections, written by such giants of the mystery genre as Ellery Queen, Cornell Woolrich, Lawrence G. Blochman, Vincent Starrett, and Anthony Boucher. **Introduction by Otto Penzler.**

Otto Penzler, ed., ***Golden Age Detective Stories.*** The history of American mystery fiction has its pantheon of authors who have influenced and entertained readers for nearly a century, reaching its peak during the Golden Age, and this collection pays homage to the work of the most acclaimed: Cornell Woolrich, Erle Stanley Gardner, Craig Rice, Ellery Queen, Dorothy B. Hughes, Mary Roberts Rinehart, and more. **Introduction by Otto Penzler.**

Otto Penzler, ed., ***Golden Age Locked Room Mysteries*****.** The so-called impossible crime category reached its zenith during the 1920s, 1930s, and 1940s, and this volume includes the greatest of the great authors who mastered the form: John Dickson Carr, Ellery Queen, C. Daly King, Clayton Rawson, and Erle Stanley Gardner. Like great magicians, these literary conjurors will baffle and delight readers. **Introduction by Otto Penzler.**

Ellery Queen, ***The Adventures of Ellery Queen*****.** These stories are the earliest short works to feature Queen as a detective and are among the best of the author's fair-play mysteries. So many of the elements that comprise the gestalt of Queen may be found in these tales: alternate solutions, the dying clue, a bizarre crime, and the author's ability to find fresh variations of works by other authors. **Introduction by Otto Penzler.**

Ellery Queen, ***The American Gun Mystery*****.** A rodeo comes to New York City at the Colosseum and the headliner is shot dead during his big performance. The police instantly lock the doors to search everyone but the offending weapon has completely vanished. **Introduction by Otto Penzler.**

Ellery Queen, ***The Chinese Orange Mystery*****.** The offices of publisher Donald Kirk have seen strange events but nothing like this. A strange man is found dead with two long spears alongside his back. And, though no one was seen entering or leaving the room, everything has been turned backwards or upside down: pictures face the wall, the victim's clothes are worn backwards, the rug upside down. Why in the world? **Introduction by Otto Penzler.**

Ellery Queen, ***The Dutch Shoe Mystery*****.** Millionaire philanthropist Abagail Doorn falls into a coma and she is rushed to the hospital she funds for an emergency operation by one of the leading surgeons on the East Coast. When she is wheeled into the operating theater, the sheet covering her body is pulled back to reveal her garroted corpse—the first of a series of murders **Introduction by Otto Penzler.**

Ellery Queen, ***The Egyptian Cross Mystery*****.** A small-town schoolteacher is found dead, headed, and tied to a T-shaped cross on December 25th, inspiring such sensational headlines as "Crucifixion on Christmas Day." Amateur sleuth Ellery Queen is so intrigued he travels to West Virginia but fails to solve the crime. Then a similar murder takes place in Long Island—and then another. **Introduction by Otto Penzler.**

Ellery Queen, ***The Siamese Twin Mystery*****.** When Ellery and his father encounter a raging forest fire on a mountain, their only hope is to drive up to an isolated hillside manor owned by a secretive surgeon and his strange guests. While playing solitaire in the middle of the night, the doctor is shot. The only clue is a torn playing card. Suspects include a society beauty, a valet, and conjoined twins. **Introduction by Otto Penzler.**

Ellery Queen, ***The Spanish Cape Mystery*****.** Amateur detective Ellery Queen arrives in the resort town of Spanish Cape soon after a young woman and her uncle are abducted by a gun-toting, one-eyed giant. The next day, the woman's somewhat dicey boyfriend is found murdered—totally naked under a black fedora and opera cloak. **Introduction by Otto Penzler.**

Patrick Quentin, ***A Puzzle for Fools*****.** Broadway producer Peter Duluth takes to the bottle when his wife dies but enters a sanitarium to dry out. Malevolent events plague the hospital, including when Peter hears his own voice intone, "There will be murder." And there is. He investigates, aided by a young woman who is also a patient. This is the first of nine mysteries featuring Peter and Iris Duluth. **Introduction by Otto Penzler.**

Clayton Rawson, ***Death from a Top Hat*****.** When the New York City Police Department is baffled by an apparently impossible crime, they call on The Great Merlini, a retired stage magician who now runs a Times Square magic shop. In his first case, two occultists have been murdered in a room locked from the inside, their bodies positioned to form a pentagram. **Introduction by Otto Penzler.**

Craig Rice, *Eight Faces at Three*. Gin-soaked John J. Malone, defender of the guilty, is notorious for getting his culpable clients off. It's the innocent ones who are problems. Like Holly Inglehart, accused of piercing the black heart of her well-heeled aunt Alexandria with a lovely Florentine paper cutter. No one who knew the old battle-ax liked her, but Holly's prints were found on the murder weapon. **Introduction by Lisa Lutz.**

Craig Rice, *Home Sweet Homicide*. Known as the Dorothy Parker of mystery fiction for her memorable wit, Craig Rice was the first detective writer to appear on the cover of *Time* magazine. This comic mystery features two kids who are trying to find a husband for their widowed mother while she's engaged in sleuthing. Filmed with the same title in 1946 with Peggy Ann Garner and Randolph Scott. **Introduction by Otto Penzler.**

Mary Roberts Rinehart, *The Album*. Crescent Place is a quiet enclave of wealthy people in which nothing ever happens—until a bedridden old woman is attacked by an intruder with an ax. *The New York Times* stated: "All Mary Roberts Rinehart mystery stories are good, but this one is better." **Introduction by Otto Penzler.**

Mary Roberts Rinehart, *The Haunted Lady*. The arsenic in her sugar bowl was wealthy widow Eliza Fairbanks' first clue that somebody wanted her dead. Nightly visits of bats, birds, and rats, obviously aimed at scaring the dowager to death, was the second. Eliza calls the police, who send nurse Hilda Adams, the amateur sleuth they refer to as "Miss Pinkerton," to work undercover to discover the culprit. **Introduction by Otto Penzler.**

Mary Roberts Rinehart, *Miss Pinkerton*. Hilda Adams is a nurse, not a detective, but she is observant and smart and so it is common for Inspector Patton to call on her for help. Her success results in his calling her "Miss Pinkerton." *The New Republic* wrote: "From thousands of hearts and homes the cry will go up: Thank God for Mary Roberts Rinehart." **Introduction by Carolyn Hart.**

Mary Roberts Rinehart, *The Red Lamp*. Professor William Porter refuses to believe that the seaside manor he's just inherited is haunted but he has to convince his wife to move in. However, he soon sees evidence of the occult phenomena of which the townspeople speak. Whether it is a spirit or a human being, Porter accepts that there is a connection to the rash of murders that have terrorized the countryside. **Introduction by Otto Penzler.**

Mary Roberts Rinehart, *The Wall*. For two decades, Mary Roberts Rinehart was the second-best-selling author in America (only Sinclair Lewis outsold her) and was beloved for her tales of suspense. In a magnificent mansion, the ex-wife of one of the owners turns up making demands and is found dead the next day. And there are more dark secrets lying behind the walls of the estate. **Introduction by Otto Penzler.**

Joel Townsley Rogers, *The Red Right Hand*. This extraordinary whodunnit that is as puzzling as it is terrifying was identified by crime fiction scholar Jack Adrian as "one of the dozen or so finest mystery novels of the 20th century." A deranged killer sends a doctor on a quest for the truth—deep into the recesses of his own mind—when he and his bride-to-be elope but pick up a terrifying sharp-toothed hitch-hiker. **Introduction by Joe R. Lansdale.**

Roger Scarlett, *Cat's Paw*. The family of the wealthy old bachelor Martin Greenough cares far more about his money than they do about him. For his birthday, he invites all his potential heirs to his mansion to tell them what they hope to hear. Before he can disburse funds, however, he is murdered, and the Boston Police Department's big problem is that there are too many suspects. **Introduction by Curtis Evans**

Vincent Starrett, *Dead Man Inside*. 1930s Chicago is a tough town but some crimes are more bizarre than others. Customers arrive at a haberdasher to find a corpse in the window and a sign on the door: *Dead Man Inside! I am Dead. The store will not open today*. This is just one of a series of odd murders that terrorizes the city. Reluctant detective Walter Ghost leaps into action to learn what is behind the plague. **Introduction by Otto Penzler.**

Vincent Starrett, ***The Great Hotel Murder.*** Theater critic and amateur sleuth Riley Blackwood investigates a murder in a Chicago hotel where the dead man had changed rooms with a stranger who had registered under a fake name. *The New York Times* described it as "an ingenious plot with enough complications to keep the reader guessing." **Introduction by Lyndsay Faye.**

Vincent Starrett, ***Murder on 'B' Deck.*** Walter Ghost, a psychologist, scientist, explorer, and former intelligence officer, is on a cruise ship and his friend novelist Dunsten Mollock, a Nigel Bruce-like Watson whose role is to offer occasional comic relief, accommodates when he fails to leave the ship before it takes off. Although they make mistakes along the way, the amateur sleuths solve the shipboard murders. **Introduction by Ray Betzner.**

Phoebe Atwood Taylor, ***The Cape Cod Mystery.*** Vacationers have flocked to Cape Cod to avoid the heat wave that hit the Northeast and find their holiday unpleasant when the area is flooded with police trying to find the murderer of a muckraking journalist who took a cottage for the season. Finding a solution falls to Asey Mayo, "the Cape Cod Sherlock," known for his worldly wisdom, folksy humor, and common sense. **Introduction by Otto Penzler.**

S. S. Van Dine, ***The Benson Murder Case.*** The first of 12 novels to feature Philo Vance, the most popular and influential detective character of the early part of the 20th century. When wealthy stockbroker Alvin Benson is found shot to death in a locked room in his mansion, the police are baffled until the erudite flaneur and art collector arrives on the scene. Paramount filmed it in 1930 with William Powell as Vance. **Introduction by Ragnar Jónasson.**

Cornell Woolrich, ***The Bride Wore Black.*** The first suspense novel by one of the greatest of all noir authors opens with a bride and her new husband walking out of the church. A car speeds by, shots ring out, and he falls dead at her feet. Determined to avenge his death, she tracks down everyone in the car, concluding with a shocking surprise. It was filmed by Francois Truffaut in 1968, starring Jeanne Moreau. **Introduction by Eddie Muller.**

Cornell Woolrich, ***Deadline at Dawn.*** Quinn is overcome with guilt about having robbed a stranger's home. He meets Bricky, a dime-a-dance girl, and they fall for each other. When they return to the crime scene, they discover a dead body. Knowing Quinn will be accused of the crime, they race to find the true killer before he's arrested. A 1946 film starring Susan Hayward was loosely based on the plot. **Introduction by David Gordon.**

Cornell Woolrich, ***Waltz into Darkness.*** A New Orleans businessman successfully courts a woman through the mail but he is shocked to find when she arrives that she is not the plain brunette whose picture he'd received but a radiant blond beauty. She soon absconds with his fortune. Wracked with disappointment and loneliness, he vows to track her down. When he finds her, the real nightmare begins. **Introduction by Wallace Stroby.**